THE DEVIL OF MISTY LAKE

LORESTALKER - Book 5

J.P. BARNETT

THE DEVIL OF MISTY LAKE
Lorestalker – 5
Copyright © 2021 by J.P. Barnett

All rights reserved. No part of this book may be used or reproduced in any manner whatsoever, without written permission, except in the case of brief quotations embedded in articles and reviews. For more information, please contact publisher at Publisher@EvolvedPub.com.

FIRST EDITION SOFTCOVER
ISBN: 1622536495
ISBN-13: 978-1-62253-649-8

Editor: Mike Robinson
Cover Artist: Richard Tran
Interior Designer: Lane Diamond

EVOLVED PUBLISHING™
www.EvolvedPub.com
Butler, Wisconsin, USA

The Devil of Misty Lake is a work of fiction. All names, characters, places, and incidents are the product of the author's imagination, or are used fictitiously. Any resemblance to actual events or persons, living or dead, is entirely coincidental.

Printed in Book Antiqua font.

Praise for the "Lorestalker" Series

THE BEAST OF ROSE VALLEY:
"Barnett's plot is clever and irresistible, and his book is a sheer pleasure to read. Horror, thriller and mystery fans alike will find much to their liking in this intriguing story about the unknown."
~ *Jack Magnus for Readers' Favorite Book Reviews*

~~~

"If you are looking for a fun, fast-paced creature feature set in a small town, you really can't go wrong with this one."
~ *Steve Stred, Kendall Reviews*

THE KRAKEN OF CAPE MADRE:
"It was an exciting read, and as I'm not a fan of creepy sea-creatures, it was indeed a proper horror novel to me. Novels like this make me feel validated about my hesitance to step into the sea! You never know what lurks out there."
~ *Kim Anisi for Readers' Favorite Book Reviews*

~~~

"Barnett has skills. He has the ability to take a reader anywhere and everywhere and make you feel every bit of emotions his characters are feeling."
~ *Ash, Reviews of a Fear Street Zombie*

THE WITCH OF GRAY'S POINT:
"For lovers of myths, folklore, and the macabre, Barnett is the author to follow...."
~ *Alicia Smock, Roll Out Reviews*

~~~

"...reality pervades every aspect of this horror story."
~ *Lex Allen for Readers' Favorite Book Reviews*

BOOKS BY J.P. BARNETT

The LORESTALKER Series
The Beast of Rose Valley
The Kraken of Cape Madre
The Witch of Gray's Point
The Haunt at Hogg Run
The Devil of Misty Lake
The Legacy of Rose Valley

PROLOGUE

Bent in an unnatural position, Ben's shoulder ached, trapped beneath Abby's head as she peacefully slept. He fought hard not to react to the pain, for fear of waking her. Rain whispered lightly across the top of the tent. He kept thinking about the ring in his bag, waiting, waiting for the moment.

Though he didn't have a history of being obsessive-compulsive, he couldn't help but want to verify its safety at every chance. When he'd suggested this camping trip, he didn't expect it to come with so much anxiety. They'd been together for five years. Surely she wouldn't say no. But he hadn't found the perfect moment yet, so the ring sat quietly in his jacket pocket, patiently awaiting its reveal.

Unable to find sleep, Ben slowly tried to free his arm from under her soft hair. She stirred at first, but not fully, and before long the pain of his wrenching shoulder gave way to the pins and needles of his waking arm. Moving as quietly as he could, he unzipped his sleeping bag, verified he still had the ring, then unfastened the tent door. He stepped out into the drizzle, but didn't really notice the rain. As a longtime resident of Washington, it hardly even registered.

The fire had long since died. The water of Misty Lake shimmered with an almost celestial majesty. The usually verdant evergreens stood muted in the darkness. They hadn't seen another camper in days. He felt so completely unplugged from the rest of the world, and loved it. Their cell phones were useless out here. It was just him and his girlfriend—soon to be fiancée, hopefully—and the beauty and splendor of the great outdoors. With everything going on in the world, part of him wanted to stay forever.

A ripple echoed out across the surface of the lake, drawing his curiosity. A fish perhaps, or a turtle. Nothing frightening swam in those waters. The only thing he feared out here were the bears, but he'd taken all the precautions. They'd sprayed everything down with what purported to be repellent, and they even hung their food in a bag up high enough that it would be a difficult prize for any animal to win. He'd been camping a lot, but never this deep in the woods. Never this isolated.

Fixated on the ripple, he jumped when he heard rustling nearby. He spun wildly, wishing he'd brought the flashlight. He saw nothing, but noticed that the supply bag wobbled back and forth. What could have caused that? Something from above, perhaps? He briefly wondered if a raccoon might be smart enough to untie the rope to get at the tasty morsels inside the bag, but he knew how to tie a good knot. Most humans couldn't even undo it.

Suddenly, the rain felt smothering. His skin grew clammy and cold. Why hadn't he put on his jacket? Though he couldn't see or hear anything weird, something felt off.

His eyes widened, as the forest moved behind the bag, its whole darkness somehow shifting as one. His eyes tried to make sense of it, but could come up with nothing but that. A moving, shifting shadow of the forest. It grew larger, closer. Just when he thought he might be going crazy, he saw the shimmer of wet, black fur. A bear, then?

A splash from the lake drew his attention. The ripples were large, creating small wakes. Suddenly, the forest became alive with sound. Chittering to his left. Splashing in front of him. He twirled back to the shadow to find both it and the food bag gone. A frayed rope dangled from the branch above. He spun in a circle, terrified that the shadow—something that he quickly decided could not possibly be a bear—would attack him from another angle.

As he glanced towards the tent, he saw something much smaller digging at the ground. Long and lithe, perhaps furry, but he couldn't quite tell. A smaller version of the creature in the shadows, perhaps? It nipped at the nylon walls of the shelter. Whatever this thing was, Ben had a healthy size advantage.

He stomped forward and hissed. It turned to look at him with beady black eyes, vacuous and empty, barely visible in the dim light. He made out fur, and a hulking form that he couldn't believe. The thing twittered at him. Hardly a threatening sound, but still he felt a prickling sense of danger at the nape of his neck.

The shadow appeared again, or perhaps had been there since the beginning. It came forward, hulking over the smaller creature at the base of the tent. A second pair of eyes emerged from the darkness, this time deeper and blacker. And angrier. This thing bared sharp, yellowed teeth and exhaled fetid breath, tainted with the smell of rotting fish.

Not a bear. Bigger.

It looked almost as if it were made of plastic, slick and wet from the rain. He thought maybe he saw whiskers in the darkness but didn't trust himself to make a positive identification.

Did bears have whiskers? He didn't think so, but doubt made him wonder if maybe all mammals had them.

"Abby!"

No answer from inside the tent. He surged forward and grabbed her ankle through her sleeping bag.

"What the hell, Ben?"

The fog in her voice told him she'd registered nothing of the commotion outside.

"We gotta go!"

"What? Why?"

"Just, come on. Please!"

He backed away to catch a glimpse of the monstrosity again, but saw nothing. Both the little one and the big one had disappeared from the side of the tent. Great. Now Abby would never believe him. He turned cautiously in every direction until she emerged from the tent, dressed in only a t-shirt, sweatpants and his jacket.

"Something's out here," Ben said.

"No shit, Ben." She'd never been very pleasant in the morning. "It's the woods. There's a lot of stuff out here."

Sploosh!

The sound reverberated through the forest, echoing off the trees. Nothing in the lake should have been capable of making that deep of a splashing sound. He spun to see more ripples, emanating out towards the shore.

"Wait. Where's the food?" Abby asked.

"It took it."

"It? Like a bear?"

"No. Something else."

"Ben. You're scaring me. Make sense."

Before he could answer, chaos erupted. The tent flattened. Abby spun and screamed. From the shadows above, the creature's mouth opened wide and snapped forward, causing her to stumble backward. Ben caught her just in time. The water. The woods. This thing was everywhere at once. Everything in Ben told him to run. This was no animal. This was something else entirely.

Ben grabbed Abby's hand and took off in a sprint. When she couldn't keep up, he let go, regulating his speed to ensure she kept pace just behind him. As much as he wanted to enfold her, protect her, clutch her, they'd each run faster on their own.

They ran and ran, long after the sound of the creature disappeared into the woods. Abby and Ben had both competed in marathons. Both exercised regularly. They could run for a long time, and even longer when threatened. Still, they both began gulping for air.

Ben's toe hooked on a tree root and he tumbled forward. And down. Way down. Unable to pull up in time, Abby fell in after him. Frantically, Ben surveyed the deep depression in the ground. Not quite a hole, but deep enough that he wasn't sure they'd be able to escape. He scrambled up one side, lost his balance and slid back down. How could there be such a large hole in the middle of the woods?

Maybe this was good. Maybe this hole would keep them hidden and safe.

With no gear, though, Ben realized that, even if they did manage to climb out, they'd be inescapably lost.

"What was that thing?" Abby asked.

Ben turned from the muddy wall of the depression to look at her. "I don't know."

"It was so big. Not a bear."

"No."

Ben turned to Abby. Water dripped from her hair onto her face, which she quickly blinked away.

Shivering, she slipped her hands into the pockets of her jacket. Well, his jacket really.

Wait. No!

"What's this?" She pulled out the felt box and turned it over in her hand. Whatever adrenaline raced through Ben's veins intensified. This was definitely not the right moment. He snatched it away from her before she could open it.

"Nothing."

Something crashed in the forest behind them. They both turned.

"Did you hear that?" he asked.

"Y-Yes."

"Abby?"

She didn't respond, just pressed her body against his. Something came for them. They could hear it, or maybe feel it, its sheer size quivering the earth under their feet.

Movement on the ground caught Ben's eye. Little ones. Just like the one digging at the tent. Two or three or four. He couldn't be sure. He could barely see more than the shadows.

They hadn't stumbled into a hole at all. They'd fallen into a nest.

This was it. The last moment they'd have together. No way out of the hole. No way to defend themselves against this. Abby reached back and squeezed his hand.

The creature slammed through the trees into the clearing, bearing down into the hole with unbelievable speed, its mouth open, teeth glistening in what little moonlight made it through the canopy and the clouds.

He feared he'd never have another chance to ask.

"Abby, will you marry me?"

PART ONE:
The Devil

CHAPTER 1 – Miriam

On the inside, the Portland International Airport looked a little like the scene of an unfortunate clown massacre. Miriam had rarely seen such bright colors in Texas or Missouri. Every wall and carpet fought against one another in various shades of rarely-used decorative colors—turquoise, orange, purple.

"I read once that the suicide rate up here is way higher," she said to Macy, who walked a couple of steps behind. "And that they use bright colors to keep people happier."

It wasn't working.

"Why so many suicides?" Macy asked. She carried a heavier load, partially because of random monster-hunting equipment, but mostly because she packed way more clothing than necessary.

"No sun. Lots of rain."

"Ugh. I hate the rain," Macy said with a sigh. "It destroys my hair."

With hair like Macy's, it didn't take much. At least her part of the job would keep her safe and snug indoors, or, at the very least, inside a vehicle. Miriam, on the other hand, would be spending days in the backwoods of southwest Washington, soaking up more rain and humidity than she could imagine. Her first paid job. No more stumbling into monsters. She would find this one *on purpose*.

Hopefully. If it even existed.

So few of the purported monsters actually did.

As they made their way to pick up their luggage, Miriam reviewed the facts in her head, each one hastening her pulse. She'd been hearing stories about this one for as long as she could remember, but no one had ever found it. Only a few blurry pictures and dubious eye-witness accounts. But that tended to be the kind of "facts" she had to work with in her line of work. If people had more evidence, it wouldn't be a mystery at all.

"I wish Tanner could have come," Macy said after a few minutes of silent walking.

"Me too. But Gabe needed him."

"Gabe needed you," Macy corrected. "And you declined."

Miriam didn't care for the reminder. She could have spent the weekend with her boyfriend and chose not to. Partly because she still didn't feel comfortable working with her father's company, but something even deeper pushed her away. Separated by hundreds of miles, she and Gabe had spent relatively little time together, mostly on dates or in group settings. She'd never spent the night with him—well, except for the cave back at Gray's Point. But to go on a whole weekend trip with him sounded downright terrifying. At least she could recognize that now: that she felt scared. A few years ago, she would have just been cold towards him without knowing why.

Progress.

They found their carousel and stopped in front of it. Eager to change the subject, Miriam asked, "They're sending someone to pick us up?"

"Yeah," Macy said, fishing through pockets until she pulled out a piece of paper. "They didn't give us his name. A backwoods guide, though, that'll be with us the whole time. I have a number to call if we can't find him."

Miriam nodded, just as she spotted her bag emerge from the rubber curtains into the cold white light of baggage claim. Macy's followed quickly behind, larger, pinker, and perfectly at home in the cavalcade of colors around them.

Luggage in hand, they took off towards the exit. Through the doors, Miriam searched through the sea of travelers to find someone who looked like a backwoods guide. It turned out that whether they be hipsters or lumberjacks, the Portland airport overflowed with people who could fit that description. Then her eyes caught a white sign with "Brooks" printed on it in block letters, held by someone who most decidedly did *not* look like a nature guide.

The man that Macy promised was actually a woman. Sitting patiently, just looking around, not even playing on a phone or anything. Streaks of blue hair reflected the light, in playful contrast with her shoulder-length raven bob.

When the woman noticed Miriam and Macy approaching, she stood and flashed a Cheshire smile. "Miriam? Macy?"

Miriam nodded, shifted some weight and offered a hand. The woman took it with a firm but clammy grip.

"Kimiko Akana. You can call me Kim. I'm your guide."

Babysitter, more like. Miriam hardly needed a guide to survive the woods. Kim held Miriam's gaze with almost black eyes. The stare was intense, causing Miriam to fight the urge to squirm. But also, mesmerizing. Miriam never really found other women pretty, but Kim's exotic features intrigued her.

Exotic? Don't be racist, Miriam.

"Where you from?" Miriam asked. Wanting to make sure that Kim knew the area well, Miriam truly just wanted to know if Kim had grown up in Portland, but quickly realized the question could be construed otherwise. Her cheeks flushed just as Macy jabbed an elbow into Miriam's ribs.

Kim's smile faded to quiet anger. "Portland."

Miriam stammered, "Yeah. That's what I meant. I didn't mean..."

Kim's face lightened. "I'm just messin' with ya. People ask me all the time. You get used to it." She flashed an infectious smile. "I can also help with some other burning questions. I don't speak Japanese. I hate math. And yes, of course I'm a disappointment to my parents. Backwoods guide is pretty far down the list from doctor or engineer."

"I-I-I didn't mean—obviously, you're American."

Macy placed a hand on Miriam's forearm, silently encouraging her to stop talking. This wasn't the first time—and most certainly wouldn't be the last—that Miriam stuck her foot in her mouth. Macy frequently had to save Miriam from herself.

"So, this is exciting," Macy interjected. "Our first real job. I'm so glad they hired us a guide. We've never been up here before, so it'll be a huge help having you along."

Uggh. Macy was so much better at this.

Kim switched her focus to Macy, regarded the redhead for a second, then nodded and winked.

"Honestly, you're pretty lucky. I'm one of the best."

She took hold of Miriam's suitcase and started heading for the door. Miriam was too flustered to stop her, instead letting herself fall behind to take up the rear. As Macy passed, her face telegraphed the very thing Miriam was telling herself.

Chill out.

Kim led them out of the terminal, across a few busy streets, and into a parking garage.

"Have you been a guide long?" Macy asked.

"A few years. Didn't like college. Decided to do this instead."

"So, you spend a lot of time out in the woods, then?"

"If you consider four or five days a week a lot, then yeah. Mostly I just do day hikes, though. It's rare that I have overnight clients. Should be fun."

"Oh, I'm not going with you."

"No? Just your awkward friend then?"

Kim shot back a teasing look, which Miriam felt certain she didn't receive properly.

"Uh... yeah. I don't do fieldwork anymore," Macy said.

"Why not?"

Macy didn't answer immediately. They waited in silence for an elevator.

"Bad experience?" Kim prodded.

"You could say that."

In fact, Macy had almost died at the hands of a madman and his murderous pigs. Miriam had barely convinced her to go on the hunt at all, but Macy's will seemed to overpower the fear. Perhaps all the monster hunts helped. Miriam liked to think so, to believe that her obsession had brought at least some good to her best friend's life. For the first few months, Macy had become despondent and inconsolable, crying more often, jumping at every sound. Miriam had had no idea what to do with all that, but with therapy and time, Macy had finally started to learn how to cope with the incident. Perhaps she'd never be over it, but she certainly seemed to be handling it better than before.

Kim led them to an ice-blue Prius and popped the trunk. Their stuff didn't look like it would fit, but somehow Kim made it work through an intricate game of luggage Tetris. When they went to get in the car, Macy staked a claim on the backseat and motioned Miriam to the front. Miriam tried to protest, but Macy tilted her head towards Kim and climbed into the backseat. Miriam took a deep breath and slid inside.

"So, the devil. At Misty Lake. Have you seen it?" Miriam asked.

Kim started the car, though it didn't really make a sound like a regular engine. "Of course. Lots of times."

"Seriously?"

"Yeah. If you spend any time at all out on Misty Lake, you'll see it eventually."

Miriam looked back at Macy, who shared her shock. A firsthand eyewitness to the monster in question? That never happened.

Kim continued before Miriam could respond. "You're not going to hurt it, are you?"

Miriam considered the question. She hadn't been hired to kill it, but her track record so far had forced her hand. She had no compunction with going that route if she had to, but the job was to find it. Catalog it. She doubted it would be that easy. Likely this thing came from a line of undiscovered animals, but people called them monsters for a reason.

"I hope not."

"Good," Kim said. "Because it's not dangerous."

"What do you think it is?"

Kim put the car in reverse, backed up, and got it going forward again. "Honestly? I'm not sure. My mom thinks it's a *kappa*, but she's never actually seen it."

A Japanese water demon? In Washington?

Oh. This was gonna be fun.

CHAPTER 2 – Macy

Macy tried to ignore the looming forest beside her. She hunkered into the back of the van and treated the windows as if they were solid, metal walls. She found it relatively easy to focus instead on the tech—the fancy laptop, the wires snaking up to small holes in the roof, connected to satellite dishes and antennae. She fiddled with the sturdy handsets that would connect her with Miriam and Kim as they ventured into the foreboding mists. She told herself that, within the walls of this white, nondescript vehicle, she could hide from whatever lurked in the woods—or, more precisely, whatever lurked in the memories of Hogg Run.

She'd been through therapy. God, so much of it. Almost a year, in fact. It had taken a while to find a therapist she connected with, but she'd found one and had made progress. Or so she thought. But in Rose Valley there were no ominous banks of towering trees. At Dobie Tech, there were hardly trees at all. A curious thing, to be afraid of trees. The very things that provided the oxygen she breathed. It was not the trees that had almost taken her life. Why should she blame the trees?

Behind her, Kim and Miriam sat on the van floor, their legs dangling onto the asphalt parking lot. Macy could see Kim's Prius parked alongside the van. While still inspecting the gadgets, Macy kept an eye on Miriam as she began the interrogation.

"So, what does it look like?"

Kim seemed uncomfortable with the question, wriggling her butt against the floor of the van as if she had to get situated first. She didn't look at Miriam when she answered. "Big. Hard to say. It's always at a distance."

"You haven't seen it, then?" Miriam prodded.

This caused Kim to look up. To lock eyes with Miriam. "Yes. I have seen it. It couldn't have been anything else. I haven't been up close to it, of course. That'd be dangerous. But in the water, swimming. Arching above the surface."

"Arching?"

Macy felt disconnected from the whole conversation, as if she wanted to participate but couldn't find the motivation. She was fairly certain, though, that Kim knew something more. Miriam wouldn't see it. Miriam was horrible at reading people. But Macy saw it. As clear as day. Kim may have been hired to help them find this thing, but she had a motive of her own. Macy would've bet anything on it.

"Yes." Kim spoke with hesitance now, pausing between her words. "And it's shiny. Slick."

"How many arches?"

"Does that matter?"

"Of course it matters." Miriam failed to hold back a sigh. "If it's multiple arches, then we may be dealing with a sea serpent. If it's just one arch, then maybe not."

"It's a lake," Macy said plainly. Both girls turned to look at her, neither of them amused. Macy held up a hand as if to say she was sorry for butting in.

"Of course, it wouldn't be a *sea* serpent, exactly. But there's no reason a giant serpent can't live in a lake. Actually, it's probably more likely they would live in a lake."

"Like the Loch Ness monster?" Kim asked.

Miriam gave a half-nod. Macy took it to mean Kim had it exactly half-right. "Sorta. Nessie does live in a lake. But most of the pictures and eyewitness reports describe it as more like a plesiosaur than a serpent."

Kim chewed her lip, then broke out in a bright smile. "Well I did *not* see a plesiosaur!"

"So how many arches then?"

Kim looked off into the woods in front of the van. "We should probably head out soon, yeah? It'd be nice to get to the lake before nightfall. Camping there would give us the best chance of seeing it."

Miriam shot an exasperated look at Macy, who shrugged.

"Macy, can you pull up our research?"

Macy nodded, relieved to have a job. She turned to the computer, where she navigated to their secure portal, typed a username, password, then a code from her phone. Miriam and Tanner had complained incessantly about all the extra security, but Macy insisted on it.

She brought up the folder on the Devil of Misty Lake. Most of the incident reports had been compiled by Miriam, so Macy didn't have them memorized.

"Whatcha looking for?"

"The one death," Miriam said.

Easy enough to find.

"We don't know for certain that the... devil... did that," Kim said. Calling it the devil seemed to make her uncomfortable.

"His girlfriend saw it happen. Why would she make that up?"

"Maybe she killed him and needed a scapegoat."

Glancing over the file, even Macy knew the response to that. "You think she mutilated and half-ate her own boyfriend just so she could sell the story?"

"Anything could have eaten his body after he was dead," Kim suggested. "Maybe they got in a fight or something."

"Cops never charged her with anything," Macy replied.

Miriam folded her arms across her chest and leaned back against the pillar of the door. "Kim's not wrong. We have to consider all of the possibilities."

"Thank you," Kim said with an air of vindication.

"Still, it's proof that if this thing does exist, it's dangerous. Deadly, even."

"But there's only the one death," Kim said. "Most of the other stories are mundane. Comical even."

Macy took the cue and closed the current file, bringing up instead a few of the lesser sightings. Mostly ripples in the water, or strange shapes running along the surface. No pictures of anything that Miriam hadn't deemed explicable. Despite it being Miriam's whole job to find monsters, sometimes it seemed like she looked for any excuse to prove they didn't exist. Macy supposed that was good science, but sometimes it only took the wind out of their sails.

Kim continued, "Like, one family reported that it came to their camp in the middle of the night and rooted through all their bags. Ate their food. Played with and deflated their football. That's not dangerous. Just curious."

Macy popped open a few more files until she found the account that Kim had referenced. "Only the kids saw it. Said it was a teddy bear."

Miriam nodded. "Right. So just a bear. Bears are weird. People get confused by them all the time, especially if they're mangy or walking on their hind legs."

"But they said it had whiskers," Kim added. "Bears don't have whiskers."

"True..." Miriam said, trailing off in thought.

Macy could almost see the wheels turning behind Miriam's clouded eyes. No doubt the entire catalog of cryptids now shuffled through her head, making comparisons and connections. She'd figure it out eventually. She always did. In truth, Macy worried much more that Kim would be Miriam's undoing.

As Miriam thought, Kim started unloading two backpacks from the front of the van. They were stuffed full, bedrolls and tents squished inside the nylon bags.

"It's getting late," Kim said. "We should head out so that we hit the lake before nightfall."

Macy turned back to her paltry watch station and grabbed two radios from the charge banks. She handed them both to Miriam, trusting one would make it to Kim.

As Kim worked, Macy tried to speak privately with Miriam.

"Don't let her get under your skin," Macy whispered. She felt a little like a mother sending her kid off to school.

"It's fine," Miriam said. "I just don't trust her. She's being obtuse."

Miriam always thought people were being obtuse, but in this case, she might have been right. Clearly, Kim had a motive of her own, and Macy wasn't entirely sure that motive included actually finding the devil in the lake. Still, taking Kim along was part of the contract, so Miriam didn't really have a choice.

"I'll be here on the radio for you, if you need anything."

Miriam nodded curtly, casting a sideways glance towards Kim. Macy felt a swell of dread in her chest. She was more than happy that it wasn't her going into the woods, but for her that same trepidation now extended to Miriam, as well.

Without thinking, she wrapped Miriam up in a hug.

"Be careful, okay?"

Miriam squirmed in her grip at first, but eventually relented and melted into the hug. Miriam hated such things, but Macy needed the reassurance. She knew she was being silly. Miriam could handle herself. She always managed to find the way out. She'd do the job, escape the monster, and be back to the van in no time.

Or she wouldn't.

"I'm always careful," Miriam said as she gently pushed out of the hug. "You know that."

Macy nodded sheepishly.

Kim strode over and offered a pack to Miriam. "Ready?"

"Ready."

The two women hoisted the backpacks over their shoulders and took off down a dirt path, marked only by a small stone pillar with no text. Macy sighed, climbed back into the van, and turned on some music.

Loud music.

CHAPTER 3 – Abby

Abby threw his arm off her like it burned. She never felt good the morning after giving in to her baser instincts. He barely stirred, mumbling something before rolling over in bed. She dressed quickly, sat down at the small desk, and powered up her laptop. The cheap hotel chair creaked. She checked the news, her email, then her "special" email in that order.

Nothing of note in any of those places. She hated waiting.

Spinning in her chair, she found Beatty still sleeping, his muscled chest exposed, reminding her why she always called him when she felt lonely. She grabbed a pen from the desk and threw it at him. It bounced off one of his biceps. He blinked wearily.

"You slept over," she said.

He pushed up on his elbows. "Yeah. So?"

"Get out."

He smiled at her. His smile wasn't particularly inviting or warm. She didn't even find him that attractive. He had a nice body earned from years of hunting in the most remote areas of the world, hauling guns and camping equipment up mountains and through forests. And he was always nearby. Abby couldn't really think of anything else redeeming about him.

Actually, he was loyal. She had to give him that. Maybe that meant something.

"Seriously?"

She nodded. "Seriously."

Beatty pushed himself out of bed, making no effort to dress quickly like she had. Wilson didn't demure, enjoying the tight lines of his body until he managed to slip on his boxers.

"This is dumb, you know."

"It's not dumb," she said. "It's setting a boundary."

"I'm not going to force you to marry me or something because we had sex. You know that, right?"

She didn't answer, but neither did she turn away. After he slipped on his t-shirt, he headed for the door. No shoes. He'd come barefoot.

"Breakfast?" he asked as he opened the door.

"Of course. One hour."

"You got it, boss."

Abby cringed slightly at the honorific as the hotel door slammed at Beatty's exit. She sighed. This always happened when the jobs got light. She preferred to keep moving. Keep hunting. Keep killing. Keep amassing wealth that she had absolutely no use for.

She stared at the closed door for a few minutes, lost in thought. Sometimes the briefest glimpse of the future she never had played across her mind, often in the oddest of times. She sighed and stood, then threw off the clothes she'd just put on and started the water for a hot shower. Just before she stepped into the tub, her laptop dinged.

She had a ding for everything, and this ding was the most important of all. Not bothering to cover herself, she scuttled back over to the chair, sat down, and unlocked the laptop, quickly scanning the email that had come in. Her heart sank.

A job was a job. It's what she did and what she'd do.

She responded tersely: *On it. Will be at location within 24 hours.*

Wilson leaned back in the chair and breathed deeply, the mesh poking and prodding her bare back. Back to her past, then. Somehow, she always thought this might happen. It was her past that led her to this line of work in the first place. She'd tried this job before—back before it was a job—back when it was a passion. She'd failed then, but now she had experience... and money.

She grabbed her cell phone from the desk and dialed up Beatty.

He answered almost immediately. "I know you don't want me back in your bed this quickly."

"We got a new assignment. Check your email and make the arrangements."

"Oh shit. Really?"

"Yep."

"Where to this time?"

"Washington."

A slight pause on the line. She knew why.

"How long's it been?" he finally asked.

"Fifteen years."

"That's a long time."

"Yeah. Long enough. I gotta go back eventually."

"You really don't."

She didn't answer, as her mind took her back to memories she couldn't shake. He didn't know how close to home he'd hit. How close to home she'd have to go for this mission.

"Make the arrangements. Breakfast in an hour still."

"You got it, but..."

She didn't need this. She didn't need Beatty to be... human.

"Abby. Seriously. We can take the next one."

"Don't call me that. We'll take this one. It's fine."

It wasn't fine.

CHAPTER 4 – Miriam

Miriam did not often become disoriented. Kim kept a steady, clipped pace, leading them down a path not quite wild, but certainly unkempt. Miriam couldn't be sure she'd be able to follow it without a guide, certainly not without any knowledge that the path existed. The dense trees, creeping moss, and cloying underbrush created the illusion of an endless abyss of green, stretching unbroken in every direction. Not exactly the type of woods to which she had become accustomed, but then, Miriam trusted herself to adapt to any situation.

There *was* a path. Sort of. But often, Miriam didn't see it until they'd already stepped foot onto it. She took in every nuance of the forest. Every tree. Every stump. She studied the way the moss changed from a bright green to an almost gray. This gave her a clue about the way the sun came in. A clue that probably provided her absolutely no actionable information other than to keep her mind occupied, to make her feel as if she could navigate this maze on her own if she had to.

"So, mostly there's only black bears out here," Kim said suddenly. "Occasionally some grizzlies, though. They roam really far, and it's happened."

"Okay," Miriam said flatly. She already knew that, of course. One did not venture into the woods without understanding the local predators.

"Black bears are smaller. If you run into one, you should make yourself as big and loud as possible. It'll probably run."

"I know."

Kim glanced back with a smirk. "Oh. Well, of course you do. So, you also know that for grizzlies, you should—"

"Curl up in a ball. Play dead. Hope they get bored."

The back of Kim's blue hair bounced in a nod, but she didn't slow her pace. "Sorry. I usually spend the hike out to the lake educating people on how to survive out here. I've never had a client that already knew everything."

Miriam didn't reply, instead ruminating on whether she knew everything. Not everything she decided, but probably more than this girl.

When Kim offered no further topic of conversation, Miriam returned to the stillness of the forest. At first, she thought it quiet. Society didn't hum here. No road noise. No thrumming of factories or whirring of electricity. But the forest wasn't really quiet; just filled with much more pleasant noises. Birds chirped above. Unseen animals skittered across the tree branches. The *whoosh* of the foliage against their legs sounded alien and foreign, and Miriam suddenly became hyper-aware of how unwelcome they were here. She'd never had that thought before. That maybe she didn't belong among the wild animals.

After a few more minutes of silence, Kim asked, "Dating anyone?"

Miriam responded quickly, as if on autopilot. "No." She backtracked. "Yes. I mean yes. Gabe. His name is Gabe."

For the first time, Kim stopped walking and turned. A huge grin painted her face. "You sure about that?"

Miriam felt the blood rush to her cheeks. Small talk was the absolute worst, especially about this. About Gabe. It made her skin crawl.

"It's still new."

"Uh-huh. Well, I'm sure he's a nice boy." Kim said.

Kim stared at Miriam as if she expected something else, but Miriam froze, staying silent until Kim resumed the march into the woods. Ahead, a barely worn path veered to the left. Kim didn't take it, but Miriam slowed as she approached, embarrassment urging her to maybe take the left, get lost in the woods, and become a mountain-woman. She thought better of it and hurried to close the gap instead.

Searching for a way to cut through the awkwardness, Miriam tried to turn the tables. "What about you? Got a boyfriend?"

No slowing this time, so Miriam couldn't see Kim's face when she said, "How do you know I like boys?"

At that moment, Miriam decided that Kim was what Macy would call a troll.

"Well. I... I guess I don't. How did you know I like boys?"

"Gabe is usually a male name, but I suppose it could be short for Gabriella. Are you dating a Gabriella?" Kim said, still moving forward, one foot in front of the other, as if the ground were smooth and flat and easy to traverse. To be sure, the conversation provided a tougher path than the forest for Miriam.

"But you asked if I had a boyfriend first."

"Did I? I'm pretty sure I just asked if you were dating anyone."

Miriam rewound the conversation, trying to remember exactly how it'd started.

Unprompted Kim continued, "I just think love can't be constrained by gender labels. When I do find someone, it doesn't matter to me what gender they are. It matters *who* they are. Ya know?"

Miriam didn't know and she didn't want to know—she wanted to exit the conversation as soon as possible. Though a part of her did find the notion interesting. Miriam had spent zero time thinking about love or what it should mean or how she should choose it. Did she love Gabe? She decided not. Not yet anyway. Maybe she was incapable of love. She had a complicated relationship with her dad that she'd be hesitant to call love. Maybe Tanner or Macy. Maybe she loved them. Maybe.

"Yeah," was all Miriam managed, before asking, "Are there any wolves out here?"

There weren't any, of course, but wolves were preferable to love.

"No. There are some in the east, especially as you get closer to Yellowstone. But not down here."

"That's good."

Whether because she took the hint, or because the conversation had run its course, Kim fell silent again, still trudging through the underbrush as if it parted specifically for her. Miriam followed, thankful for the silence, trying to keep her mind from nagging her about love and what it meant and whether she was normal. She turned her focus to the monster they were out here to find. The devil.

Surely no devil. Probably an animal. If lucky, maybe a rare or undiscovered one. Miriam believed in the supernatural even less than she believed in love. As time had gone on, however, she found that money started to be the bigger focus. She'd graduate soon, and her attempts at monetizing her skillset had largely failed, with only a few odd jobs, none of which paid enough to sustain her in the long term. This job, though. This one paid well. And she hoped with success she'd find other clients.

After another fifteen minutes of walking, Kim slowed up. So lost in thought, Miriam didn't even register why until they stepped into a clearing with a view of a huge, mossy lake. The forest surrounded it on all sides, giving it the feel of some secret grotto, though not an attractive one. Debris littered the edges, mostly sticks and moss and leaves and, largest of all, a few entire logs—as if the trees had come here to die. She wondered briefly how that even happened, but Kim jumped in before Miriam could ponder it too long.

"So, this is it." She spread her arms out, twisting right, then left to encompass the entire body of water. "Misty Lake. Home of the..."

She trailed off. Miriam had noticed that Kim didn't seem to like calling it a devil, but she also didn't appear to have an alternate word for it.

"Home of the anomaly," Miriam offered.

Kim smiled. "Yes. The anomaly. I like that."

Hopefully not an anomaly for much longer.

Miriam looked around to the small patch of dry land before them, the grass smoothed out and even worn bare in places. "So, is this where we make camp?"

Kim nodded. "Yup. This is where I usually set up. It provides a great view of the lake, and we can use the trees to hang our stuff."

Miriam went straight to work without any more prompting, unrolling her one-person tent and setting up with expert ease. She took the food she had and shoved it all in a bear bag before tying it to a rope and looping it over the nearest tree branch. Hopefully, she pulled it high enough that bears wouldn't be able to get to it. Kim did her own thing during this, mostly ending at the same result. Miriam appreciated the focused quiet time.

In the end, the entrance to Kim's tent faced Miriam's, with only a few feet between them. The charred firepit from Kim's previous expeditions sat between them at a safe distance. This would do nicely.

Miriam was ready to work. "So, I assume the devil-thing is nocturnal, or at the very least crepuscular. Most animals are. We should get some rest now, so we can stay up to watch for it."

Kim nodded blankly.

"What times of day have you most often seen it?" Miriam asked.

Kim glanced out over the lake before answering. "All times of day. Morning most often. When my campers are still sleeping."

"So crepuscular, probably. Good to know. That means we might catch it at dusk, or shortly after nightfall."

"Yeah... maybe," Kim murmured.

"Okay. Well, I'll see you in a few hours then," Miriam said, crouching into her tent.

She zipped up the door and rolled out her sleeping bag. She laid down on top of it, and propped her hands up behind her head. She listened. To the trees. To the birds. To sporadic splashes of water. And for Kim, who seemed eternally silent. But Miriam knew one thing.

Kim never entered her tent.

CHAPTER 5 – Abby

The small plane banked, giving Abby a full view of her past. The water only shimmered in a few places, the sun mostly muted by the moss or reflected by the rotting, slime-covered logs. Acid burned in her throat as she actively worked to force the memories away. This is why she'd gone into this business in the first place. She couldn't afford to get angsty about it now. Secretly, she'd hoped that she'd have this opportunity one day, but somehow it always seemed far away, like she needed to do one more thing first.

Now, as she stared out over the forest that took her future from her, she realized she'd been avoiding it. She should have done this long ago.

Beatty's voice echoed in her headphones: "You okay, Wilson?"

Abby only grunted. Beatty, thankfully, took the hint.

After a full circle around Misty Lake, the pilot's voice came next. "I'm gonna put us down a mile out. There's a farm out there with a makeshift runway. That okay?"

When Abby didn't answer, Beatty took control. "Yeah. That's good."

She could feel him staring at her, his eyes boring into her soul, seeing the parts that she tried so hard to hide. Almost instinctively, Abby reached down to her left hand and felt for the ring. She rotated it around, pointing the diamond inward, then squeezed as hard as she could. Sharp pain flooded into her palm as she took a deep breath and let the physical pain crowd out the emotional. She preferred physical pain. Perhaps that was why she'd taken up with Beatty. He was good at that.

As the plane turned away from the lake, Abby felt her breath slowing, her heartbeat calming. She was always an out-of-sight, out-of-mind kind of gal. With most things, anyway.

She turned away from the window and forced a smile. "This one should be fun."

Beatty didn't look at her. "Or cathartic at least, I hope."

She regretted ever telling him about her past. It just happened on one of those lazy mornings after a job, before the next one. Being that physically vulnerable, she supposed, encouraged emotional vulnerability, as well. Other than being overly concerned about her well-being, he'd taken it well. Didn't seem to doubt her resolve or strength. Still seemed to trust her. In their line of work, a lack of trust could easily lead to a lack of life.

She felt the pressure in her ears as they began to descend. Slight from the already-low altitude, but still there all the same. Before long, the plane touched down in a patch of flattened grass, the frame squeaking and rumbling, indicating it may not have been flight-worthy to begin with. After it rolled to a stop and the engine ceased, Abby threw off her headphones and stepped out into the damp Washington air.

No rain. Yet. But it would come. It always did.

Beatty dutifully started unloading their gear, while Abby approached the pilot.

"You'll be here when we get back?"

He took off his sunglasses to reveal cobalt eyes—a young, cocky looking man that fit the exact description of a fighter pilot. But this plane was about as far removed from a fighter jet as a house cat was from a tiger. She wondered what kind of mediocrity he'd exhibited in his earlier years to have earned this gig. She had to admit, though, that landing on makeshift runways in cleared-out forestland probably wasn't all that easy. Maybe he was actually a savant.

"Contract says I don't leave until you do," he said with a bleached-white smile. Crow's feet near his eyes indicated that maybe he was older than she first suspected.

"Interesting. Well, you're not coming with us."

"Of course not. I don't even know what you're here for," he said. "Also part of the contract."

Abby nodded curtly. "Good."

"I'll just hole up here until you get back. We've got enough fuel to get us back to Seattle at least, and from there you're on your own."

Abby never stayed for the aftermath. She'd do the job, radio her location, and let the company handle extraction. After something like this, all she ever wanted was a long shower and a day of sleep. Maybe more.

"What's your name again?" she asked.

"Radley."

With his response, she realized she'd never known his name.

"All right. Thanks Mr. Radley. We'll be back as soon as we can."

"Oh no. Radley's my first name. Last name is Furey."

People actually had the last name of Furey, outside of comics books? Wait. His name was Rad Furey? What kind of parent...

"Ok. I'll remember that."

How could anyone forget it?

"Good luck, Ms. Wilson. With whatever you're doing."

"Thanks."

Abby trudged to the back of the plane and lifted her pack onto her shoulders. Beatty did the same before handing her a rifle, which she hung from her right shoulder. The weight didn't bother her anymore. When she'd started, Beatty carried more than his fair share, but now they split the gear evenly. Far more than a typical hiker, but then they were here to do more than relax. These missions were anything but relaxing.

Without a word, they headed towards the tree line, shoulder to shoulder. Beatty stole glances at her but didn't talk. She could tell that he was worried about how this mission might affect her. At least she had him. At least he would see the mission complete even if she froze up. She didn't think she would. Not this time. What was all the training for, if not to exorcise her fear?

She could never get back what she'd lost. But she sure as hell could take revenge for what was taken.

CHAPTER 6 – Macy

Macy put her phone down next to the laptop and leaned back in the chair to stretch her back. Instagram, TikTok, Twitter. She'd exhausted them all, and boredom had started to set in. She even checked Facebook, which she hardly did anymore. Only old people hung out there. Though she did get a glimpse of yet another romantic getaway for her mom and Jake.

Ew.

Dutifully, she'd liked the post anyway, then scrolled down, sparingly giving just one more *Like* to a picture of Kat and Olivia. She missed Olivia sometimes.

She'd tried having a conversation with her boyfriend, Tanner, but the boy was hopeless when it came to texting. Technology hadn't been coveted in his house growing up, and he could never remember to keep his cell phone anywhere nearby. She found it endlessly frustrating, but whenever he came around with those blue eyes and bulging biceps, she forgot to be mad at him. He was old-fashioned, uninterested in technology, and always on the go. They didn't have any other jobs, but if he wasn't helping Gabe, Tanner would surely just go make something up: looking for some local monster that would turn out to be a possum or an owl.

Macy looked over at the small cot in the back of the van, considering just going to bed. The moody, cloud-muted sun, however, pierced the windshield and warned her away. Sleeping during the day would mean being wide awake in the middle of the night. Nothing worse than that. Especially when right next to a creepy forest. She pushed away the memories and the fear, not permanently, but long enough for her mind to move on to other things.

They'd talked a good game when getting the job. How they had a field operative and an operations specialist. But really, the former just meant "looks for monsters," and the latter had no concrete definition. They'd never had a well-paid and organized job like this. So far, *operations specialist* seemed to mean "surf the internet and try not to go insane with boredom."

Desperate for some fresh air, Macy opened the sliding door and looked out into the wet parking lot. She sunk down to the floor of the van and sat with her legs hanging out. The sky didn't look very threatening as it had when they'd arrived, but clouds still monopolized the view, with precious few breaks in between.

It was kind of peaceful when she could disassociate it from Hogg Run.

A low humming interrupted the peace, growing in intensity until a plane flew overhead. A small one, awfully close to the ground. It sped away over the forest towards where Miriam and Kim had gone, before banking back and flying over again. Macy didn't really care what it was up to, but it gave her something to pay attention to for the short time that she could see it. Maybe people took sightseeing tours or something.

Behind her, a radio crackled. Miriam's voice echoed out into the walls of the van. "Hey Macy, you there? Over."

Macy scrambled back to her table, grabbed the handset, and depressed the button. "Hey Mir. How's it going out there?"

Several seconds passed before Miriam finally responded. "You have to say 'over' so I know you're done talking. Over."

"Why?"

A bigger pause this time. "Because that's how it works. Over."

Macy laughed quietly. She'd always seen people do it in the movies, and surely there must have been a reason, but Miriam's strict adherence to the rules amused Macy anyway.

"Fine. How's it going out there?" She took special care to emphasize the next part. "Over."

"Good, I guess. Just some downtime before nightfall. Over."

"How's Kim? Over."

"You can just say 'over.' You don't have to make a production out of it. Over."

Macy laughed, vowing to be even more over-the-top with it going forward.

"Ok. Sorry. How's Kim? Ohhhhhh-*verrrrrr*."

Miriam sighed dramatically on the other end. "Wouldn't know. She disappeared. Over."

Disappeared? That seemed odd.

"Do I need to call someone?"

Several seconds passed with no response, then Macy remembered to say: "Over."

Instant response. "Nah. I'm sure she'll be back. She knows her way around. She left all her stuff, but I feel like she's up to something. Over."

"Maybe she just needed to pee. Over."

"Maybe. Over." Miriam didn't sound convinced.

"Any sign of the devil yet? Over."

"Not yet. We're going to look for it at dusk, when it's more likely to be active. Over."

"Sounds like a plan. It's been pretty quiet here. A plane flew over pretty low, but it left again. Haven't seen any hikers. No chatter on the internet about any sightings recently or anything."

Macy waited for a response, then sighed. "Over."

"Okay. Well, keep us posted if anything happens. Kim just got back. I'll check in later. Over."

Feeling especially cheeky, Macy replied, "Ten-four, good buddy. Copy that. Check. Check. Over and out."

She could actually feel Miriam rolling her eyes on the other end.

***

After talking to Miriam, Macy felt a little bit more upbeat. She decided to take a walk, carefully locking up the van with the keys Kim provided. She didn't dare venture into the tree line, so instead walked aimlessly around the parking lot, up the road a bit, and back a few times. The temperature really was lovely, and without any rain, she sort of liked it. Texas basically never got like this except maybe one or two days a year. Mostly it was hot or pouring rain, most commonly at the same time.

On her third lap through the parking lot, Macy detected voices. Up the road, she thought. She stopped and listened, but couldn't make out the words yet. Hikers, probably. It was bound to happen. Surely lots of people came out here. Why else would there be a whole parking lot?

Still, she owed it to Miriam to report any hikers headed their way, so she stopped and waited. She pulled out her phone to act disinterested.

Before long, two people came into her peripheral. She glanced towards them, careful to turn back to her phone quickly. Her eyes didn't even register what she saw before her heart started pounding. She'd seen hikers before, and these two weren't hikers. They looked more like military.

Out here, though? Why?

Macy looked back and mumbled a greeting as they grew closer. The woman ignored her. The man smiled and nodded. Not a word from either of them. She let them pass, remembering as much as she could. Probably nothing to worry about. Some hunters went a little overboard with their gear. Did they allow hunting here? Maybe.

Once they passed, Macy looked closer. They each carried a scary looking rifle, and black backpacks with lots of metal on them. The word *tactical* came to mind, with all sorts of things swinging from the clips along the back. Binoculars, some sort of goggles, knives. A lot of dangerous stuff.

When the woman glanced back, Macy quickly looked back to her phone. She listened to their boots crunching against the gravel parking lot, waiting until she could hear them no more. She scrabbled for breath as her chest heaved.

Calm down, Macy. Why do you always have to assume the worst now?

Indeed, she had once been an eternal optimist. After Hogg Run, though, she saw danger in everything, no matter how mundane. And two hikers armed to the teeth could hardly be described as mundane.

She idly scrolled around her phone for a few minutes before turning back towards the van. No sign of anyone else. Taking a deep breath, she headed back to the van, not quite in a sprint, but certainly a vigorous power-walk. She fumbled for the keys, unlocked the door and scrambled inside to reach for the radio.

She pushed the button.

"Miriam. You there?"

She waited.

"Who's Miriam?"

Panic rising, Macy spun to see the two hikers looking into the van. The woman's eyes darted around, soaking up every piece of kit. The man smiled at her. The kind of smile that might appear friendly enough in any other circumstance.

Macy didn't answer the question.

"For that matter, who are you?"

She decided to play dumb, a skill she'd honed quite well over the years. She forced a smile, as radiant as she could manage. "I'm Macy. So nice to meet you. And you are?"

She offered a hand. The man smirked and took it, giving it three quick pumps before letting go.

"Name's John Beatty. People call me Beatty."

Macy didn't expect that. Dangerous people didn't freely give their names out.

"This is Abby Wilson."

The woman met Macy's gaze with a cool stare before quickly nodding a greeting. Something about the name rang in her head. It seemed significant. Important. Something she knew but couldn't quite remember.

Abby spoke, "This is a lot of gear. What are you and Miriam out here for?"

"Umm..." Macy scrambled for a plausible excuse. She wasn't doing anything illegal. In fact, they were hired to do it. She had no reason to lie, but something urged her to do so anyway. "On our way south to run some exercises with a platoon there."

A platoon? Macy tried not to visibly wince as she realized how ridiculous she sounded.

"Exercises, huh?" Abby's lips turned up slightly at the edges. "You military?"

Macy knew she couldn't pull off a lie like that. Not in jeans and a t-shirt that showed off her midriff. "No. Just contractors."

"I see. So..." Abby trailed off, her eyes scanning the inside of the van again, this time for show. "Just stopping here for a rest?"

Macy nodded.

"Is Miriam out there?" Abby thumbed to the tree line.

Macy didn't respond.

As if her eyes could produce deadly lasers, Abby stared into Macy's eyes. Macy withered at the gaze, regretting ever trying to lie in the first place. They'd been invited. She had nothing to hide.

"Fine," Macy said with a sigh. "We're cryptozoologists... monster hunters, kinda. We're here to look for the Devil of Misty Lake. It's a local legend."

The two interlopers shared a look. Macy thought she might have seen surprise on Abby's face, but it disappeared too quickly to know for sure.

The radio crackled. "Sorry, Macy. I'm here. Forgot the radio. Heard you from across the lake. Over."

Macy spun to grab the handset, but she never made it. A cold hand grabbed her wrist, easily keeping her from completing the task. Abby didn't look particularly happy to be holding onto her when Macy turned to meet her gaze, but that didn't cause Abby to release the grip.

"I don't think it's in our best interest for you to do that," Abby said.

Something inside Macy fell away. Her confidence. Her strength. It all melted in an instant. She sat frozen in fear. It was happening again. Her eyes burned. Tears streamed down her hot cheeks.

Abby motioned with her head towards the forest. "Let's take a walk."

CHAPTER 7 – Miriam

Miriam matched eyes with Kim across the extinguished campfire.

"The Loch Ness Monster is certainly the most famous lake cryptid," Miriam said. "Name another."

With dusk quickly approaching, they were just killing time now. Macy hadn't answered since she'd radioed earlier, but Miriam didn't give it much thought, assuming she'd just gone on a walk, or to use the bathroom. Macy didn't always take these things as seriously as Miriam would have liked, but the frustration from that was only a minor annoyance at this point. If something important came up, Miriam felt confident that Macy would radio again.

Miriam still hadn't forgotten Kim's vanishing act. When Kim had returned, Miriam had asked where she'd been, but Kim only offered a vague reply that didn't bring comfort. *Walking.* But why? They'd just walked so far to get to the camp. Why walk more? Miriam didn't feel right bringing up any more such questions, though.

"Champy?"

Miriam smiled, impressed. She liked this conversation. She could command this one.

"Yep. In Lake Champlain, between New York and Vermont. Basically the same as Nessie based on eye-witness accounts."

"Do you think that's what you're gonna find out here?" Kim asked, a strangely amused look on her face.

Miriam glanced out across the water, considering the question. "Not really. Not enough water for something that big."

"What if it could walk?"

Miriam nodded. "Maybe then. There are some people who claim to have seen Nessie walking at least. I'd expect anything that big living in this lake would have to move to other waters occasionally for food. There are other types of lake monsters, though. They aren't all purported to be plesiosaurs."

"Well, that's about all I know," Kim said, her teasing eyes glittering. "I'm not a monster nerd like you."

Though Kim had proven quite adept at getting under Miriam's skin, this particular jab didn't do the trick. Though Kim implied that being a "monster nerd" was an insult, Miriam actually wore the distinction with a badge of honor. She'd yet to meet anyone that could match her encyclopedic knowledge of cryptids. It honestly felt like the only topic of conversation she ever felt comfortable discussing.

"Well, maybe you should be if you're going to live out here with one."

"I don't live out here," Kim said.

"Might as well." The comment came off a little sharper than she intended, colored by Kim's strange disappearing act earlier.

"Well there's the Monster of Elizabeth Lake. It's a real weird one down in California."

"How so?" Kim asked, her lips turned up as if she were about to laugh. Ever-teasing, ever-playful. It unnerved Miriam.

"If witnesses are to be believed?" Miriam asked rhetorically. "Bat wings, giraffe neck, six legs. Supposedly smells really bad."

Kim made a show of sniffing the air. "Smells great here."

"True. Probably not our cryptid, but California is reasonably nearby, and sometimes these descriptions are off."

"Do you really think the... anomaly... is a cryptid that's been seen elsewhere?"

Miriam shrugged. "Sure. Stands to reason. I suspect a lot of these cryptids are the same, just in different parts of the world. Eyewitnesses are unreliable and colored by their own culture. Ogopogo, Nessie, Mussie, Champy. I think they're all the same, or at least closely related. Sure, you've got the outliers like the Dobhar-chú in Ireland, but most everything else is described as something approximating either a plesiosaur or an eel."

When Kim didn't respond with anything other than a nod, Miriam realized she had hoped to be questioned on the Irish water hound. Perhaps Kim had grown tired of the conversation. Miriam sometimes had a hard time reading the cues, especially when talking about her favorite subject.

After a few beats of silence, Kim chimed back in. "What about a kelpie?"

Miriam made no effort to hide her disdain. "A shape-shifting river horse? That's just folklore. Not a real cryptid."

"How do you know? They can take human form, after all."

"Because it just doesn't make sense."

"I could be a kelpie," Kim suggested with a quick wink. "Maybe I'm the devil of Misty Lake."

"Well, we're not in Scotland for one." Miriam looked down at Kim's sneakers. "And you don't seem to have hooves. Also, you're not trying to seduce me."

"Am I not?"

Miriam felt the blood rush to her cheeks, hopefully masked by the dim light of the waning sun. "I hope not. I'd rather not have my entrails eaten."

Kim's smile grew so big that it glowed, her deep brown eyes twinkling. Miriam had given the troll some bait, hadn't she? She could muster no better response than to awkwardly stare at the ground.

"Almost dusk," Miriam said, motioning to the sky.

Only a hint of the sun peeked out above the trees. Miriam looked longingly at the black ash of the previous campfires. The warmth would have been nice, but they'd intentionally not started the fire, hoping to be as discreet as possible. Better chances of an encounter, Miriam figured.

"Ok," Kim said, backing off her playful assault. "What do we do?"

Miriam got up and rummaged through her backpack until she found two pairs of small binoculars. She tossed one pair to Kim, easily and gracefully caught.

"Now we wait."

***

Though the moon remained elusive, the clouds allowed more of its light to filter through than Miriam might have expected. The trees stood as silhouettes, guardians of the lake. Miriam and Kim had sat through dusk without so much as a ripple. They'd need to start a fire soon if they intended to start one at all, but she worried doing so would ruin their chances.

Kim sat diligently beside her, sending her twinkling gaze across the lake. She seemed content. Happier as the minutes turned into hours.

Reluctant to give up for the night, Miriam whispered. "Should we make a fire?"

Kim looked at her, the whites of her eyes apparent in the dim light. "Sure."

The suggestion seemed to be enough. Kim took to work immediately, clearly practiced at the ritual of stacking the sticks and logs just right. Flames shot up in only a matter of minutes, and within ten, they had a small, cozy campfire, perfectly built so as not to rage but to crackle, to throw dancing shadows across the wall of trees. Miriam hadn't realized how cold she was until she sat next to that fire.

"We still have dawn," Miriam said. "We need to be up early."

"*You* need to be up early," Kim replied. "I'm just a guide, remember?"

Miriam looked at Kim across the fire, trying to determine whether Kim meant it as a joke. She couldn't tell.

"Okay. Well, I'll be up early then."

Kim nodded, a stern and serious look across her face. Too stern. Too serious. The kind of forced expression someone might use when they were attempting to...

That Cheshire grin spread across her face again, her white teeth striking against the darkness. "I'm kidding. Of course I'll get up with ya. Geez. I'm not that mean."

Maybe not mean, but certainly obtuse at times. Did Kim get this way with everyone, or was there just an incompatibility of personality? Miriam didn't get along with that many people. She had to at least entertain the possibility that their communications difficulties stemmed from her, not Kim.

Miriam's heart jumped at the crying of an animal. She couldn't immediately place what it was—it sounded like a baby mammal of some sort. Her head spun towards the sound just as it dissipated. It sounded close. And loud. Especially for a baby.

Kim just shrugged when Miriam turned back to the fire.

The cry echoed through the forest again, sending Miriam to her feet. Certainly not the cryptid she came to look for, but something in trouble. Curiosity overtook her as she reached down for a flashlight and headed towards the cries.

"Hey, wait up," Kim hollered. Miriam didn't slow down.

Miriam tried to be relatively quiet, but the underbrush whooshed past her legs, snapping back into place. Branches slapped against one another, creating enough sound that any creature would be able to hear them coming.

She stopped. She needed another clue. Miriam became aware of her heart beating. Of her chest rising and falling. She quieted herself as best she could.

Kim caught up, somehow moving through the underbrush more quietly, but not in total silence. She stopped behind Miriam.

Miriam held up one finger meant to keep Kim quiet. Kim obeyed.

After thirty seconds, Miriam's breathing had slowed. She listened for the sounds of the forest, but heard barely any. Something had spooked the local wildlife into silence.

Again, she heard the cry. She crept forward for its length, following her ears. Ahead she saw a clearing. The sound had to be coming from there.

Trying hard not to rush and make more noise than she had to, Miriam advanced to the edge of the tree line, stopping at the lip of a depression in the forest floor. A big one, by the looks of it. If she'd fallen in, getting out would have been challenging. She tried to tease out the purpose of this thing. Of where it had come from, why it was there.

"A trap," she whispered to Kim.

Having not yet employed her flashlight, Miriam switched it on, the beam shining downward. Slowly she lifted it, the spotlight inching across the floor of the depression. All manner of detritus littered the floor. The light reflected brightly back into her eyes as it crossed over... aging bone.

Yes, surely a trap, though not the deep, perfectly dug type she might have imagined. This thing was far too large to cover over with leaves and twigs to fool a passerby into stumbling into it. It seemed more like the work of a giant doodlebug—more appropriately called an antlion. She remembered fishing the small insects out of their conical traps as a child, though the floor of this trap lay mostly flat.

The cry rang out again, this time so close that Miriam instinctively snapped her flashlight to the sound. She expected an infant, but instead saw a full-grown otter. It skittered quickly around the opposite edge of the depression, with no way out.

Kim squealed, somehow in a whisper. "Awww. We have to get it out of there."

Miriam ran the flashlight around the edge of the hole. It didn't look to be more than six-foot deep. Certainly, with the help of someone up top, she'd be able to get out. She gave a sharp glance back.

"Okay, you'll have to help me back up," Miriam said, abandoning the whisper entirely. This otter couldn't run away from them, and even if it did, it wasn't the creature they were looking for, anyway.

Kim nodded. Miriam turned and tested the edge of the depression with the toe of her sneaker. Not sandy and loose like a doodlebug hole. Turning her ankles at painful angles, she shuffled down, almost in a full sprint to keep her footing. Once on the bottom, her heart fluttered with a brief jolt of panic.

She inched across, using the flashlight to avoid some of the larger chunks of leftover animals and accumulated foliage. The otter ahead skittered. She could hear its feet pattering across the dirt. Flashbacks of saving a cheetah cub in Rose Valley bounced around her head—the memory of the day her brother died. She twisted back towards Kim, driven by a need to verify the woman's safety. Kim was safe, of course. Why wouldn't she be? Miriam crouched down and shined the flashlight towards the otter. Its bright eyes curiously judged her.

"Hey fella. Did you fall in?" she said, feeling kind of dumb. The otter couldn't understand her.

She held out a hand, the way she might when approaching a cat or dog. She didn't know a ton about otters, but knew enough to know they could be dangerous if threatened.

The otter crept forward, stretching its neck to sniff the air. When it got close enough, she'd snatch it up, sprint to the nearest edge, and toss it into the woods. Hopefully she could do all that before it could cause too much damage. She remained patient as it sniffed the ground, slowly taking one step at a time. Like cats, otters were often slaves to curiosity, and Miriam surely made for an interesting investigation, especially if this one had never seen a human before.

The otter took another step and Miriam's ears perked up. Leaves moved nearby. Knowing she couldn't afford to move, she whispered back at Kim. "Is that you?"

"No. It's..."

The way her voice fell off told Miriam all she needed to know. She stood up in a flash, the otter breaking away towards the darkness. She drove her beam up ahead just in time to see something emerge from the undergrowth, coiling and slinking. It moved almost silently. Miriam stumbled backwards, pointing the flashlight towards Kim. Towards her escape.

The ground shook as the thing moved into the pit. She could hear the otter crying again, its high-pitched whine cutting into the night. Then, from behind her, she heard a sound that she'd never heard in her life. Not a growl, or a bark, or a roar, but it rumbled into her bones. She could feel its hot breath.

She'd found the devil.

Also a slave to curiosity, Miriam spun around, backpedaling towards Kim and shining the flashlight at the devil. The beam didn't illuminate its entire frame. She didn't see a face. Only its back as it turned around, stepped out of the pit as if it were a rain puddle, and crashed through the brush away from her.

She fell, her foot catching on a rotting femur, then quickly scrambled to her feet. Kim crouched on the edge of the pit and offered a hand. Miriam took it, borrowing some of Kim's strength to walk up the sloping wall. Slight in frame, Miriam felt sure that the twenty pounds of muscle that she had over Kim would prove challenging. Miriam looked up to see Kim's bicep straining, a grimace on her face. She didn't falter though, and Miriam soon found herself standing beside her trail guide.

Sweeping the area with the flashlight, Miriam searched for any sign of the otter. It was gone. Survival instinct made way for excitement as Miriam realized this trap might have been made by the devil itself.

"Where is it?" Kim said, her voice shaking.

"I don't know," Miriam replied. "Eaten, I assume."

As big as that thing was, a single otter would hardly make a meal. Miriam's mind raced, collating information.

"This is so great," she said. "We can rule out so many cryptids now."

"You almost got eaten," Kim said, the usual twinkle of her eye diminished. "And you're thinking about classifying it?"

Miriam might have blushed if her cheeks weren't already flush from the encounter. She wouldn't apologize for geeking out over this. It's why she'd come. Sifting through everything she wanted to do and think about and plan for, Miriam never once considered packing up and leaving.

The devil was real. And she was going to find it.

CHAPTER 8 – Macy

The walk had turned into more of a hostage situation.

Macy couldn't really decide, though, if it fit the classical definition, as her captors didn't seem interested in any sort of payment. They dragged her through the woods, not caring much when she stumbled over an exposed tree root. She managed not to fall, and kept her word to not scream, which, she assumed, was why they didn't gag her. Only her hands were bound, and in front.

They stopped in a small clearing, where they pushed Macy to the ground, up against a tree. Her two captors exchanged words that Macy couldn't make out, then the man—Beatty—stalked off alone. The woman came over and knelt in front of her. Macy tried to hide the fear in her wide, green eyes, but knew she couldn't.

What did the universe want her to learn, that it kept dumping her in forests with crazy people?

"We're not going to hurt you," Abby Wilson said. Macy didn't really know whether to think of her as Abby or Wilson, or Abby Wilson. *Bitch* was probably too strong a name... to utter out loud anyway.

Macy didn't respond.

"You can call me Abby. And, like I said, we're not going to hurt you."

Something in Abby's eyes seemed genuine. This woman was big and strong and carrying enough weapons to kill Macy fifteen times over, but she didn't seem terribly threatening—other than the whole kidnapping thing.

Abby continued, "Look, I'm not going to sit here and threaten you. You don't have to tell us anything if you don't want. We'll figure it out on our own if we have to. But this will be a lot easier and a lot faster if you just fill us in on some details. Who else is out here? What exactly are they looking for? Have they... found it?"

Macy considered the offer, if one could call it that. Though soft and veiled, this still kind of seemed like a threat. If Macy didn't answer the questions, then what would happen? She weighed whether she wanted to find out.

"Ok. Let me start then," Abby said, slipping off her backpack and taking a seat across from Macy in a strangely childish cross-legged position. "I'm Abby. I grew up around here. I work for a man—a company—that finds things for people. For clients with expensive, sometimes quasi-legal tastes. I like to get paid, and I'm a little worried that you and your team present a bit of an obstacle for me."

The more she talked, the more Macy realized that Abby wasn't really that old. If she squinted and forgot about the rougher exterior, Abby might not have even been much older than her.

Abby paused to see if Macy wanted to talk, and continued when she didn't. "And I don't want to hurt you—I'm not going to hurt you. Or your team. I just need you out of the picture until we're done, and then you're free to go."

Interesting plan. Macy had seen her and would report her to the cops. Macy ran her eyes across Abby's sitting form, trying to remember as many details as she could. Brown eyes. Brown hair in a ponytail. No scars or identifying marks on the face. Muscular and toned, but not in a freakish way. Pretty enough. A diamond ring on her left hand. But no band. An engagement ring. Who the hell would ask this woman to marry them?

The brassy part of Macy's personality really wanted to spew threats about how she'd tell the cops, how they'd catch Abby and she'd regret this. Given the current power imbalance, though, Macy didn't figure that would help anything. Unlike Hogg Run, Macy didn't currently feel as if her life was in mortal danger, and somehow that kept her head clearer.

"Are you here because of the devil?" Macy finally asked. Abby appeared in the sharing mood, so questions seemed safer.

Abby looked at her, frowned a bit. "Yeah."

Macy gave a slight nod.

"Well, Macy. There's only one devil. And we can't both have it."

Macy had spent enough time with Miriam to know that there was likely more than one devil. A breeding population would require lots, in fact. Maybe not all here at Misty Lake, but somewhere on the western seaboard within roaming range. Close enough to get together and screw every now and then, at least. Unless, of course, the devil was actually *the* Devil, in which case they'd made a horrible mistake and Macy would have to take up the Catholic faith and learn how to perform exorcisms. Or something like that. Whatever one did when confronting Satan.

"We're only here to observe it, catalog it, take pictures," Macy said. "We don't want it."

"See, though," Abby said. "If you do that, then people will believe it exists. And then it's a much bigger hassle for me when it disappears. People start asking questions, cops grill you. You'll probably give it all up to them, and then I'm a fugitive."

"What makes you think that's not going to happen anyway?"

"It might, I guess. Always a possibility in my line of work." Abby leaned back on her hands and looked up at the towering tree behind Macy. "But I'm not going to hurt you. Or your team. And sure, you can tell the cops about me and Beatty, but I doubt they'll have much motivation to do anything about it when there's no fallout. Especially if you start spouting off about some mythical creature that no one's ever proved the existence of. And my employer, he tends to keep us safe. Deep pockets and all that."

The brush rustled, parted, and Beatty broke back into the clearing. He looked down at Abby, then Macy.

"Having some girl time?" he asked with a grin.

"Something like that."

Abby sprung to her feet with a nimble quickness and dusted off her hands and butt.

"Did you get through?" she asked Beatty.

"Not to HQ, but to Radley. He's gonna forward the message. The van and the Prius will be gone by morning."

Macy couldn't hide a frown. Her cell phone was in that van. Not that she stood much of a chance of finding her way back to it, even if she did somehow rid herself of these two.

Abby turned her attention to Beatty. "Okay. Well, she's gonna slow us down."

Beatty shot Macy a look. "Should we, you know..." He drew his thumb across his throat.

The blood drained from Macy's face. She held her breath without thinking, not sure what to do or say.

Abby had promised her no killing. If death was an option, then screaming seemed like it was worth the shot, but before she could get it out, Beatty reached down and grabbed her under the arm, a big grin spreading across his face.

"I'm kidding," he said. "We're not here to kill people."

He pulled her to her feet as if she weighed nothing.

Abby loaded back up with her gear and started walking. Beatty followed, dragging Macy along with a force neither rough nor tender.

"I don't suppose you know where your friends went," Abby said. A question clearly aimed at Macy.

"Not exactly. The lake, I think."

"Good. Once we find them, we'll get you far away from here and let you go."

Macy couldn't bring herself to believe the promise. Whatever drove this woman to a life of... well, whatever she meant to do... must have been one hell of an experience.

CHAPTER 9 – Abby

Abby's first kill was a Sumatran rhino. She told herself that the rhino would have died either way. She wasn't the only poacher on the market, after all. Only a few dozen such rhinos existed, in populations too small to even provide enough genetic diversity to save the species. At the time, she relished in the hunt, desperate to prove herself and intent on sating the rage in her veins. After the rhino, it became even easier. Just a job. The rage had dissipated into a simmer, and she racked up kills fast enough to earn some renown among those in the know about such things.

It wasn't until she started working for her current, secretive employer that things got really interesting, though. She'd never met him, but he clearly had a penchant for the truly exotic. So far, that had meant hunting and killing animals no one even knew existed. Some of them survived in modern folk tales and rumor, and still others had only been discussed by technology-starved locals whose stories had never ventured out of their small villages. Abby had no idea how her employer caught wind of these fantastical creatures, and the organization wasn't too fond of questions.

Perhaps she'd always meant to pursue this path. Perhaps she'd always meant to learn how to hunt and kill large, dangerous animals. It certainly seemed like it now that she was back here. Back to where she almost lost her will to live, and veered from any kind of normal or decent path, never to return. But maybe she could. Maybe if she did this one thing, her soul would find solace and she could escape this life. She didn't really have much use for all the money, so it sat safely in a foreign bank account, ready to provide for a retirement when she'd finally exorcised her demons.

The last demon was surely the devil itself.

So lost in thought, she didn't think about the branches scraping at her boots, or that her flashlight barely provided visibility through the shadow-soaked forest. She wanted to push on. To finish. To finally be done. But this Macy girl had slowed them down and making it to the lake in the dark seemed increasingly unlikely.

"Hey, Abby. We should probably call it a night soon."

Abby nodded into the darkness. "Agreed. We just need to find some flat ground. Somewhere to set up."

They walked in silence for a few more minutes before they found a suitable location. Tight, but big enough for the two tents. Beatty lowered the girl to the ground, and Abby went to work on the tents, with Beatty jumping in shortly thereafter.

"How are the sleeping arrangements gonna work?" Beatty asked as they worked.

Abby didn't think this girl would be brave enough to try to escape, especially in the darkness without a flashlight. By the time Macy could possibly make it to the parking lot—assuming she could find her way— she'd have no car or van to retreat to. She'd have to walk miles to the nearest gas station, or flag someone down on the small park road. Seemed unlikely.

Still, better safe than sorry.

"I'll keep her in my tent, perv."

"That's not—"

"It's a joke."

Abby just needed time. She needed to find the other interlopers, round them up and keep them out of her way until she found the devil. Assuming she could. It had eluded detection for years, obviously. But she'd never failed a contract yet, and she certainly didn't intend to fail this particular one.

She didn't have a plan. She didn't know how she would keep Macy and her "team" out of the way without them going to authorities before Abby skipped town.

"All right. Let's get some shut-eye," she said to Beatty. Then to Macy: "Come on. Time for bed."

"I'm not going to sleep," Macy said plainly.

"You wanna stay out here and keep watch, then?"

Macy didn't answer, but there could only be one answer to that question. Even without the devil, Macy would still have to contend with bears, at the very least. Possibly cougars. And then the bees and wasps. Even a large deer could cause enough trouble if put in the wrong situation. The pine-filled woods of southwestern Washington did not provide the most hospitable place for sleeping out in the open.

Beatty made a move to help Macy back to her feet, but she leaned on her bound hands and pushed herself up. She shot a glare at him, sharp enough to elicit a subtle grin.

"This one's stubborn."

Unamused, Abby held open the door of the tent and motioned inside. "After you."

Macy crouched and duck walked inside. Abby followed, zipping up the tent behind her. The quarters were tight. They were almost in each other's lap, but they'd have to make the best of it. Abby unzipped her sleeping bag into one big blanket.

"Here. We'll lay on the ground. Use this is as a blanket. It gets cold here at night."

"I'm not sharing a blanket with you," Macy said.

Stubborn indeed.

"Suit yourself." Abby rolled to her side, facing away from Macy and pulled the sleeping bag over herself. She left enough that Macy could get under if she changed her mind. And she certainly would.

What a mess this was turning out to be. It was supposed to be get in, get out, get paid, retire. Maybe. If she could stomach giving up this life. Her mind wandered, trying to paint the picture of how she'd live when she wasn't living in hotels, helicopters, and tents. The scenes came in murky and amorphous as sleep started fraying her thoughts. Her heart fluttered when the shape of a man appeared in a nondescript kitchen.

Ben?

She moved closer.

Not Ben. Beatty.

Her heart sped up. She couldn't pull out of sleep enough to know if it was real, or only in the dream. Emotion replaced logic. Sorrow filled her.

Ben was dead.

Killed by the devil.

And she'd let it happen.

CHAPTER 10 – Miriam

Miriam's mind buzzed. She'd think about Macy a few times, wondering why she hadn't heard from her, but then she'd think of another cryptid, another possibility, another avenue of research or tracking, and so lose thoughts of Macy to all the noise. Adrenaline caused her mind to scatter, but Miriam knew from experience that eventually her focus would narrow on a single directive. She would solve the problem, find the answer, and win.

Win.

Kim sat in front of the smoldering fire, her chin propped up on her hand, her glittering green nail polish chipped and aging. Dark circles hung under her eyes, her blue hair tied back in a messy ponytail. Her glow had dissipated. Miriam wasn't sure it was due to lack of sleep or fear.

To be fair, Miriam knew that no one could handle her when she got like this. She'd turned into a laser-guided missile, her coordinates locked in, with only one singular focus. She could no longer be a generalist. Only a specialist. She hadn't slept much herself, but she didn't care how that made her look, and didn't care if her body tried to stop her with fatigue. If Miriam had one skill, one strength, it was that her will could out-vote her body every time.

She paced and mumbled and talked at no one. She wanted to go back to the trap in the daylight. She wanted to find the tracks. Those alone might give her some insight, but even if they didn't, she could follow them until she found the lair of the devil. Kim insisted on breakfast first, though she'd hardly eaten anything, and seemed intent on staring into burning embers instead.

"So..." Miriam said, trailing off, hoping Kim would snap back into focus. "Ready to go?"

Kim looked up. "Um. Yeah. I guess. Maybe we should stay here, though? People see it in the lake most often, you know."

"Yeah, but we saw it out there. In that hole, or trap, or whatever it was."

It seemed as if Kim wanted to say something else, but instead she stood up. "Fine. But shouldn't we fill Macy in on what happened?"

Of course, that made sense.

Miriam walked to her pack slouched up against the side of her tent, pulled out the radio, and depressed the button. "Hey, Macy. We've got some news. Are you there? Over."

Nothing.

"It's been a while," Kim said. "I hope she's okay."

"I'm sure she's fine. Girl sleeps like a rock. She's probably inches away on the cot. It's still pretty early."

"If you say so."

On Kim's reluctance, Miriam tried one more time. "Macy. Come on. Wake up. Over."

Still nothing.

"We'll try again later, and we'll take the radio with us this time."

She should have had it with her last time Macy checked in, but they never left eyesight of the camp, and before they knew it, they'd rounded a bend in the lake and put a significant distance between themselves and their gear.

As Kim walked away, Miriam stuffed the radio into her pack and hefted it over her shoulders. Kim had done the same by the time Miriam turned around.

"Camp'll be okay, right?" Miriam asked.

"Yeah. Should be fine. We're not leaving anything except our food and bedding."

"Speaking of which." Miriam used a rope to lower her food bag and fish out a few protein bars. "Might be a long day. Make sure your canteen is full."

"Full enough," Kim said.

Miriam tested her own and decided the same. She didn't want to take the time to boil water, anyway.

As they started walking, Miriam attempted to quench her curiosity. "So are otters common around her?"

"Yes. River otters, anyway. Sea otters were wiped out during the fur trade and reintroduced in the late 60s. They're more rare, but, in general, otters tend to be elusive."

"Well, the one we saw was in a trap, so I guess we just got lucky."

Miriam tried to picture the otter from the night before, but the image had been hazy even then. With nothing but a flashlight, she couldn't really remember many of the details of the creature. Something nagged at her, though. Something about the dimensions or the size, or...

"What did the tail last night look like?" she asked Kim.

"I don't know. I didn't get a good look."

Miriam knew a few things about otters, of course, just as she knew things about most animals. Even without Kim's concurrence, Miriam felt sure that something about the thing's tail didn't match what she expected from a river otter. Vague recollections formed, as she considered obvious differences between river and sea otters.

"I think it was a sea otter, not a river otter. But a sea otter this far inland and out of the water? That's unheard of."

"Maybe the anomaly brought it here," Kim suggested. "It seems pretty big, so it's not crazy that it would have a huge territory."

"Maybe."

The conversation just made Miriam all the more eager to find the truth. It didn't really make sense that the devil would have brought a sea otter inland just to dump it into a trap of its own making. But it had been dark, and creepy, and Miriam could easily believe that they'd misremembered the dimensions and traits of the otter they'd seen. Until proved otherwise, Miriam was cautiously willing to believe it was a full-grown river otter, unfortunately caught in a trap, then eaten by a mythical monster.

And so, she marched on, never doubting that she'd find her quarry.

***

The "trap" seemed completely different in daylight. Miriam slid her way to the bottom for a more thorough inspection. The ground had been worn away almost perfectly flat. Though present, the carcasses and bones weren't nearly as plentiful as she remembered from the night before. It was pretty large, but not as big as she remembered. Some of the sides weren't nearly as steep, low enough that she'd easily be able to climb out on her own.

Kim stayed on the edge, watching cautiously. Miriam

didn't think she seemed scared, just tired and uninterested.

The mostly-smooth ground was disturbed with the claw marks of the otter. It had trampled over its own tracks so much that she had a hard time picking out any one footprint, which she really wanted to find to verify its probable size. No luck there, but she had another thing to look for. The devil had stepped into the trap, and that meant...

There. She practically ran over to the giant depression in the mud. A well-formed track sat before her, five clawed toes and an almost triangular foot. It looked like a clawed human footprint, except that the toes were splayed a little far apart for that.

And it was huge. Easily larger than her head.

"Hey, Kim," she hollered. "Can you look in my pack? I've got some plaster in there. We can mix it with some water and take a mold of this."

Kim knelt next to Miriam's pack and unzipped it. "You came prepared."

"Of course, I did. I'm not an amateur."

"I didn't mean to..." Kim trailed off, searching through the backpack before she stood up with a plastic bag filled with white powder. "This it?"

Miriam nodded. "That's it."

She walked to Kim, took the bag and a canteen before making her way back to the track. She hadn't brought enough plaster to do this more than once, so she felt pressure not to mess it up. Opening the bag, she poured in the water until it looked about the right consistency, then zipped it back up and shook it, until she had uniform sludge to work with.

She opened the bag and dumped the contents over the track, careful to fill every hole until she could see nothing but the white of the plaster. In a perfect world, she would have used a mold to ensure a better distribution of the plaster, but this would do. She patted the plaster gently, ensuring it packed neatly into the track.

"Now we wait."

"How long?" Kim asked.

"Probably half an hour or so."

Miriam climbed up one of the shorter sides and moved around to Kim. She sat on the edge of the hole and let her legs dangle. Kim took a seat beside her, closer than Miriam would have liked. It bothered her that Kim had deflated so much. As much as she got annoyed at being trolled, she'd grown accustomed to it.

Miriam bumped her shoulder against Kim's. "Not bad for our first full day, eh?"

"Yeah," Kim said. "I guess so."

Miriam had hoped for a more interactive response, so she just sat in silence for a few minutes. Eventually, her mind wandered away from Kim back to the task at hand.

"It doesn't deserve to be killed," Kim finally said, glumly.

"I'm not going to kill it."

"I know you don't want to. But, if you had to, you would."

"I guess," Miriam replied. "If it was about saving my life... or yours."

"But that's not really the point." Kim looked up from the ground and over to Miriam. Miriam tried to meet her gaze but withered under the passion. Is that how people felt about her when she was wrapped up in something?

"What is the point, then?"

"Look, if you find this thing—if you bring hard proof to the world—then you're putting it in danger."

"If I can prove its existence, then we can protect it."

"You and what army? People are horrible, Miriam. They'll come for it, either on purpose or accidentally. There'll be tours set up just to get a glimpse of it. We'll destroy its habitat, if nothing else."

Miriam looked away, unable to take anymore of Kim's dark judging eyes. She tried to grapple with Kim's perspective, but ultimately, Miriam believed that science and truth would always win, that it was better to know than not. Sure, it would take effort and money, but whatever this thing was, it would likely die out anyway if not properly protected. Anything seen so infrequently couldn't possibly have much of a population.

"What do you want me to do, Kim?" Miriam came off sounding a little more frustrated than she meant to. "How can we be sure to protect its habitat if we don't know anything about it?"

"I..." Kim kicked her feet against the side of the trap. "I don't know, Miriam. I'm just worried."

Miriam didn't quite know what to do, so she took a note out of Macy's playbook and placed her hand on Kim's shoulder. "Hey, it'll be okay."

Would it, though? Miriam didn't like lying.

Kim looked up at her, those dark eyes watery, almost cartoonish, as if at any moment buckets of tears would gush out. She lunged at Miriam and enveloped her in an unexpected hug. A tight one. Miriam patted Kim's back. Despite having slept in the woods, Kim's hair smelled good. Natural and earthy. Miriam blushed for even thinking about that, for even noticing such a detail at all.

After an interminably long time, Kim backed away, but still leaned in too close.

"I like you, Miriam. I really do. You're like badass and everything." A smile finally peeked out. A glimmer of mischief back in her eye. "But..."

Kim finally pulled away, leaving Miriam confused and uncomfortable. Not too surprising. Miriam never did like human contact much. Macy could be emotional, sure, but rarely passionate like this. Miriam respected passion, and for the first time, she saw Kim as more than just a troll. Beneath the quips and the prodding, Kim cared about all of this. She wanted to protect it.

Unsure of how to continue the conversation, Miriam slid herself back down into the pit. "I'm gonna check on the plaster."

Kim sniffled. "Ok. Sorry for all that."

Miriam didn't turn around to respond. "It's okay. I get it."

She really didn't.

Miriam tapped on the plaster. A hard, hollow *thunk*. It had cured. She grabbed the edges and lifted carefully, turning it over to see the results of her handiwork. It was a perfect cast. With some time and research, she'd be able to match this with the track of something. If not that, at least she could compare it to known animal tracks for similarities. One thing she felt certain of: whatever this thing was, she could rule out reptiles or birds.

Definitely a mammal.

As she stood up, she looked out towards the back of the pit at the trampled greenery. That's where it had gone. Now that she had her first piece of hard evidence, she needed to find more.

Despite her small victory, the hunt was far from over.

CHAPTER 11 – Macy

By the time the new day dawned, Macy had already spent most of the night psyching herself up. Sure, this wasn't the best situation, but no one and nothing was actively trying to kill her, so that put the situation considerably ahead of Hogg Run. Against her will, she nodded off for a few hours, but when she woke her adrenaline kicked in and she began studying everything she could, desperate to find an escape route. If she could get away, then she could warn Miriam, or the police... or maybe get hopelessly lost in the woods. But at least then Miriam would eventually find her.

Beatty and Abby packed up camp with truly impressive speed. They threw Macy a foil pouch, which she only figured out was food once they started eating their own. She fumbled with the packaging, her hands bound so close that she couldn't really get a grip. Her stomach rumbled, eager to eat anything, even as her senses told her she surely wouldn't like this.

Macy held out the pouch once Abby started in her direction, but Abby didn't take the pouch. Instead, she pulled a small knife from her belt and cut the cuffs off Macy's wrists.

"You're not gonna murder us in our sleep or anything, right?" Beatty said with a laugh, his mouth full of whatever food he slurped out of his own foil pouch.

Macy certainly didn't intend to. She'd killed one person too many in her life, and no amount of fear would push her into repeating that.

With her newly freed hands, Macy went to work on her food, wondering if it was a military MRE or something else. The packaging didn't say anything about being federal property, so she assumed the latter. She recoiled as the smell hit her nose, reminding her of some cross between dog food and lunch meat. She didn't know when she'd get to eat again, so she choked it down. Surprisingly, it seemed to settle pretty well, despite the horrible taste.

They only spent about five minutes eating before they struck out into the woods. Given the ground they'd made the night before, Macy figured they would surely be at the lake soon. Her heart tied itself in knots trying to imagine what might happen then. On paper, these soldiers surely held the upper hand, but Macy hadn't seen Miriam fail yet, so she remained optimistic.

Cautious. But optimistic.

They didn't drag her today, instead letting her follow behind. Beatty frequently checked her progress. Macy knew she couldn't outrun them. If she took off, they'd be on her in a heartbeat, and if she provoked them, they might reach for the rifles, the knives, the handguns—maybe even blow darts or some exotic weapon Macy couldn't fathom. They seemed to have it all.

They walked in silence, changing direction seemingly at random but always in sync with each other. Macy could discern no trail. Neither Abby nor Beatty ever pulled out a compass, or GPS device. They just seemed to intuit the correct direction.

Suddenly, Abby stopped and held up a hand. Beatty halted, and Macy stopped only inches short from plowing right into his back, unable to contain a quiet yelp.

Abby whispered, "Do you hear that?"

Beatty nodded. Macy redirected her attention to the strange chirping sounds. Not a bird, she didn't think. Almost more like a baby cat. The sounds came quickly, overlapping each other, surely coming from more than one animal, but all the same for sure. She didn't even try to guess what sort. With the exception of maybe livestock, Macy knew precious little about wildlife.

Abby broke off towards the sounds, Beatty close behind. Was this Macy's chance? With her captors hyper-focused, she could run. Disappear into the woods before they could find her. Macy suddenly felt hot, her heart thumping in her chest. Her leg muscles tensed. The scars from Hogg Run burned.

"Hey, girl, come on," Beatty said, pausing to look back at her.

Macy's heart fell. She'd missed her chance.

Beatty didn't turn back until she started towards him. Abby pulled ahead. When Macy finally stumbled into the small break in the underbrush, Abby stood looking at the ground, a half-smile on her face. Macy's eyes caught up, revealing the prize. A small hole in the ground, the chirping mews pouring forth from it, piercing and loud. Inside, a nest of baby animals, though Macy couldn't tell what kind.

"Otters?" Beatty asked. "How many?"

Abby peered into the hole. "Two. Maybe three." She knelt, reached a hand inside and pulled one out by the scruff of its neck. Definitely an otter. Even Macy could tell that. Not nearly as small as she'd imagine a baby, though.

Holding the cub at eye level, Abby studied it. "I don't think this is a pup."

The otter shivered. Its mews quieted.

"It's in a nest," Beatty said. "Crying like a pup. Giant river otter, maybe?"

"Up here? How would it have even gotten here?"

Beatty only shrugged.

"At any rate, it's not what we're here for."

"True. But otter fur still fetches a decent price. Could sell it off the books, keep the money."

Macy's eyes moistened at the thought of watching them slaughter this cute little thing. Beatty looked at her, studying the look on her face, or maybe the tears in her eyes. Appearing stoic couldn't be listed among Macy's many skills.

"What? Can't handle a little blood?" He laughed, as if life meant nothing, before pulling out a large knife. Macy kept quiet, too scared that he'd use it on her if she protested.

Abby sighed and held the baby otter towards Beatty. "Fine. But make it quick. We've got more important things to do."

Beatty roughly took the animal, then all hell broke loose. At first, Macy couldn't process it. Out of nowhere, the underbrush parted and something big—something huge—broke out into the clearing, ramming into Beatty and knocking him to the ground. Macy backed away, stumbling and falling on her butt, before finally getting a chance to look up.

To see... it.

She couldn't tell where it began and ended, just one long stretch of muscle and fur. The business end thrashed towards Beatty, fangs bared, fetid breath stout enough for Macy to smell from where she sat on the ground. Beatty still brandished the knife, but the pup had broken free, skittering away. Blood. On the knife. From Beatty or the pup or the devil, she didn't know.

The thing roared at Beatty, snapping at him just as he shuffled away. Macy scrambled to her feet as Beatty pulled his rifle around and pointed it up at the monstrosity. Macy couldn't see Abby and stopped looking when she heard Beatty scream as one of the huge, clawed feet of the devil stepped on his chest, forcing him prone. The rifle fired into the air, hitting nothing.

Macy stood frozen in fear, unsure of what to do or how to help.

Help?

Why would she help?

This was her chance.

Her chance to run.

CHAPTER 12 – Abby

Abby's body reacted more strongly than she expected. Her heart pounded; her mind unable to stop itself from upchucking sensations and images of that night. The ring on her finger suddenly felt like it burned. She swallowed. Drew her attention to her breathing. Her heartbeat. Her racing mind.

When Beatty screamed, she snapped into action.

Her rifle was out and ready to go in a matter of seconds. She pointed the muzzle in front of her and pulled the trigger. Missing a target this large at this range would have been impossible, so she didn't have to worry about aiming, really. She was so close that the rifle almost sounded like it had a suppressor on. Blood from the devil spattered across her face.

It turned on her in an instant. She'd only made it mad. Just over the shoulder of the animal, she saw Beatty on the ground. He didn't get up. Why wasn't he getting up?

Abby turned and scurried away, not to flee, but to get some distance so she could aim better. This thing was at least as big as a grizzly, but longer and sleeker. Bigger than even she remembered. It crashed through the trees after her, and she knew in an instant that she had no hope of outrunning it. She'd have to outsmart it.

Scanning the forest floor in front of her, Abby searched for any advantage. Her mind worked as if it were driven by silicon, analyzing, naming, and discarding her options. Climbing a tree. Impossible to do fast enough, with the length of her pursuer. The lake was too far away. The devil could surely swim anyway. Undoubtedly far better than her. She had to turn her size disadvantage into an asset.

She could feel the thing behind her. The ground subtly shook with its every step. She could smell it. Feel its breath.

There!

She threw her pack off in full stride before sliding to the ground, like she was racing a baseball to the base. She didn't completely make her target, but at least she was already down enough to crawl into the huge hollowed out log, before army-crawling to the middle as fast as she could. She left her rifle behind. It would only slow her down.

No sooner did she trap herself into a cocoon of wood than the entire frame of the log shook with an ungodly force. The creature huffed and snorted behind, trying to get in. Her hiding place started rocking. Dust and debris rained down on her head. The devil intended to crack her hiding place like an egg, to eat her as the yolk. The old Abby, the one from Ben's death, came to light. For months after, she'd told herself that dying at the hands of the devil with Ben would have been better than living. And now the ghost of her former self wanted her to take up that position once again. There'd be a certain poetry to it, she supposed, but...

She started army-crawling towards the other end of the log. She popped out the other end, pushed to her feet, and sprinted forward without looking back, the log shaking and rattling behind her. It gave her time to gain ground. She was crashing through trees and underbrush, no longer able to see the devil, by the time she heard the splintering crack of the wood finally giving way. Now she had time to climb a tree, but these trees were tall and straight, nothing like the kind kids climbed in their backyards.

A quick survey gave her a path, up a half-fallen rotting log, over to a low-hanging branch, up higher to another. She worried that a path for her meant a path for the devil, but she saw no better option. Without all her gear, the climb proved quick and easy. She sat almost twenty feet in the air by the time she finished, straddling a branch that probably wouldn't hold her weight for long.

The devil was big, but not twenty feet. Maybe ten—fifteen tops—from head to tail. She felt safe up here.

As she caught her breath, Abby listened. She didn't hear the brush disturbance of any giant animal. No snorts or huffs or growls. She waited, still, certain that maybe it would sneak up on her. She and Ben hadn't heard it coming back then, so it was capable of being quiet.

Seconds turned into minutes.

Then half an hour.

Her heart never stopped racing. Beatty needed her. She had to get back to him. And the girl had surely run away. Abby silently wished Macy well, fairly confident the girl would die out in the woods, either to the elements, the devil, or starvation. But Abby wouldn't accept responsibility for that. She had enough to worry about.

After almost an hour, Abby finally shuffled down from her roost, easily sliding back down from branch to branch, then to the fallen log, and finally to the soft wet ground of the forest. Not easily disoriented, she quickly found the direction she came from and retraced her steps back to the hollowed log, now just a mess of splinters. If not for Beatty, she would have followed the tracks leading away, but she had no time for that. She took solace in the fact that they didn't lead back towards him.

She gathered her gun and her pack on the way, neither looking worse for the wear, then continued forward until she came into the clearing where it had all started. There, Beatty sat with his back against a tree, his shirt covered in so much blood that she couldn't tell where it came from. He looked up at her with a ragged breath and forced something that resembled a smile, though it ended up closer to a wince.

She rushed to him and collapsed to the ground.

No. Not Beatty. Not to this monster.

Not like Ben.

"Hey, Wilson," Beatty said, his usual rugged voice sounding distant and thin. "Took you long enough."

She carefully lifted his shirt, surprised to find denim wrapping his wound.

Beatty looked down, let out a mirthless chuckle. "That little girl came back. Cut her own pants legs off and wrapped me up like this."

"Where is she?"

Beatty let his head fall back against the trunk of the tree behind him. "Gone."

Abby nodded and gingerly pulled the denim away from his chest. Four puncture wounds oozed blood. It looked painful, but she didn't think the worst of his problems came from the claws. The sheer weight of the devil could have crushed his ribs, and if one of those punctured a vital organ, Beatty might not have long. She didn't have the first aid experience to do anything about internal bleeding.

"We need to get you back to the plane," Abby said, trying hard not to show her dismay as she wrapped the denim back into place. The girl didn't matter anymore.

"How bad is it, doc?"

"I'm not gonna start lying to you now. It looks bad. Can you walk?"

Beatty shrugged, winced. "I don't know."

"You have to try. We have to get you out of here."

He nodded.

Without thinking, Abby leaned in and pressed her lips to his. She'd done it a thousand times before, between missions when they had nothing better to do than occupy each other's beds, but this time felt different.

"You're gonna be fine. It's gonna be fine."

Beatty smirked. "Is that why you're crying?"

She wiped the tears from her face with the back of her hand. "Shut up. Come on. Let's get you back to the plane."

She stood, reached under one of his armpits and slid him up to his feet. The tree trunk provided support to ensure she didn't lose control of him. Abby was not a small woman, but she couldn't carry Beatty outright. If he couldn't walk on his own, they stood no chance of making it out.

"Motherfu—" Beatty groaned.

She managed to get him all the way up, his arm draped around her neck. "Oh come on. Don't go soft on me now. I can handle a little language."

He let out an exhalation of air that might have been a laugh under normal circumstances. She wished it had been a laugh. It would have brought her some comfort that he'd actually make it.

She looked down at the packs, the rifles. She wanted to take them, but she couldn't carry it all and Beatty had to be the priority. She reached for the beaten cell phone in her pocket and clicked a button to mark the location. She'd fetch it all later. They'd left spare gear back at the plane, so she'd bring some of that on her way back out.

The first step elicited a sharp hiss from Beatty, the second more of a low moan.

"Word of advice," Beatty said, taking a deep breath before continuing. "Try not to get stepped on by that thing when you come back."

Abby couldn't help but smile. He never questioned that she'd come back. Never expected her to stay with him. He'd always been like that. Always just accepted her for what she was. Never balked or judged. Maybe he wasn't so bad.

Each step became easier, but Abby had to support more of Beatty's weight than she would have liked. People recovered from worse, though, right? It would be hours before she got him back to the plane, but after that, Radley could get him to Seattle in no time. If Beatty needed surgery, he'd be under the knife by the end of the day and well on his way to recovery by tomorrow.

It would be fine.

It had to be.

CHAPTER 13 – Miriam

Miriam scrambled up a log that had fallen to form a ramp. Eager to gain ground, she stopped at the highest point and listened. Somewhere ahead of them, she heard the most amazing sounds, guttural and rumbling, with a mix of high-pitched clicks, almost as if it had all been mixed together in a sound studio.

"Do you hear that?" she asked Kim.

Kim nodded.

Miriam dug through her backpack until she found her cell phone. She hit the record button on her audio app in plenty of time to catch a significant sample of the calls. These would be invaluable in her report.

Then—a loud *pop*. A gunshot.

"No," Kim whispered, bringing her hand up to her mouth. Her face had gone pale, her eyes moist. Her hand visibly trembled.

Seeing Kim's reaction, brief panic for Macy's safety blurred through Miriam's head, but she quickly dismissed the concern once she ascertained the direction of the commotion. Macy sat safely in the parking lot, which stood in the complete opposite direction. No, Macy was fine; just derelict in her duties as the *operations specialist*. Still, the gunshot might have frightened her. Miriam made a mental note to check in as soon as she got the chance.

Miriam rushed back down to ground level and squeezed Kim's shoulder. "Don't worry. One shot isn't going to kill that thing."

As if to confirm her point, the sounds of the devil echoed again through the trees.

"See."

Miriam was less concerned about the safety of the devil and more interested in who held the gun. They hadn't seen another soul since they'd arrived. Odds were that whoever fired that shot was just a random hiker, spooked by a giant monster. That meant an eyewitness, and a trail to follow.

She took off without even a thought to whether Kim would follow, but of course she did. Pretty quickly, actually, and a little less reticent than before. The distance between them and the vocalizations proved to be further than Miriam expected, but it didn't surprise her. A creature that big could certainly project its voice great distances, and gunshots tended to be much the same.

For the first time on the expedition, it was Miriam who led the charge with Kim trailing behind. Though considerably less adept at pushing through the foliage, Miriam couldn't afford to trade positions. She moved on the memory of a sound, and her mind wouldn't be able to hold the information forever. She worried that every time she cut around a tree, she'd lost her vector on their destination.

Of course, the bigger problem with the greater distance was that they would have no way to know they'd arrived. If the shooter or the devil weren't still there, then Miriam would have to rely on other evidence to stop her track. And she couldn't be sure what she'd even look for. Not everywhere was as muddy as the trap, so footprints weren't guaranteed. If the shooter had missed, there wouldn't be blood. If they'd been a random hiker, they'd surely have run away. Unless...

She pushed the grislier possibilities out of her head and focused on staying alert, her perception on overdrive.

After a while, her ears slowed her down at the possibility of a sound. When she confirmed it, she stopped entirely. It was faint, but unmistakable. Almost the same sound they'd heard the night before, from the mewing otter that had lost its life to the devil. She re-vectored towards the sound and soon stopped at a small growth of underbrush.

Kneeling, she quickly saw the source of the sounds. Laying on its side, she saw another otter, similar to the one they'd seen earlier. This one was injured, a jagged cut across its abdomen. Blood oozed from the wound, but it hadn't been gutted.

Kim appeared beside Miriam in an instant, a soft coo in her voice as she suggested saving the animal. Maybe, but Miriam didn't like the odds. Neither of them were veterinarians.

Nonetheless, she felt enough empathy to help Kim fish the otter out for a more thorough examination. The injuries were bad enough that the creature didn't protest or fight them off. Certainly not a good sign. The cut didn't look particularly deep, but it was long, almost the full length of the otter's body.

Kim fished a handkerchief out of her pack. Why she had that, Miriam had no idea, but it worked well as a bandage to staunch the bleeding. The white cloth didn't turn red immediately, which Miriam took as a good sign. Extensive blood loss would surely spell doom for this little thing.

"You stay here," Miriam said. "Take care of him... her... it. I'm going to look around."

Kim nodded and offered a half-smile.

Miriam moved away, looking for the direction the otter was likeliest to have come from. Maybe this had something to do with the devil, or maybe it didn't, but she knew from the previous night that the devil ate otters, so it stood to reason that this might have been a meal that got away.

Careful examination uncovered the trail of blood left behind, which she followed to a small clearing. Her breath caught in her chest when she looked over the scene. A lot more blood littered the leaves of the ground. Two rifles and two backpacks were scattered nearby. She had no way to be sure, but the amount of blood either meant the devil had been grievously wounded, or a human had. Given the odds, she'd bet on the human. Few people would be prepared to fight something like this monster.

She surveyed the scene again, looking for clues other than the blood, and noticed a hole in the ground, relatively wide. Clearly a den of some sort. She peered inside and saw nothing moving. Best guess was that the wounded otter lived here, and the devil had come to fish it out. And...

Some campers happened to be in the wrong place at the wrong time? A closer inspection of the nearby packs suggested they weren't campers, though. The rifles were intended to kill big game. The tightly bound packs were built to survive any encounter. These backpacks weren't those of day hikers. These people, whoever they were, had meant business. They came to kill.

And there could only be one thing someone would come out here to kill.

They weren't alone.

Though, maybe that problem had taken care of itself. The blood and the gear left behind hinted that maybe they hadn't survived their encounter with the devil.

Miriam's heart pounded as she heard a noise behind her. She spun to see Kim break into the clearing, cradling the injured otter in her arms. When she looked up, her eyes went wide.

"Is this the place?" she asked.

Miriam nodded. "Looks like it. I'm not sure the shooters survived the encounter."

Kim's chest exhaled. Weird thing to be relieved about, but clearly Kim loved animals more than people.

"So, what now?" Kim said, with a glance at the dying animal in her arms.

Miriam considered the question. Her preference would have been to follow the trail. The devil had left a lot of smashed shrubbery in its wake, and she felt confident that she could follow. Now, though, they had an injured otter, as well as new information that implied the devil might be more dangerous than they first believed.

"Back to camp. It's gonna get dark soon. We need to check in with Macy," Miriam said, her heart falling as she admitted defeat for the day. "I'm not quite sure what to do with all this gear."

"We've already got our stuff. It'd slow us down to carry this, too."

"True. But maybe the rifles. We didn't bring anything with this much firepower, and it might protect us if things go south."

"Those rifles are meant to kill it, aren't they?" Kim asked, not really seeming to want an answer. "That's not what we're here for. We don't need them."

Miriam looked longingly at one of the rifles. "I know, but..."

Kim's nostrils flared. "Look. I was hired to guide you through these woods. To help you find it and prove its existence. I wasn't hired to help you kill it, and that's not what the University wants."

Miriam's gaze drifted up to Kim's. Damn that passion and conviction. Miriam recognized it. Respected it. But, unlike Kim, Miriam had never been a dreamer, never had that luxury. She had to look at things realistically, for both her safety and Kim's. Still, she could see that pressing the issue would cause a rift between them that Miriam wouldn't be able to mend.

Without a word, she took off towards camp, leaving the gear and guns behind. If Kim reveled in her win, she showed no signs.

On the way, Miriam dug the radio out of her backpack. It seemed as good a time as any to catch up with Macy and fill her in on the many developments. She pressed the button, "Hey, Macy. Miriam here. Checking in. Lots to report. Over."

No answer. Miriam turned the radio over in her hand, checked the dials and the battery and cycled the power, ensuring that the small indicator light flashed when she did. Everything seemed to be in order.

"Macy. Are you there? It's been a while. Starting to get worried. Over."

Still no answer.

"Maybe something in the van broke," Kim offered.

"Maybe."

They moved on in silence, Miriam keeping the radio in her hand just in case Macy checked in. Miriam's mind felt jumbled and confused. The variables only kept increasing, when she'd hoped the equation would have moved towards a solution. She had more to worry about now than before.

Was the devil deadly?

Could they save this otter?

Was Macy okay?

Miriam started to entertain a possibility that she could barely stomach.

Her first high-profile expedition was proving to be far more difficult than she'd imagined.

CHAPTER 14 – Macy

Hopelessly lost.
Not that Macy should have expected anything different. She tried to remember all the wisdom she'd heard over the years—find a river and follow the stream. Look at the moss to tell the east from the west. Use some sticks to build a makeshift sundial. Offer an acorn to a friendly squirrel and ask nicely for directions. That last one might not have been a thing. She couldn't remember.

She wrapped her arms tightly around her chest, her one leg colder than the other, as she trudged along through the waning light. If she died out here, she'd surely kick herself for running away from her captors, but she also couldn't judge herself too harshly. Though the man had been taken out by the devil, the woman would have come back, and who knows what she would have done then. Probably make Macy carry Beatty on her back or something. As if that were possible.

She did want him to live, though. She wouldn't wish death on anyone.

Macy really did think she was heading back towards the parking lot, but now she questioned her conviction. She hadn't seen water yet. Only trees. So. Many. Trees. She seriously hated trees now. She vowed that she'd move to a desert as soon as she got back to Texas. So what if trees sustained life on the planet? Wasn't worth it.

She wandered aimlessly, trying at least to stay in a straight line. Surely it all had to end eventually. She would have felt a lot better if Miriam at least knew she was out in the woods alone. As it stood, Miriam probably just thought she was being lazy or something, texting Tanner instead of answering the radio.

This made her plight all the more complicated. If no one was looking for her, then no one could find her, and if no one could find her, then she'd surely die out here eventually. She didn't know the good berries from the bad. Didn't know how to hunt (especially with her bare hands). Couldn't fish. Hell, she wasn't entirely confident that she could build a fire without lighter fluid, though she had at least seen that done by her father and Miriam on multiple occasions.

So wrapped up in trying to find her way, it took Macy a while to actually give herself some credit. A lot of emotions coursed through her, but fear was among the least of them. She didn't know whether to thank the therapy or the repetition of being lost in the woods, but being more focused on survival than fear helped make the situation manageable. She hadn't lost hope, and though she steeled herself for a cold night in the woods, she felt confident that her luck would turn around by daybreak.

Giving up on actually finding a way out, Macy started to turn her attention towards shelter. The canopy far above did provide some, but it wouldn't stop the cold stinging rain if—no, *when*—it started to fall. She imagined maybe a tree that had fallen, to form a lean-to.

After a bit more wandering, just as the sun started to disappear entirely, she stumbled out into a surprisingly large area without trees. Across from her, the land rose sharply, almost straight up. Not a mountain by any means, but definitely a solid rock wall. It wasn't wide. She could easily skirt around it and climb up the sloping forest floor if she wanted, but instead her eyes were drawn to the large, gaping maw in the middle.

A cave. Nature's best shelter.

She moved towards it cautiously, trying to imagine what might live inside. She'd seen a giant monster earlier in the day, so she couldn't rule that out, but she'd walked a long way, and nothing had passed her, or even seemed out of the ordinary. There could be a bear, she supposed. Either way, an animal wouldn't answer a knock, so she'd have to take her chances.

On the threshold, she stilled her breath and listened. Nothing. She peered inside but could see only darkness, pitch black that would not abate from moonlight alone. That was fine. She'd just stay near the entrance where she could see out, and when the sun came back up, she could explore further in the unlikely event that she'd need a second night of shelter. Surely, in the relatively flat forest, the cave couldn't go back that far. It couldn't be *that* deep, right? Just because she couldn't see the back didn't mean it wasn't near.

She heard the *plop, plop, plop* of the rain before she felt the first drop against her scalp. If she got drenched, she'd be too cold to sleep. She took a deep breath, put one foot forward, and stepped inside the lip of the cave. She stopped. Listened.

Nothing happened.

She pressed herself against the side, taking comfort from the smooth rock poking against her back. She slid down to the ground and sat, the cold wet seeping through her jeans, chilling the skin underneath. No avoiding that. She pulled her knees up against her chest and hugged her legs. The cave seemed at least a few degrees warmer, and she wasn't actively getting rained on, so it would have to do. If she could have her way, she wouldn't sleep. But she knew she'd lose consciousness eventually, and this seemed as safe a place as she'd seen.

The panic tried to crowd out her optimism. Her mind unhelpfully reminded her of the consequences of getting lost permanently in the woods. Unlike her experience in Hogg Run, though, she felt stronger, surer that, as soon as the sun came up, she'd be able to orient herself and find a way out. She was young and healthy, and more resourceful than she usually gave herself credit for. She'd already escaped from...

What were those two even doing here, anyway? After the devil, yes. But what a strange coincidence that they'd show up at the same time. Macy didn't generally heed coincidences, so she instead considered the one variable she couldn't predict.

Kim.

Macy turned her mind to replaying every interaction she'd had with Kim. Sure, she'd been a bit subversive on first meeting, but she'd done nothing that screamed "this girl definitely works for mercenaries" or anything like that. No, it just didn't make sense. Unless Kim was some sort of secret agent, it made way more sense that Abby and Beatty had come for the devil at this time by pure happenstance.

Her mind wandered back to the clearing, how she'd used Beatty's knife to turn one half of her jeans into cut-offs. She didn't know much about first-aid. Had she even helped? Hopefully Abby had come back to save him, but maybe she'd been killed by the devil. Maybe now both bodies were rotting somewhere in the woods.

Oh well. Not her circus, not her monkeys. In the past, she'd been unable to control her rampant empathy, but if she'd learned anything over the past few years, it was that there just wasn't enough room for everyone. And if anyone deserved to be sidelined, it would surely be paramilitary kidnappers.

Fatigue crept up on her, and her head drooped against her chest. She jerked awake, fighting as best she could, but every time she tried to focus on something new, it wandered into nonsensical weirdness until, eventually, she started to doze. Not completely. Some part of her still knew that she was in a cave in the woods. Some part of her still knew that she needed to watch out for danger. It made her sleep fitful.

At one point, she detected a sound that didn't come from the rain, or from wildlife. A scraping against stone came from her left, deeper in the cave. All vestiges of fatigue evaporated as the sound came a second time. She swallowed, her heart racing. The pattern of the sound reminded her of a dog getting up to circle its bedding.

Okay. Probably an animal. Not weird. If it was good shelter for her, then it was good shelter for Smokey the Bear or whatever.

Macy slowly rose to her feet, focusing intently on remaining as silent as possible. Whatever stirred back there could certainly outrun her, so moving quickly didn't seem prudent. She stood with her back against the cave wall and took a slow, deep breath. The scraping sound came again. If her ears were to be trusted, it had moved closer.

She took a sideways step towards the entrance, unable to stop her shoe from making a noise as it crunched against the rock underneath. She looked left to see a silhouette coming from the darkness, slender and long, moving towards her like a giant snake. Before she could take another step, it closed the gap between them and stopped in front of her, its face dipped down, level to hers. She could see very little in the dim light, but she couldn't mistake the beady eyes. The whiskers. Sleek, shiny fur.

The creature huffed, its fetid breath blowing back the wispy hair that had escaped from her ponytail. It sniffed, running its head down her body before coming back up, staring at her face to face.

Macy swallowed hard, suppressing a scream.

The devil chittered and was answered by higher pitched sounds from the darkness.

So much for optimism.

CHAPTER 15 – Abby

Radley took some of the weight and helped Abby lift Beatty into the plane. Beatty hadn't talked the back half of the trek. His head lolled against his chest, his eyes flittering open occasionally, but for no length of time, and never focusing on any particular thing. It was bad. Very bad. A part of her wanted to go with him. To be by his side. Hold his hand. Make sure he recovered.

But that wasn't the job. And Beatty wasn't her husband or boyfriend or even her friend, really. Only her business partner. A partner who counted on her to get the job done.

"What the hell happened?" Radley asked. Abby noted that he didn't sound nearly as incredulous as she'd expect of someone who didn't know why they'd come. He didn't even look particularly shaken when he looked up at her with those shrewd, piercing eyes.

"Bear." The lie came easily.

She expected some pushback from her pilot, but instead he just flashed a shit-eating grin, wiped it off his face quickly and replied, "Bears can be assholes, that's for sure."

He didn't believe her. She didn't care.

Abby moved to the cargo hold of the plane, pulled it open and fished out some new gear, identical to what she'd been carrying earlier. She always traveled with backups, but this would be the first time she'd actually needed it. Further up the body of the plane, Radley shut the door to the backseat, and opened the door to the front.

"I'll radio ahead to SeaTac and make sure they've got an ambulance waiting."

Abby looked at him, more sincerely than she intended. "Thanks, Radley. I appreciate it. Still radio silence, but I'll check in when I'm in a safe spot."

Radley lifted himself into the plane and leaned out, looking back towards Abby. "Sounds good. He's in safe hands. You just go out there and finish the job. It's what he would have wanted, I'm sure. I'll come back and wait here after I've passed him off. And of course, I'll keep in touch with the hospital for you, fill you in when I hear from you."

Abby didn't respond, even with Radley staring at her a few seconds. Instead, she got lost in thought, swimming in possibilities, none of them particularly inviting. She'd gone on solo hunts before. That wasn't the problem. That hopeless feeling in her gut came from somewhere else. A bad somewhere.

Radley ducked inside and slammed his door shut. Abby took the cue and backed away from the plane. She watched as the engine revved up and the props started spinning. The plane lurched forward, before rolling down the flattened land. Soon it lifted off the ground and disappeared above the tree line. Abby stood silently and watched, knowing that she should head back yet somehow glued to her spot, her motivation draining by the second.

No way out now. Only through.

***

She walked through the night, passing up multiple safe opportunities to make camp. Abby knew from experience that she could skip one night of sleep without serious consequences, and she didn't want to waste any more time than she had to.

People had been injured before. It was a dangerous job. But never this grievously. And never her partner.

The parking lot sat empty when she came to it, the van and Prius gone. Abby stopped at the edge of the pavement and stared into the dark abyss of trees. Somewhere in there, her quarry hid. Waited. Was it scared that she might return for vengeance? It helped her to think so, even if she knew better.

The forest stared back at her. With a shiver, she stepped towards it, let the darkness envelop her. On her wrist, she wore a small LED flashlight that she flicked on, giving her just enough light to take the next step. And the next. She lost herself in the monotony of it, pecking her way between the trees with an occasional check of her phone's GPS, completely unfazed by the rain starting to fall.

Like any good hunter, she knew the best place to hunt was wherever the prey had last been seen, and she knew exactly where to start. She'd set up camp there. Risky, sure, but also the fastest way she could come up with to complete the mission and get back to Beatty. Back to her life. Not Beatty. She shook her head, tired of Beatty worming his way in. It was normal to be worried about his safety. They'd worked together for years, after all.

Moderately successful in clamping down her wandering thoughts, she focused on the path ahead, immersing herself in the sounds of the night. Chirps and chitters and the rustling of branches overhead. Before long, she found her spot. She'd left in a hurry, but it seemed like someone had gone through the gear.

Probably that Macy girl. Abby couldn't begrudge her looking for some survival tools, especially since it might have been her actions that had stemmed Beatty's bleeding.

The small hollow was empty, no signs of the otters that had been inside. She avoided shining her light towards the tree that Beatty had leaned up against.

Looking up at the canopy, she could barely see the moon above. She'd made good time without carrying Beatty. Enough time for a few hours of sleep before continuing on.

Abby made camp quickly, climbed inside her tent, and waited sleeplessly for a new day to dawn.

CHAPTER 16 – Macy

Macy didn't move a muscle. The devil smelled her from head to toe, over and over, backing away, then coming back. Its long sinewy body gave her no confidence that she could escape without it catching her, probably solely by stretching out and clamping down. After what seemed like an interminably long time, it exhaled one last breath, and retreated back into the darkness of the cave.

Macy finally released the air in her lungs.

Could it not see her? Was it like the T-Rex in *Jurassic Park*? Was anything like the T-Rex in *Jurassic Park*? Or did that get made up by a crazy writer to enhance the plot and give the heroes a fighting chance against a prehistoric monster?

She took a step out of the cave, the rain instantly chilling her. She looked up, let the raindrops hit her face. Then back down to see nothing but darkness, haunted by the silhouettes of towering trees. Inside the cave was a mythical creature that she'd seen violently attack another human, but out in the woods, she saw only a black void of uncertainty.

In Hogg Run, she'd come face to face with a mutant pig that wanted her dead. Despite what she'd seen earlier in the day, she didn't think the devil wanted her dead. Somehow, she felt it in her bones.

She took a step back inside and waited. The chitters from before had quieted. She could hear nothing, not even the breathing of the beast, or the rustling of its feet against the cave floor. Staying here was surely a gamble—one that could end in her death. But all her choices were a roll of the dice, a shuffle of the cards.

Macy slid to the ground, pulled her knees up and hugged them against her chest. She lowered her head, focused on her breathing, and, eventually, fell sleep.

***

She woke with a start. Chirping birds. Pale sunlight leaking through the cave mouth. No more rain.

Macy had stayed balled up all night, and her shoulders ached. Her butt throbbed from sitting on hard rock. She blinked into the brightness, then turned back to look further into the cave, still unable to see the very back. She could make out a mass of fur, though, spiraled in on itself, its body heaving up and down with every breath.

A whole night in a cave with the devil. Other than a few sore muscles, she was no worse for the wear. Her gamble had paid off. She sat relatively dry, less tired than she might have otherwise been, and filled with the hope that had kept her from giving up the day before. Still not entirely confident that she wouldn't be eaten—the devil might have just been full, after all—Macy quietly got to her feet, her eyes on the creature in the back of the cave the whole time.

When she finished the maneuver, its large head lifted, high enough for its beady eyes to look at her. Its whiskers twitched and, for the first time, Macy didn't see a monster. It buried its head back into its spiral of fur before she could get a good enough look.

Her stomach rumbled. The pre-packaged food she'd eaten the previous day could only hold out so long. She'd need food. Water, more importantly. She didn't know how to get either of those things. Vaguely, she knew she should boil any water before she drank it, but starting a fire was a daunting task that she didn't feel up to, given her resources. Just glancing around, she spied a large pitted rock, where rainwater had collected in a divot.

Surely better than river water, right? She moved to the rock and cupped some water in her hand, bringing it up to her mouth, bracing herself and swallowing it down. Tasted like dirt with a pinch of grass. Not the worst thing she'd ever put in her mouth. She took a few more scoops until her parched throat felt a little better, then dried her hand off on the longer leg of her jeans. Probably she needed to get some sort of shot or something when she got back to civilization. She'd worry about that later.

She found a fallen tree nearby and used it as a bench, the seat of her jeans already so wet that it didn't matter that the log had been soaked through in the night. Now entirely unconcerned with the devil in the cave, Macy turned her thoughts towards bigger problems. She had to find a way out of the woods, or a way towards Miriam. Either would save her. Miriam could be anywhere, and if Macy had learned anything so far, it was that these woods were a maze of confusion. The chances of finding Miriam seemed infinitesimally small. She'd just as likely get eaten by a bear, or break her ankle, or get stung by some sort of bug. Or a snake. Did they have snakes up here?

She considered yelling. Perhaps she'd stayed close enough that Miriam would hear her cries. But, Abby...

if she was still alive, she'd certainly be able to hear. Macy couldn't take that risk.

Macy needed something more than risk or hope. She needed to know the future. She needed to know where Miriam would be, where she was going, where she could be found.

But wait.

She had that.

She knew exactly where Miriam would be. Eventually anyway. Miriam had come to Washington for one reason, and one reason alone. To find the Devil of Misty Lake. And since Macy had already done that, it was only a matter of time before Miriam showed up. Maybe not in this exact place, but if Macy just followed the devil, then she'd find Miriam. Or, at least, that was her best shot.

Her chest warmed at the thought. It made sense. It didn't require her to stumble through the woods. It just required her to shack up with the devil for a little while and, based on her first night, that didn't seem too terrible.

Not the best plan, she realized, but also not the worst.

Content to stay put for the time being, Macy wandered back into the cave and took her spot against the wall. Without a phone, time seemed insufferably slow, but it wasn't more than a few minutes before Macy heard skittering from the devil's den. Then chitters and chirps. High-pitched. Not from the devil itself.

Then, a small silhouette appeared from behind the fur and hopped towards Macy, its back arching with every step. When it came into the light, she beheld the cutest little otter.

"Hey, little fella. What are you doing here?"

She held out a hand for inspection. The otter sniffed it.

What *was* an otter doing here?

Eager to pet the cute little creature in front of her, Macy moved her hand a little faster than intended and caused the otter to jump, to back up several feet. The devil stirred at the commotion, its head sticking up again, regarding Macy with those same beady eyes. Large eyes, but also familiar. She looked down at the otter, who had begun creeping back towards her. And back up again.

The eyes.

The whiskers.

The shape of the head.

For a monster, this thing looked strangely similar to her new little friend.

Holy crap.

The devil wasn't a monster at all. It was a humongous frickin' otter.

CHAPTER 17 – Miriam

Digging a grave with a foldable spade was no small task, but Miriam persisted. Kim stood above her, tears trickling down her face, dripping onto her blood-streaked shirt. The otter hadn't even made it through the night. Moving it seemed to have re-opened its wound, but Miriam didn't feel bad about that. It wouldn't have lived where they found it, either. For Kim, burying this creature would bring some sort of closure, but for Miriam, burying it just made sense. Scavengers would pick up the scent of a dead otter quickly, and from very far away.

She'd been at it for a while, and had finally reached a depth that felt safe enough. From her knees, Miriam put her spade on the ground and reached her hands up to take the otter's carcass. Kim sniffled and pulled it away from her body, the outline of its form starkly drawn in blood against the belly of her shirt. Miriam took the animal gingerly. Its head and tail fell limp, not stiff yet—as arduous as the task was, she'd dug quickly.

The hole she'd dug wasn't quite as long as the otter, so Miriam had to curl it just slightly to make it fit. She used her body to block Kim's view until she could get it looking natural, then took up her spade again.

"Any last words?"

Kim sniffled and shook her head. Miriam went to work filling in the hole.

When done, she stood, her hands covered in mud, her spade hopelessly dirty.

"Let's head back to camp," Miriam said. "Get you cleaned up." She was doing her best to be understanding and supportive, but honestly, it was just an otter. She wouldn't have wished death on it, but nature was cruel, and animals died all the time. Otters didn't have much of a problem re-populating. Not like the fur trade was still in full swing.

Even for someone who obviously cared very much for animals, Kim's overreaction was perplexing.

As they walked, Kim grabbed Miriam's hand. Miriam bristled at first, but allowed it, understanding that such a gesture could provide comfort to those in such distress. They hadn't strayed far from camp to dig the grave. Just far enough. By the time they made it back, Kim seemed to have calmed down considerably.

"So what do we do now?" Kim asked, as she started digging through her bag.

"I know it'll take a while, but we should head back to the parking lot. I wanna make sure Macy's okay."

Kim pulled a fresh shirt from her bag and sat it on top. She stood and peeled the blood-soaked one off and over her head. Miriam quickly averted her eyes.

"I've got a bra on, ya know," Kim said, some of her playfulness creeping back in.

Indeed, she did. A no-frills, functional lilac one. Kim walked towards the shore and scooped up some water in her hand, using it to scrub her stomach and chest, getting off any blood that had seeped through. Miriam spent the time fetching the clean shirt, offering it to Kim as soon as she returned from the water's edge.

Kim laughed as she took it. "You're a weird girl, Miriam Brooks."

Miriam didn't answer, and relaxed only after Kim had dressed. Miriam didn't know why such things bothered her. She could autopsy an animal without breaking a sweat, but stuff like that made her acutely uncomfortable. Always had.

"Ready?" Miriam asked.

Kim nodded. They started the walk, leaving camp set up and taking only a few essentials. It was early enough in the day that they'd be back before nightfall, and they'd make better time without all their gear.

They walked in silence for a while. Miriam's brain worked on putting all the pieces together, sifting through the facts she had, the ones she didn't, and the ones she thought she could find. She'd started to form a theory, but she couldn't quite fill in all the gaps. She suspected Kim could fill those in for her, though, and Miriam intended to use her working theory to draw out the truth.

"Ever heard of the dobhar-chú?" Miriam asked.

"Nope. I've heard of Bigfoot, the Loch Ness Monster, and the devil here. That is the entirety of my cryptid database."

"It's from Ireland. Dates back to the 1700s. A lady—her name was Grace Connolly—went out to do her laundry in a nearby lake. When she didn't come home after a while, her husband, Terence, started getting worried about her, so he grabbed his gun and set out to find her. When he got to the usual spot, he saw her dead, disemboweled body, blood everywhere."

"Ew."

"Yeah. And beside her, a huge animal slept, working off the human-sized meal it had recently consumed. In a sorrowful rage, Terence lifted his gun and fired a well-aimed shot into the animal, killing it. Before it died, though, the creature let out a high-pitched scream that echoed across the lake.

"Almost immediately, the waters churned and another of the creatures rose from the depths, angry and looking for revenge. It moved surprisingly fast, almost catching Terence before he managed to mount his horse and gallop away."

"That was close." Kim asked, enthralled.

"Oh the story's not over. The creature kept pace with the horse, with Terence only able to stay a few steps ahead. He rode over two counties, it's said, before finally gaining enough ground to stop at a blacksmith for shelter. The blacksmith, being a local man of some age, knew of the dobhar-chú. He advised Terence to set a trap, offering his horse as bait. Terence could hide behind the horse, and when the creature attacked, take his chance to kill it for good."

"So what happened?"

"Terence did as the Blacksmith instructed, putting his horse on the road, sideways to provide as much visual cover as possible. When the dobhar-chú arrived, it jumped at the horse, tearing its way through the horse's belly almost instantly. Terence saw the head of the creature poke through the horse and saw his chance. He bound forward and, using a sword provided by the blacksmith, beheaded the dobhar-chú."

"So what was it?"

"Well, dobhar-chú is actually old Irish for otter. So, if you're asking my opinion, I think it was some sort of oversized otter. Some people say it's more like an alligator. Others, some weird mix between the two. There've been a few more sightings over the years in different lakes, but no definitive proof, of course. It's hard to know how true the story is. The Irish, well... they like their legends. Could just be Terence wanted to get rid of his wife without being accused of murder, and so made the whole story up. Probably equally likely, honestly."

"Have you ever gone there? To look for it, I mean," Kim asked.

"To Ireland?" Miriam laughed. "No. I can't afford to go anywhere I can't drive. Dad got a few exotic jobs when we were little, but he never took us on those trips. And he never got a call to find the dobhar-chú. I don't imagine the Irish actually want it found. Probably worth more to them as a folktale."

Miriam fell silent, letting the story sink in. If her theory held, this tale would prick at Kim's conscience, subtly letting her know that Miriam had started to catch on to the deception. Miriam had a hunch that Kim knew exactly what the devil was.

"So, uh... how recently has it been sighted?" Kim spoke with self-consciousness.

"I'm not an encyclopedia," Miriam answered.

"Are you sure? You kinda seem like one."

Miriam ignored the insinuation—yet another comment meant as an insult that she actually took as a compliment. "Twenty years ago or so, I think. Which is relatively recently, all things considered."

"And..." Kim's questions were coming slower now, more carefully chosen than before. "It's only ever been seen in Ireland?"

"Yep. Only in Ireland."

"Is that normal? That cryptids are only in one place?"

"Yeah. For the most part. The big ones, like Bigfoot, seem to show up everywhere. But most are confined to their local legends."

Kim laughed. "Well, this is the real home of Bigfoot, though."

"Folks in Nepal may disagree with you, though they call it the Yeti."

After a pause, Kim asked, "So, this dobhar-chú. Is it really dangerous? Otters aren't terribly dangerous if you leave'em alone."

"Who knows," Miriam said with a shrug. "Cryptids are their own things. Their own species. Might not even be very closely related to whatever they look like. If the legend is to be believed, then they're dangerous and have a taste for human flesh. But... there aren't really any animals that naturally have a taste for human flesh, so it's unlikely. Still, when an animal gets hungry enough..."

Kim grew silent. They walked on.

"Miriam?"

"Yes?"

"I have something to tell you."

Miriam stopped. She could tell by Kim's tone that it was something serious. The ruse had worked.

"I may not have been entirely honest with you." Kim looked down. It was the first time Miriam had seen her so uneasy. "The reason that I got so, um, emotional about that otter is because..."

Miriam remained outwardly patient, but her mind started reeling, so sure of what Kim would say that she could hardly focus on the words coming out of her mouth.

"It's not an otter."

"What?" Miriam asked, not really asking for a repeat as much as an explanation.

"I mean, it looks like an otter. I know that. And maybe it is, kinda. But it was just a baby."

Miriam knew exactly what it was. Her theory was correct, and Kim had known all along.

Kim looked up, some resolve having crept its way back in. "Ya know, I've been out here a lot. Like a whole lot. Not always with others. Alone too. Probably more alone than not, actually."

"Ok..."

"The devil isn't dangerous. It's sweet. Gentle, even."

"That otter... it was the devil's pup, wasn't it?"

Kim bit her lip and nodded.

"And that means..."

Kim smiled. One of those smiles not meant to convey happiness so much as awkwardness. "I think maybe that cryptid you were talking about—the dobhar-chú. I think it might be here. At Misty Lake. I've actually spent a lot of time with it. With them. With the whole family, really."

She'd worked out that the monster they hunted was the dobhar-chú. Even that Kim had known about it. But she never expected this. Miriam had always believed that the idea of one's jaw dropping was just an expression. But in that moment, her jaw actually dropped.

CHAPTER 18 – Radley

Radley Furey touched his plane down on a private runway nestled in the Cascade foothills. He didn't taxi long before coming to a halt, stepping out and smiling at the middle-aged nurse next to a wheelchair.

"Hello, Ms. Coleman," he said. "Nice to see you as always."

She nodded curtly as he opened the back door and unbuckled the seatbelt holding Beatty in place.

Radley was a short man, easily underestimated, but he picked up Beatty without strain and lowered him into the chair.

"W-w-where are we?" Beatty asked, his question barely above a whisper.

Radley looked up across an expansive green field at the sprawling estate on the other side. "This, John, is the home of your employer—the Director."

"Never met him," Beatty forced out.

"Sure you have."

Radley took the handles of the wheelchair and started down an asphalt path that cut across the field.

"Is the infirmary ready?" he asked the nurse trailing behind him.

"Of course, sir."

"Good. Thank you."

Radley rolled the wheelchair up a ramp near the entrance and threw open the massive door leading into the mansion. He rolled Beatty through a grand foyer, down winding hallways, and through a number of rooms not designed for any particular purpose other than their grandeur. Radley never slowed down, but he also didn't shy away from admiring each and every trophy hung high on the walls, some so large as to be unbelievable. Glass boxes, tastefully placed around each room, housed still more, intricately taxidermied specimens of fantastical and exotic creatures.

The collection was truly a sight to behold. Its value in both dollars and to the scientific community could not be calculated.

Soon they came to a smaller room, sterile and white with marble tile floors. In the middle stood a hospital bed. Wires snaked out in different directions from the machines crowded around. Radley rolled Beatty alongside the bed and locked the wheels in place.

Radley bent down and lifted Beatty, shuffling him around until his head rested on the paper-covered pillow.

"Ok, Ms. Coleman. Do your thing."

The nurse flitted about the room, turning on equipment and choosing supplies. She placed a heart rate monitor on one of Beatty's fingers, and flipped a switch on a nearby machine. It made no noise, but Radley watched the line rising, slowly but consistently, with no signs of atrial fibrillation. Beatty was weak, but not on the verge of death yet.

Ms. Coleman used a pair of surgical scissors to cut what was left of Beatty's shirt off, peeled back the blood-soaked denim, and inspected the wound. The claw-marks were clearly visible, and, as Radley already suspected, they were certainly not from a bear. He wondered if Ms. Coleman could tell that.

After pressing her hands against Beatty's bare chest, Ms. Coleman looked up at Radley with a furrowed brow. "It's not good. He definitely has some fractured ribs. If any of them punctured an organ, he could have internal bleeding. We should get him to a proper hospital. I'm not a surgeon."

Radley looked down at Beatty, whose chest rose and fell with shallow breaths.

"Can't do that. Not right now. Just make him comfortable."

"But, sir, I can't guarantee he's going to make it."

Radley couldn't help but smile at this same argument, the same argument they'd had multiple times over the past twenty years. "That's for me to worry about. Just make him comfortable. Keep him alive if you can."

Ms. Coleman sighed and rolled over an IV cart. She expertly tapped a vein and got the drip flowing. Fetching a vial from a nearby refrigerator, she withdrew the liquid into a syringe, then tapped it twice to ensure there were no bubbles.

As she injected the drug into Beatty's IV, Radley put a hand on his shoulder. Beatty looked up through half-closed eyes.

Radley spoke softly. "The organization wants to express their heartfelt appreciation for your work over the years. You always were one of our best. Ms. Coleman is going to take excellent care of you."

Beatty didn't respond, of course, and Radley didn't expect him to.

"Let me know if there are any changes in his condition," Radley said.

He didn't wait for a response before storming out the door. As he walked back through the grand hallways and massive rooms, he gave no thought to whether Beatty might live or die. He'd been through this routine a hundred times before, with varying results. He couldn't afford to dwell on each one.

Radley simply crossed the field, refueled his plane, and headed back to Misty Lake.

PART TWO:
The Dobhar-Chú

CHAPTER 19 – Miriam

Miriam didn't handle transitions well. Sure, she seemed to always be calm and in control, but that was only because she had an uncanny knack for anticipating every eventuality, no matter how unlikely or mundane. Her entire mind worked as a flow chart, constantly pruning unused paths and creating new ones to be used at a later date, once she had enough information for one logical conclusion.

But now... now there were too many unexpected inputs, and her mind struggled to reform the flow chart into something usable.

"I don't understand," Kim said, wandering through the adjacent parking spaces. "Where did our cars go?"

Miriam collapsed onto a nearby curb block and stared out across the empty asphalt, not listening to Kim. Miriam had come to Washington to find the mysterious devil of Misty Lake. She'd completed that task earlier than expected in a way she couldn't have imagined. The final report would be better written by Kim than by her.

And now, Macy. Where had Macy gone?

"I did leave her the keys, so she could have driven them away, but both of them? Why go through that much effort?"

Paths started to materialize. Decisions started forming. Years of experience, terabytes of data, and a heap of intuition combined to focus Miriam on her new task. Her new mission. She hadn't ignored Kim. She'd simply buffered everything Kim had been saying. Now she could afford to process it, and now she had a pre-formed response ready—along with every branch that might result from going down the only logical path.

Miriam stood up suddenly. "You're right. It doesn't make sense."

Instead of pontificating more on that point, Miriam walked back to the trailhead, its wide muddy mouth inviting hikers into the depths of the forest. Her eyes scanned the imprints left there, cataloging each. To the untrained eye, it was indeed a mess: footprints atop footprints, boot treads crossing other treads. She could make out her own boot prints coming out, along with Kim's smaller ones just behind. Using that as a reference, she could make out pieces of their original prints heading to the lake.

They'd seen the gear out in the woods, so she expected to find prints other than their own, and they were easy to spot. The largest of them she guessed to be a men's size thirteen, with the ones nearby a lot closer to Miriam's own shoe size. Different brand, though, so not her or Kim. Four sets of prints.

No... five sets of prints.

Miriam knelt in the mud, giving little thought to dirtying her jeans. At first, she could only see a hint at the fifth set of tracks, but she followed those until she found a place that hadn't been trampled. Five sets of tracks. Four sets of boots. One set of sneakers. Brooks running shoes by the look of the print. Exactly the kind Macy wore.

Miriam searched further in for any proof that Macy had come back from the woods, but found no evidence for that. She did, however, find the smaller tracks of the two strangers headed out of the woods, along with muddled, straight lines. Something—or someone—being dragged. It could have been Macy. Or it could have been the size thirteens. She needed some proof for that.

Kim stood at the end of the trailhead, watching Miriam as if she'd grown a third head. "What are you doing?"

Miriam held up a finger to shush Kim's questioning. She had to focus. Following the prints and the line, she finally found what she wanted. At some point, the dragged one had put some weight down on their boots. On their very large boots.

"Macy's in the woods," Miriam said as she stood up and brushed off the knees of her jeans. "And the owners of that gear that we found are gone, I think. Or at least, they left. Hard to know if they came back after."

"How the hell do you know all that, Batman?"

Miriam grinned. "Because I'm the world's greatest cryptid hunter."

"More like world's greatest detective."

"Same difference," Miriam replied with a shrug. "Tracks are tracks."

"Have you considered calling yourself something other than hunter?" Kim asked.

"What do you mean?"

"Well, maybe it's just me, but 'hunter' seems nefarious. Like you mean these cryptids harm, and that's not really what you're all about, is it?"

Miriam regarded the look on Kim's face, as if her trail guide needed that to be true more for herself than for Miriam. Certainly, she never explicitly went out to kill the things, but they were often dangerous, and fighting them was really what her father taught her to do. For the first time, Miriam wondered if she'd been taught wrong. Perhaps she really was more of a detective than a hunter—or, at least, perhaps she should have been.

Expertly changing topics, as Kim tended to do when things got serious, she turned towards the parking lot. "Ok, but what about the cars?"

"Well, two strangers. Maybe they took the keys from Macy and drove away. I don't know."

"What? You can't read tire tracks and somehow tell who was driving? I thought you were good at this."

Miriam didn't know how to respond to that, but she'd started to believe Kim wasn't being mean with all her poking. It was just her form of being friendly. A fine distinction that Miriam couldn't always see the difference in.

"Well, we found the devil," Miriam said. "Now we have to find Macy."

"Do you think she's okay?" Kim asked.

Miriam replied without hesitation. "Of course she is. She's tougher than she looks, and it's not the first time she's been on her own. She wouldn't have gone out there without a reason, either. So something's going on that we're not understanding."

"Maybe she saw the devil. Felt obligated to follow for the sake of your job."

"Maybe."

Had Macy really become so invested in their little venture that she'd take on the cryptid hunting duties for herself? If so, Miriam would be very impressed.

Kim took a deep breath. "Should we call the cops or something?"

Miriam had already considered it and dismissed the idea, perhaps a little out of hubris. "We don't really have any hard evidence, and you know these woods better than anyone. With your knowledge of the terrain and my knowledge of Macy, we should be able to find her in no time."

"All right," Kim said as she marched past Miriam. "Let's go find Macy, then."

Miriam turned and followed Kim back down the trail, shoving aside thoughts of the darker ramifications of Macy being lost in the forest. Aside from the dobhar-chú that Kim insisted wasn't dangerous, Miriam didn't really worry too much about Macy being in danger. Black bears hardly ever attacked humans, and not much else could kill a human even if it tried. Macy might be hungry and thirsty and tired, but she was unlikely to be dead.

Unless the strangers had killed her. Also unlikely, Miriam decided. Why would murderers be hanging out in the woods? Whoever they were, they hadn't come to hunt humans. They'd come, at the very worst, to hunt the devil. Still, with the cars gone, it was hard to believe that Macy hadn't at least run into the strangers. If they hurt Macy...

Miriam's face flushed, and her heart sped up just thinking about it. She suddenly noticed that her fists were clenched. Over the years, Miriam had become good friends with Macy, yes, but she'd also developed a need to protect her. Not for the first time, Miriam briefly wondered if she had a savior complex, but really, if she did, it was probably the least of her many complexes.

Shaking the self-psychoanalysis, she turned her mind back to the task in hand. Lost in thought, and desperate to fill out her flowchart as deeply as she could, Miriam followed Kim as they headed back to camp.

CHAPTER 20 – Macy

At first, Macy kept to herself, only staying in the cave when she needed to escape the rain, or to rest. Other than that, she stayed outside, close enough to observe her hosts, but not so close as to give them any reason to lash out at her. She was a bit surprised that the devil hadn't left. It had stayed nestled in the cave with its two pups for the entirety of her stay thus far.

Now she sat on a fallen log, passing the time by staring up at the sky and watching the clouds. They'd dispersed greatly since the night, and the rain hadn't fallen for a few hours. She knew the area was known for its rain, but really, they'd been incredibly lucky for the most part. The nights were uncomfortably cold, but the sun during the day warmed her up enough to get by. Still, she would have loved a fresh pair of pants.

Though sometimes feeling the edges of her mind cloud with panic, she had, for the most part, been able to enjoy the quiet. There was tranquility in these woods, and her trust in Miriam lessened the fear. Macy could hardly believe that she'd been bored the previous day even with a cellphone, and now she felt at peace, drinking in the towering trees, chirping birds, and, of course, the legendary creature in the cave. She really had encountered some seriously insane stuff since she'd met Miriam back in Rose Valley, and, in this quiet moment, she felt better for it.

Something like a groan echoed from the cave. Macy looked up to see the devil at the entrance, regarding her carefully. She waved without thinking, then giggled at herself for the absurdity of such an action. She didn't know how to make it feel comfortable with her, but she felt certain that human pleasantries wouldn't mean much.

"Hey, mama," she said quietly, careful not to gaze too long into the creature's eyes. She worried that would indicate aggression, the way it did with cats. "How are the pups doing?"

The creature huffed and turned back into the cave, only to come back out. It took just a few seconds for Macy to realize that it was turning around, looking for a comfortable place to lay. In the end, it curled up at the mouth of the cave, its head resting on its tail in a way so it might keep an eye on her. She couldn't blame the thing. She wanted to keep an eye on it, too.

The devil pups peeked out into the sun, blinking their tiny, beady eyes, before looking back at the devil. Mama, as Macy decided she should be called, didn't stop her offspring, instead watching them carefully as they ventured out into the mud and grass. The pups were timid at first, but quickly turned on each other, faux-attacking in turn and rolling around on the ground in a fearsome ball of fur. Macy watched with delight, a smile painted across her face.

After the death match between the siblings, they both started creeping towards the fallen log where Macy sat. Her muscles tightened as they grew near. She remained still and quiet. If Mama thought Macy meant harm to the babies, things would surely not end well. Curiosity seemed to be a driving force of the little guys as they both became enamored with her sneakers, sniffing them before climbing over them and rolling off. The braver of the two found a way up the log and sniffed at Macy's jeans before climbing into her lap and standing on its hind legs to peer at her face.

Unable to stop herself, Macy let out a laugh as the whiskers tickled her cheeks. The pup recoiled into her lap, but didn't run. Mama lifted her head, her eyes alert, shrewd.

"Sorry, Mama. It tickled." Macy was no stranger to talking to animals. She'd always had conversations with her dad's dog, and friends' pets. And, as alone as she was, talking to Mama just made her feel more comfortable with her situation.

When the pup didn't leave her lap immediately, Mama seemed to calm down a little, but not entirely in the relaxed state that she'd started in. It seemed odd that she wouldn't object more, and perhaps even odder: the pups didn't seem scared of humans at all. Had they encountered a human before? Possibly, but Macy was hardly a wildlife expert, especially of an animal that had never been discovered.

The second pup took courage from his brother and climbed the log as well, though it took a little more effort. The second was smaller than the first. Macy decided they were boys with absolutely no evidence to support her claim. She wasn't about to lift their tails to make sure.

Before long, she had two otter pups vying for her lap, with barely enough room for even one. The battle commenced as they treated her lap as a Sumo ring, and Macy delighted in every second of it. Her instincts about the devil not being evil seemed to be true, though if they hadn't been, she'd be dead.

Mama watched carefully, but didn't try to prevent the pups from their game, and Macy was careful to keep her hands to herself. As much as she wanted to pet the little fellas, she didn't want to take any chances. Not to mention, their teeth looked very sharp. She found it miraculous that neither brother had drawn blood yet.

Just as play time started to become more comfortable than scary, the pups skittered off the log in a hurry and ran back to the cave, where they disappeared behind Mama. For her part, she got to her feet and stepped out of the cave, lowering her head. The trees rustled. Worried about what was coming, Macy stood, considering hiding with the pups.

Glued in place, Macy's eyes widened as a second monstrous otter emerged from the woods. This one, almost twice as large as Mama, walked slowly towards the cave entrance, stopped, laid on the ground, and opened its jaw as something tumbled out to the ground. From her angle, she couldn't see exactly what it was, but Mama immediately ducked her head to inspect it.

At first, Macy suspected food, but Mama didn't make any move to eat whatever the new otter had brought. Instead, she lowered her chin all the way to the ground and let out a wail that sent a shiver up Macy's spine. No matter the species, there was no mistaking the tone of that wail. Sorrow. Sorrow that Macy couldn't have imagined from an animal.

Macy froze as the new, larger otter turned to stare at her. It showed no signs of aggression, though, instead walking past Mama into the cave, and finally clearing Macy's view. On the ground, limp and unmoving, lay another pup. Mama laid next to it, curling around it as if she could warm it back from lifelessness.

Macy's chest clenched. From her vantage point, she'd only seen dried blood, but she pieced enough together to decide that this pup was the one Beatty had threatened to skin. In the confusion, he must have cut the poor thing, intentionally or not.

Nonetheless, this was all the proof Macy needed to know that these otters weren't dangerous unless provoked. And Beatty had made the first move. He'd started the war when he reached into that den and pulled out one of these defenseless babies. Whether Mama or Papa, it had all been in service to their family, and now they'd been forced to retreat to this cave.

Was that why Mama and her pups hadn't left?

The forest wasn't safe anymore. These gentle creatures, who had evaded detection for decades, were now afraid in their own home. Her heart broke for them. This wasn't what Macy wanted. And whether Miriam knew it or not, it's not what she wanted either. They'd never hunted a monster that didn't outright attack them on sight. They'd never had the choice to walk away. But if ever there was a reason, this might be it. What kind of havoc would the world wreak on these creatures if she and Miriam brought them to light?

Regardless, it wasn't just them that threatened the otters. Though Beatty had been badly injured, Macy hadn't seen Abby again after the otter had chased her away. Macy didn't know Abby well, but she knew enough to know that the hunter would be back, if able.

This added a new dimension to Macy's safety. Though she felt comfortable enough staying near the otters, and still believed it was her best chance to eventually find Miriam, she didn't want to be caught in the crossfire when Abby returned to kill these things.

But she also couldn't abandon them, so she had to protect them.

From a well-geared, expertly trained hunter.

No big deal.

CHAPTER 21 – Abby

Abby had woken up feeling like she had a hangover. She hadn't gotten very much sleep, but somehow she knew that wasn't the reason for the way she felt. She'd become so adept at controlling her thoughts that her body had taken on the weight of her emotions instead. At one point, after the death of Ben, her therapist had told Abby that she had to confront the trauma, or else it would manifest physically. Sounded like a bunch of horseshit to her, so she quit therapy and immersed herself in her new job.

Much healthier.

She was slow to pack up camp, stumbling around, expertly avoiding any of the evidence that might remind her of Beatty's mishap. She was good at avoidance.

As she tried to formulate a plan for the day, her radio crackled.

"Good morning, Ms. Wilson." A beep followed, letting her know Radley was done talking. Bastard wasn't supposed to call her. He was supposed to keep radio silence until she contacted him. She preferred that. It gave her control of the situation, let her dictate when she wanted to confront Beatty's condition.

Still, he had information she desperately wanted, so Abby moved with the greatest speed she had mustered since waking, scooped up the radio, and pushed the button. "How is he?"

"Alive."

"Is he going to be okay? Did he get surgery?"

"He's comfortable," Radley replied. "They're doing everything they can. I'm sure he'll be fine. He's strong."

Abby collapsed onto the ground and pulled her knees up. She took a deep breath, her shoulders growing lighter. He would be fine. He hadn't been killed.

After a few minutes of silence, Radley's voice came through again. "How are you doing, Ms. Wilson?"

She replied immediately, automatically. "I'm fine. Just glad he's going to be okay."

"Ya know what he told me on the flight?" Even with the waning frequency, the concern in Radley's tone carried through. She barely knew the guy, but she so desperately needed someone—anyone.

She wiped her nose on the back of her hand before replying, "What's that?"

"He told me that it didn't matter that he'd been taken out, because you're the one who always gets the job done anyway. He seemed confident you'd succeed."

Abby's eyes felt itchy, watery. "We're a team. We do it together."

"Well, do it for him, then."

She didn't answer immediately, instead drinking in the directive, really thinking about it for the first time. This devil had taken the love of her life, and now the best friend she'd ever had. At what point should she just admit defeat? At what point was it no longer worth the cost? For the first time, she considered that maybe she pressed forward on pride alone. She wanted to know that she could kill the devil, if only to banish that hollow feeling of helplessness.

She pushed the button. "Yeah. I'm on it."

"Good, Ms. Wilson. Beatty would be very pleased. Talk later?"

"Yeah. But radio silence, remember? Nothing until I call you."

"Even if there's significant news on Beatty's condition?"

Abby put the back of her hand to her mouth and leaned on it. She wanted to say no. She wanted to tell Radley to contact her the second he heard anything. But that wasn't protocol, and if he radioed at the wrong time, he could give away her location or spook her prey.

"Not even then. I'll check back when it's safe."

"As you wish. Radley out."

She lowered her head into her knees. She took a deep breath, then exhaled, over and over, as if breathing alone could solve her problems. She hated the way she felt. Fatigued. Confused. Every step a mountain. She hadn't felt this way in a long time. Not since...

She hadn't gotten this far by giving in when her mind and body tried to give up. And she sure as hell didn't intend to start listening to herself now. Like she'd done for ten years, Abby shoved aside the emotions threatening to burst out, and went back to work.

After packing, she looked over at the gear they'd left behind. She had three sets now, but could only carry one. Her new pack had plenty of supplies and rations. She wouldn't need these others unless something happened to hers. She couldn't rule out the possibility, so she decided to stash away the other supplies in the event that she'd need them later. She knew just the place.

She secured the packs back together, then lifted one with each hand, her primary on her back. Her biceps strained, but Abby didn't buckle under the weight. She'd spent enough time in the gym to know her limits, and she hadn't spent all that time building up muscle for nothing. She followed the path she'd taken before, when she'd run from the devil.

That run was etched into her brain. If she'd stayed and fought, maybe she could have done more for Beatty.

She turned at all the same places, skirted the same trees, trampled the same underbrush. When she arrived, she walked to the hollowed-out log and sat the gear alongside. It had saved her life once, and if she needed the extra supplies, it may well save her life again. The devil had popped it like an egg in an attempt to flush Abby out, but some parts of it still remained. Enough that she was able to stuff each set of gear inside.

Now to do the work. She didn't care if it got messy. She didn't care if those cryptid hunters got in the way. None of that mattered anymore. She was out after this last kill. She'd leave the country and never come back, thus never risking arrest or prosecution, even if they managed to pin something on her.

Maybe she'd convince Beatty to retire as well.

No. She'd go alone. Safer that way.

Abby turned and headed back to the fateful clearing, ready to follow the clues to her prey. Once there, she tried to discern anything that would give her a hint at a direction. She had some skill in seeing trace evidence, but no one would have called her a proper tracker. When she couldn't find anything concrete, she instead chose to go off memory. She closed her eyes and replayed the event in her head, dispassionately.

Confident in the direction the devil had originally come from, she struck out that way. She walked tirelessly, barely drinking, the morning melting away. Occasionally she'd see something awry. A branch broken. Mud disturbed. After a while, she realized she wasn't tracking the devil. She was tracking the girl. The overnight rain had scrubbed any clear tracks, but what little remained was diminutive in comparison to the devil's massive paws.

Abby considered breaking off. Finding the girl wouldn't accomplish anything. But she had no other tracks to follow. Nothing else to go on. She persisted, happy to have purpose.

And then luck broke her way. The end of her journey shone upon her. Just ahead, near the mouth of a cave, she found the girl, yes. But also the devil, curled up at the entrance. She took barely any time to process the odd juxtaposition of this monster so near the girl, without any sign of fear. Abby couldn't allow the thought that perhaps these creatures were anything but vicious.

Most important was that neither of them had noticed Abby yet, so she stilled her movement and breath. She wasn't a tracker, but she had mastered stealth. One did not hunt big game without it. Slowly, and surely, she retrieved her rifle. She kept it well-oiled. Handling it barely produced a sound.

She put the butt of the gun against her shoulder and lifted the barrel, looking through the scope until she lined it up with the head of the devil. No chances this time. A straight kill. If the girl knew what was good for her, she'd run.

Abby took a deep breath, and as she exhaled, she slowly and evenly pulled the trigger.

So much happened in just a fraction of a second. The gun fired. The devil moved. The girl jumped to her feet. Another devil emerged from the depths of the cave.

Abby lowered her gun, certain that the smaller of the two devils would collapse at any moment. Certain that her aim had been true enough to pierce its skull.

But she knew, in that same fraction of a second, that that it wouldn't happen. Despite her best efforts, she'd given away her position a moment too soon. The devil had moved. The bullet had missed.

And now she had a moving target on her hands.

CHAPTER 22 – Miriam

Miriam turned her head to do her best at echolocation, then took off in the direction of the sound, not even considering that moving towards gunshots might be a bad idea. Kim took one last look at the upturned grave of the otter pup before following behind.

Then vocalizations.

The same as they'd heard before. From the devil.

And a scream.

From a woman.

Macy?

"Macy!" Miriam yelled.

No response.

Miriam picked up the pace.

CHAPTER 23 – Macy

Macy fell backwards off her seat on the log and crouched behind it, where she caught a brief glimpse of the commotion. Papa shot out of the cave like lightning, his back arching and falling as he galloped towards the sound of the gunshot. Two more shots went off before he made it, but he never slowed down. From the foliage, someone screamed. Macy could only see rustling leaves from her vantage point, before any evidence of Papa or the shooter disappeared entirely.

Macy peeked above the log just in time to see Mama take off up the hill behind the cave, the pups struggling to keep up. The over-sized otter turned, took the larger of the two pups into her mouth and continued onward. The smaller of the two siblings stayed behind, pecking its way up the hill as fast as it could, but losing ground as much as gaining it.

If they trusted Papa, so did Macy. She left her hiding place and ran, keeping herself in as much of a crouch as she could while still moving quickly. She scooped the stray pup up in full stride, and used her free hand to balance as she scrambled up the hill.

At the top, Macy came face to face with Mama, who snarled. Macy startled and held out the pup.

"Sorry, Mama. I didn't know you were coming back."

The mother otter sniffed at the pup, looked back the way she'd come, then huffed. She turned without taking the pup from Macy's arms. She took that as much of an invitation as she'd get and hurried forward, pausing briefly while Mama scooped up the first pup from some underbrush where she'd stashed it. Mama turned again, as if to ensure Macy still had her baby, then continued forward.

Macy followed.

It quickly became clear that, despite the adrenaline, Macy couldn't keep up with a four-legged mega-monster. She lagged behind, eventually stopping entirely to catch her breath. The baby in her arms squirmed to get away, but Macy held firm, worried that if she put it down it would scamper off into a place she couldn't follow.

Behind her, the sounds of the scuffle had entirely vanished, leaving Macy with so many questions.

Why had she run instead of helping Papa?

The shame washed over her. Had she learned nothing from Hogg Run? Retreating wasn't always the answer, and hiding never lasted forever. The pup flipped over on its back in her arms, looking up at her and chirping, almost cooing, though Macy wasn't sure if that was projection or truth. She had to run, right? She had to save this pup. Mama couldn't carry them both at once, and relaying them would have taken too much time.

Given the circumstances, Macy had done the right thing. Perhaps the lesson of previous encounters was that both running and fighting were valid choices, and she had to learn to make the right choice at the right time.

Miriam would have fought, though.

Macy took off towards the path Mama had been on, able to follow for a little while before quickly getting lost among the trees. Her heart pounded, and jittery energy surged through her veins. Adrenaline. A panic attack. Some mix of both. Her lack of control started to set in. Her plan had been dashed. Without the devil, Miriam would never find Macy in all these trees. It seemed impossible, and with Abby out there, yelling would just as likely end badly, too. Though maybe Papa took care of that problem.

Hopefully.

CHAPTER 24 – Abby

had better accuracy when it was on the move. She tried to stay brave. She stood her ground and kept firing, somehow sure that she'd get enough clean shots in that this monstrous *otter* would fall down inches from her feet.

That didn't happen, though, and after the second shot didn't even seem to faze it, she realized that, if she wanted to try another day, she needed to run. Now.

Abby got up, scrambled backwards a few feet then turned. She sped forward, while searching for any hiding place she could leverage on the way. She'd shot this thing three times now in total, counting when it attacked Beatty, so she worried that it wouldn't be giving up so easily this time. She crashed through the underbrush like a bull, shattering small branches and ripping leaves to the ground, all desperate to find another vantage point. Another place that she could afford to turn and fire.

The devil gained on her, though. She could tell. The sound of its weight behind her echoed in her eardrums, and its breath became louder and louder. She could feel it now, its wet warmth buffeting her neck. She tried to run faster. Pushed her legs harder. But she couldn't outrun it this time. She didn't have enough of a lead. *Dammit*. She shouldn't have stayed to fire.

A force behind her sent her tumbling to the ground, right into a tree trunk. Hitting it knocked the wind out of her. She climbed to her feet as quickly as she could, fighting through the pain. When she planted her left leg, she winced. Something was wrong. Very wrong. No time to investigate. She had to move.

She turned and it was there, within striking distance. The tree trunk prevented her from going backwards, and no lateral movement offered escape.

The creature lunged towards her, but stopped short. A mock charge, she guessed. It lunged again, closer this time. She was finally close enough to fully take in the monster she'd been hunting. There was no doubt that it shared the phrenology of a typical otter, but its size made it almost impossible. Like when seeing bugs magnified too many times, it just didn't seem real.

Its beady eyes widened, its nose crinkled. Whiskers danced around her. Then it roared in her face. Not like a lion, exactly, but she didn't know how else to characterize the deep, rumbling sound that washed over her.

She realized that, although time felt like it had slowed down, she'd only begun to process it differently. The devil hadn't stopped its attack as it seemed. It opened its mouth and lunged again. On reflex, she rose her arms. She grunted as sharp fangs dug through the flesh of her left forearm.

Abby held firm, intent on making it eat her arm off first if it wanted to get to her. It took another lunge, this time causing her to scream as she felt the teeth further in, sinking through muscle and tendons.

Then a gunshot.

The devil spun away from her, giving her a second to look at her arm. Blood gushed from the wounds, covering her skin so completely that she couldn't tell exactly where the injury was, or how deep.

As it moved away, Abby caught a glimpse of her saviors: two girls, one of them pointing a pistol towards the sky. So she hadn't shot at the devil. All the same, she managed to distract it, and that's what Abby needed to regain her composure.

Using her good arm, she reached around to her back and swung her rifle to the front. She tried to mount it against her shoulder as she normally would, but her left arm had no interest in cooperating.

Fine. She didn't have enough time to fight with it, so she used her right arm to pull the rifle up, tried her best to get it against her shoulder without the use of another hand, and pulled the trigger. Somehow, though not surprisingly given her abysmal luck, she missed, the bullet whizzing by one of the creature's whiskers. She may have even hit one, though she couldn't be sure.

Abby ran as it turned back to her, realizing that she'd made yet another mistake. She'd never encountered a creature so resilient.

She'd also never had such horrible luck.

She tore through the undergrowth, limping along on what she knew was a sprained ankle, but the pain in her arm far outweighed the pain in her leg, enabling her to completely ignore it for a short while. The devil was behind her in a heartbeat. She zigged and zagged as best she could, hoping that erratic movement would make it harder for the creature to keep a line on her. It chirped behind her, but calling it a "chirp" didn't do justice to the weighty, low menace that accompanied its sound.

Her bad ankle turned on her, just as the toe of her good foot hit a root. She fell face first into the mud, her ribs rattling as she hit the ground. Her bad arm prevented her from properly catching herself. The creature clamped her bad ankle into its mouth, not as hard as she'd expect. Not hard enough to rip it off. Still, it hurt, especially when the creature started pulling her backwards, sliding her across the forest floor. Her gun lay out of reach. She must have dropped it when she fell.

She grabbed the branch of a bush and held tight, causing the devil to slow down briefly, but not enough before the branch broke away from its stem. This thing had babies. She'd seen them. This thing wasn't killing her...

Because she was dinner for the family.

Suddenly, the devil dropped her leg, but just when she thought she might be able to get away, it stepped forward and wrapped its huge mouth around her waist. The warm breath inundated Abby's shirt. She could feel the teeth grazing against her. But again, it didn't bite hard. It didn't mean to snap her in half. It did, however, easily lift her into the air. Her instinct was to struggle, but she didn't. She worried that doing so would cause the creature to clamp down harder.

As the devil took off in an otter-like gallop, Abby winced against the pain. It seemed fitting that she'd die like this. This thing had taken everyone she loved, anyway. Perhaps this was always fate's plan for her.

Staring at the ground, Abby watched as the mud and grass sped by, out of options and drained of the will to fight.

CHAPTER 25 – Miriam

After firing the shot, and giving the woman enough time to escape the clutches of death, Miriam tucked the pistol into the back of her pants and took off. Kim didn't move.

"Wait!"

Miriam rounded back. "What? We have to hurry. It's going to kill that lady."

"That lady was trying to kill it. Maybe she deserves what she gets."

Harsh. Miriam didn't expect that from happy-go-lucky Kim at all.

"We don't know that for sure. Maybe she was out here hunting something else."

Kim shook her head. "You didn't see the gunshot wounds?"

Miriam had seen the gunshot wounds, but that didn't prove Kim's point. Every person had a right to defend themselves, and if a grizzly-sized otter attacked her, Miriam would certainly pull the trigger. Now, more than ever, Miriam had a hard time seeing a way out of this that didn't involve hurting the dobhar-chú, no matter how rare it might be. She certainly wasn't going to let someone die.

"Besides," Kim continued. "Maybe she's the one who forced Macy into the woods. Or took our cars."

Miriam surged forward. Kim finally started to follow.

"Well, if she knows where Macy is, that's all the more reason to save her."

With no further protest, Miriam moved quickly through the forest, easily spotting the path taken by the dobhar-chú. Apparently, when it moved fast, it left more of a wake behind it. The path took them further from camp than they'd ventured yet, eventually leading to a clearing with an empty cave. From there, Miriam couldn't quite tell where to go next.

"Great, we've lost it."

When Miriam turned, Kim wasn't looking in her direction. She was looking across the clearing, at the edge of the forest on the other side of a fallen log. And beyond that, the dobhar-chú, its head down. Miriam's heart sank. They were too late.

"Kawa," Kim yelled. "Stop it!"

Kawa? Who the hell...

The dobhar-chú lifted its head to look at Kim. Its fearsome facade melted, though the blood smeared across the white furred chin still made it a terrifying sight. The air hung silent and tense. Miriam reached around behind her and wrapped her hand around the handle of the pistol. It wouldn't kill this thing. She knew it wouldn't, not without a one in a million shot. But she might be able to use it to scare the creature away — if they were lucky.

The dobhar-chú stepped one foot up on the log and... smiled? Miriam realized she was personifying the behavior, but it looked like a dog whose owner had just come home.

It charged towards them. Miriam's grip tightened on the butt of her pistol. Kim put a hand across Miriam's chest, as if she was stopping short in a car and Miriam was her passenger. Kim had been, at the very least, a bit obtuse. She'd obviously lied about the dobhar-chú, even more than she'd already revealed.

Against every instinct in her bones, Miriam loosened her grip and dropped her hand to her side.

The dobhar-chú came to a halt just in front of them and ducked its head down to Kim's chest. Kim pulled her hands up and scratched behind its ears.

"Miriam," Kim said as she continued petting it. "This is Kawa."

"You named it?"

"No. He told me his name."

Miriam couldn't tell if Kim was telling the truth. Perhaps this girl was completely off her rocker.

Kim's face broke out in her signature smile as she giggled. "Of course I named him, dummy. Animals can't talk. As an expert in animals, I'm surprised you didn't know that."

Miriam didn't even know what to say. She just watched as Kim ran her hands across the otter's fur as if it wasn't a giant, mythical creature from another country. As if she'd just found a stray cat who needed attention. Miriam had so many questions.

Before she could ask them, though, she heard moaning. Lost in the moment, she'd forgotten about the lady that had been attacked. Or, perhaps, Miriam had already decided that the hunter must be dead. Leaving Kim to tend to the dobhar-chú, Miriam rushed over, deftly hopped over the log and knelt beside the woman.

She wasn't dead. If anything, she looked only a bit banged up. She had a gash on her arm, and her clothes looked snagged and torn in places. But her guts were still inside of her body, and Miriam saw no signs of worrisome bleeding. Broken bones, on the other hand, might have been a possibility, but none were in such bad shape that they sat at funny angles. That seemed promising.

Miriam put her hand on the lady's shoulder and looked down at her. "Are you okay?"

What a dumb question. Of course she wasn't okay.

The lady moved slowly, but managed to lock eyes with Miriam. She moved her lips as if to speak, but no words came out. Miriam wouldn't be able to carry this woman, not even with Kim's help. She was stout, with impressively tight muscles and a dense build. They'd have to get help into the forest for her.

Miriam started to stand, but a hand gripped her wrist.

"Is it gone?" the lady asked.

Unsure how to answer, Miriam looked over at the dobhar-chú and Kim, contently hanging out together as if Kim's pet hadn't just almost killed this woman.

"You're safe now." Not an answer. Not a lie. As inexplicable as it seemed, Kim somehow had control of this thing.

The hunter tried to get up, lifting to her elbows before stopping. "You're Miriam, right?"

Miriam couldn't hide the shock on her face, confused as to how this random hunter could possibly know her. The idea that maybe she'd garnered a few fans crossed her mind, but she quickly dismissed it. Not many people became fans of cryptozoologists. Most people didn't even know the word existed. There had to be another explanation.

Actually, Miriam found only one.

"So you met Macy."

The lady nodded. "Feisty."

"You have no idea," Miriam said. "Where is she?"

"I don't know. She ran off."

"Why did she go with you? She was supposed to stay in the van. And now the van is gone."

The lady pushed to a full sitting position before not giving an answer. "I'm Abby."

The fact that Abby had changed the subject wasn't lost on Miriam. There was more to this story.

"Did you hurt her?"

"No."

"Why was she with you then?"

"We were looking for you."

"Why?"

A pause. Miriam couldn't tell if Abby was searching for answers, or making them up.

"We have an aligned interest."

So not just a random hunter who had an unfortunate run-in with the devil of Misty Lake. Abby had come to find it.

"What do you want with the dobhar-chú?" Miriam asked.

"The dobhar what?" Abby asked rhetorically. "I was hired to find the devil."

"By who?"

"Does it matter?"

Of course it mattered. Abby was being cagey, but regardless of her motives, she needed help.

Giving up on the interrogation for now, Miriam asked, "Can you walk?"

Abby stretched her legs, bent her knees, then tried to flex her ankles which caused her to cry out in pain. No matter what Abby was lying about, she wasn't lying about that. Miriam could see the agony on Abby's face.

"Your arm looks pretty bad, too."

It was hard to tell for sure how bad. Abby's entire left arm was covered in blood. Under it were surely cuts, but Miriam had no way of knowing exactly how deep they might be. Likely a bite from the dobhar-chú. It was entirely possible that the saliva of the creature might contain bacteria that could prove deadly if the wound wasn't properly cleaned. Miriam hadn't brought her pack. Just the gun.

She stood. "Hey, Kim. You got a first aid kit?"

Miriam got the answer without Kim's reply. Kim had already taken out the first aid kit and was using it to tend to Kawa's wounds, making it quite clear where her loyalties stood. Miriam had been taught to always prefer people over animals, no matter how exotic or special. She didn't want Kawa to die exactly, but if resources were limited, there was only one logical choice of where to spend them.

"There's enough," Kim said, almost as if she could sense Miriam's concern.

Miriam hopped over the log again, gathered up some basic supplies, and returned to Abby.

"This is gonna hurt."

She didn't wait for Abby to reply before pouring alcohol over where she guessed the wound to be. Abby hissed, but didn't scream. The bite looked bad. It needed medical attention beyond what Miriam could provide with her limited first aid skills. She did her best. Abby remained impressively stoic until her arm was wrapped in gauze. Miriam could already see blood seeping through.

"We're gonna have to get you some help."

"No."

"I can't carry you, and you can't walk."

Abby glanced at the ground. "I have a guy. If you can get to him, he'll make sure I'm taken care of."

"Are you sure?" Miriam asked. "We should probably call an ambulance, or—"

"I'm sure."

Abby interrupted so emphatically that Miriam didn't even try to press the issue. She just sighed.

Pulling out her phone, Miriam voiced the new plan. "I'm marking the location here, and of Abby's contact on my phone. We'll go and get him, then come back."

"I'm not leaving her out here alone," Kim said. "I don't trust her. She wants to kill them."

Miriam couldn't argue with that. Though she didn't have all the facts, evidence did suggest that perhaps Abby meant to kill it. Or perhaps, she'd just been studying it and it attacked, giving her no choice but to fire.

"Well, she can't walk. We have to get her help."

Kim finally stopped tending to Kawa and stood up. She approached Miriam, then held out her palm.

"I'll stay here," Kim said. "Kawa can keep me safe. Just leave me the gun."

That seemed like a monumentally bad idea. Miriam's flowchart provided a dozen reasons that could go wrong, and only one narrow path of actual success. As much as Kim had grown on her, Miriam wasn't even sure that Kim wouldn't just shoot Abby, given the chance.

No. That was preposterous. Kim loved these dobhar-chús, but she wasn't a murderer.

"I don't think that's the best idea."

"Well, she's not leaving my sight," Kim replied, about as defiant as Miriam had seen her thus far. "So you can figure out how to carry her, or I can stay here and guard her."

It briefly occurred to Miriam that she could somehow use Kawa to transport the body. Given his size, it would be trivial for him to support Abby's weight. Nothing felt real anymore. Miriam had killed a kraken, fought off a cult, stopped a genetically mutated killing machine. But she'd never been in this situation. Kim's relationship with these things seemed impossible, yet here they were, Kawa comfortably stretched out on the ground. Miriam realized for the first time that she'd even started to refer to it as Kawa in her head. She wondered about the pups, the inevitable mate, and the names Kim undoubtedly had given them, but figuring that out didn't seem to be the highest concern of the moment.

Miriam sighed and pulled the pistol from her waistband, offering it to Kim. "Fine. But I've got questions when I get back. A lot of them."

"Once she's no longer a threat, I'll answer them." Kim paused and fixed her black eyes on Miriam's, drawing out something personal and honest. "I promise."

Miriam regretted not bringing Tanner. They would have finished this job by now. People were unpredictable, and Miriam had no control over what they did. So irksome.

"I'll hold you to that."

Kim nodded and headed back towards Kawa, while Miriam used Kim's phone to mark her location. Luckily (and impressively), Abby knew the coordinates of her contact by memory. Whatever gear she'd had, including her gun, was now strewn about the forest.

"Okay. I'll let your guy know and then I'll be back."

Abby nodded and winced as she used her good arm to drag her closer to the log until she could lean up against it, making it easier to keep upright. The two shared a look, and Miriam turned to leave.

"Miriam," Abby said. "Thank you."

Miriam turned and nodded, then struck out. It might have been a bad idea to leave two strangers and a mythical creature together in the woods, but now Miriam was committed to this path, and all she could do was move down it as quickly as she could.

CHAPTER 26 – Macy

Macy trudged on. Further from the cave seemed preferable to staying in place, and even if she couldn't find where Mama had gone, she needed to find somewhere safe. Occasionally it felt like her life was on a loop. Was running through the woods her thing now?

What a thing to be known for.

Something moved up ahead, coming at her from the side. Macy moved quickly, ducking around the nearest towering tree and easily concealing herself behind its trunk. She waited until it seemed especially close, then slowed her breathing, taking as much time between each as she could without having to gasp for the next. She tried to analyze what she heard. The breaking twigs. The rustling leaves. The most likely threat would be Abby.

The pup chirped in her arms, loudly, followed by a prolonged chitter. She tried to quiet it, but the damage had already been done. The intruder moved closer. Macy frantically looked for a new hiding place, but then froze in her tracks at the sound of Mama's rumbling, purr-like sound. Not Abby. Macy turned just as Mama's massive head twisted around the tree, her head lowered to smell her baby. Macy held out her arms.

Mama nimbly took the baby into her teeth, with an impressively gentle touch. It seemed impossible that the cute little pup was going to grow up to be as big as its mother. It looked tiny in her jaws.

Mama turned and slithered off, moving slowly this time. Macy watched, wondering if she'd overstayed her welcome.

But then Mama turned and locked eyes with Macy. They stared at one another for a few seconds before Mama turned back, but didn't move forward. When Macy didn't move, Mama turned to look again.

Okay. So the giant otter was telling Macy to follow it. Not strange at all.

Macy took a step forward and Mama finally started moving, walking slowly enough that Macy had no trouble keeping pace. They walked and walked, Mama turning periodically to ensure Macy hadn't fallen behind. Though this monster looked like an otter, Macy couldn't shake the feeling that some of this behavior deviated from what an otter might do. She didn't know that, of course, but Mama seemed smart. Like a dog. Maybe even smarter.

Hyenas looked like dogs, but were more closely related to cats. The animal kingdom was weird, man. Who knew what this thing might actually be, or where it might have evolved from. Maybe it'd even been mutated because of some sort of man-made invention.

Were there nuclear power plants in the area, or something? That was how popular culture usually explained mutations, anyway. And, of course, she couldn't ignore the possibly of a science experiment gone wrong. She'd already dealt with that before.

Mama stopped, and Macy, lost in thought, almost barreled right into her backside. Ahead lay dense underbrush. A wall of greenery. Macy thought the forest dense before, but this took it to a whole new level. For as far as she could see left and right, she saw nothing but unnavigable vegetation. She looked up. If they were meant to climb this tangle of trees and plants, this would be the end of the line for her. She couldn't even see the top.

But they weren't going to go up, apparently. They were going through. Mama moved to her left, found a place that didn't look like it would even come close to fitting her huge form, then pushed with her nose. The branches flexed and moved enough for her to squeeze ahead. Macy followed, easily crawling through the giant hole left by the devil.

After just a few feet, the underbrush opened to reveal a tree-formed grotto, lit by sun streaks through the canopy. Half the large space was filled with water that lapped against the far edge, going somewhere Macy couldn't see.

It had to be connected to Misty Lake.

The larger pup was already there, splashing and dashing in the shallower water, when Mama sat down his brother. The two pups sniffed one another and immediately started playing, rolling around, in and out of the water, behind rocks, over tree branches. Whatever danger they'd been in, they didn't seem to understand it.

For her part, Mama moved to one side of the drier land and circled in space before lying down, her body collapsing with a *thud*. She made a noise like a sigh.

"Me too, Mama. Me too."

Macy sat on the ground, facing the water and watched the pups play. This grotto seemed so remote and so hard to get to that surely it would provide the safety they'd need. Places like this probably existed all over the forest surrounding Misty Lake. It was easy to see how these monsters had managed to stay hidden for so long. But these woods were the home of the devil, not the people, and already Macy had watched as humans flushed the devils out of one place after another. These mega-otters couldn't be expected to survive their whole lives in grottos such as this.

Papa.

Her thoughts took a sharp turn to the larger of the two devils. Macy tried to remember how many gunshots she'd heard. Two, three, maybe. Would that be enough to kill him? She looked towards Mama, who hadn't yet closed her eyes. Macy stared into those large dark orbs, and wondered whether Mama was wondering about Papa as well.

"I'm sure he's fine," Macy said. Mama's ears twitched as if she were listening, but otherwise she stayed still, sad eyes carefully watching the pups.

Macy felt the same way. Everything certainly wasn't fine.

CHAPTER 27 – Abby

Given her vantage point, Abby couldn't see behind her. She vaguely knew the devil hadn't left, and that made her uneasy. In all her hunts, she'd never been injured this badly. Every inch of her hurt. The pain radiating from her arm made it such that she couldn't pinpoint where the actual bite was. It could have been anywhere in that side of her torso, and she would have believed it. She shouldn't have been terribly surprised. This thing had killed the love of her life, and severely injured Beatty. Why did she think she'd fare any better?

When she'd first started in the business, she made it her priority to learn as much about the animal kingdom as she could. She focused on big game. The animals that could really hurt you if you didn't play your cards right. Lions, tigers, elephants, rhinos. Things like that. She'd never really studied otters, but did remember coming across an article talking about some of the more dangerous animals, pound for pound. Ones that didn't pose a serious threat to humans, but only because of their smaller size. At the top were things like the wolverine, the honey badger and Tasmanian devil. And somewhere, further down – the otter. Not surprising really. It was in the same family as the wolverine and the honey badger.

Even a tiny river otter could cause some serious damage to a human if it felt threatened, and now Abby found herself squaring off against one the size of a grizzly. Easily six hundred pounds or more, and a length far exceeding any bear thanks to the long, slender form. Probably ten feet at least. Clearly, Abby was no match for it. She'd lost two encounters now. The first cost her Beatty and the second might have cost her the whole job. She'd be okay. Whatever damage she'd taken was mostly superficial, something that would heal over time. But in the here and now, she had a hard time seeing how she was going to kill one of these things.

She'd never failed a job. The rumors about those that had weren't pretty.

Abby heard feet crunching against the ground, moving towards her, long before the girl arrived. When she did, she stayed behind Abby, looking down and making it difficult for Abby to get a good look at her.

"If he dies, I'm going to kill you," the girl said.

Abby didn't try to hide a chuckle. "If he doesn't die, I'm dead anyway."

"That sounds like a no-win situation, then."

"Yes it does. If I have to choose, I'd take my chances with you killing me."

"Why's that?"

"Have you ever killed anyone?" Abby asked. "Or anything, for that matter?"

The girl didn't answer, which served to confirm Abby's suspicions. Most likely, she was dealing with the type of person who took spiders outside and shooed cockroaches away instead of stepping on them. Despite her harsh profession, Abby wasn't completely without empathy for animals. But they were, in the end, animals. Humans had hunted and killed them for hundreds of thousands of years. If anything, Abby had just joined a grand tradition of the *Homo sapien* experience.

"How is he?" Abby asked, trying to fully size up her situation.

The girl looked back for a few seconds, then back down. "I think he's okay. I think at least one of them was just a graze, and the two others didn't seem too deep."

Made sense. With all the muscle, and undoubtedly strong bones, Abby would need to get much closer to fire a shot that would seriously injure the thing. Her plan had been to slow it down enough with the first shot to eventually overtake it and finish it off. That plan clearly hadn't worked—yet. If it was injured enough, perhaps she'd have the upper hand in her next encounter. The pain quickly reminded her that another encounter was extremely unlikely.

"What'd you call him?"

"Kawa."

"So, what's your story? You the devil whisperer or something?"

The girl finally came around and sat on the log, facing the same direction as Abby. Now it felt more like a real conversation.

"These are my woods. I spend a lot of time out here, and over time, I guess they grew comfortable with me."

Abby suppressed a smile. *They*. It's not that Abby didn't suspect there were more devils out in the woods, especially after having found what seemed to be babies, but now she wondered exactly how many there were. Perhaps Abby didn't have to kill this one. Maybe there were smaller ones, or weaker ones. Or less aggressive ones.

"Why Kawa?"

"Kawauso," the girl said. "It's Japanese for otter."

"I'm Abby, by the way." She considered offering a handshake, but the pain would be unbearable. Either way, she didn't think this girl would take her up on the offer.

"Kim."

"Well, Kim. This has been one cluster of a mission."

"You're telling me. If I'd had it my way, no one would have seen them at all. And now..."

Abby waited for Kim to finish the thought. When she didn't, Abby replied, "Seems like no one's getting what they want so far."

Kim nodded without reply. They sat in silence for a few minutes until Abby heard the unmistakable sound of rain, *plops* hitting the canopy above. Behind her, she could hear—no, feel—the devil moving.

Kim stood and moved away.

"You okay, Kawa?" Then: "Good idea. Let's stay dry in the cave."

Abby looked up and let the drops splash against her face. It was cold, stinging, uncomfortable. But somehow refreshing, as if it could wash away the failure and give her new hope. Or maybe it could wash away her sins and give her a new lease. The things she'd done could never be forgiven, though, and, as she'd always told herself, it would be worth it—if only to get closure for Ben.

Not revenge. Closure.

As Kim and Kawa sat nice and dry inside, Abby resigned herself to the cold, wet rain.

"Come on," Kim said suddenly. Abby was surprised to hear her so close. "Can't be good for you to get this cold in your condition."

Kim knelt and threw Abby's good arm around her shoulder. Kim lifted, but Abby barely budged. Kim was a wisp of a girl. By comparison, Abby looked like a mountain.

"Gonna need your help if we're gonna get you inside."

Abby didn't think she could do it. She couldn't take the pain of moving. One ankle was beyond useless, and the other didn't seem like it was at full strength. Kim pulled again, and Abby pushed against the ground anyway, grimacing against the onslaught of hot needles shooting up her leg. Yes, her "good" ankle wasn't in the best of shape either.

"You clearly eat your Wheaties," Kim said as she started to move.

The going was slow, Abby being dragged more than helped towards the cave. Her pulse raged, working to give her all the power it could to complete the task. Her head swam. The forest started to spin. She forced her eyes open, even as they desperately wanted to close. The cave grew closer. Abby blurred in and out of consciousness. Maybe moving wasn't such a great idea.

The next thing Abby knew, she felt the stone against her butt, jarring her eyes back open. In the back of the cave, Kawa showed his displeasure at her presence.

"It's okay, Kawa," Kim said, holding up a hand as if she could physically keep Kawa away.

The reassurance only calmed the beast a little. It would certainly be ironic if all of Kim's work to get Abby dry ended in Kawa eating Abby for dinner. Though at least then, the pain would end.

So. Much. Pain.

Kim knelt in front of her. "You all right?"

Abby nodded. At least, she thought she nodded. She was having a hard time distinguishing between reality and fever-dream. Kim was nice. Nicer than Abby probably deserved. But it didn't change anything. Abby still had a mission, and that mission was in direct conflict with Kim's.

After a little rest, Abby told herself, she'd be able to think straight and formulate a better plan. And her ankles would be better. And the sting of the bite wound would lessen. Yes, she just needed to sleep.

And sleep she did.

CHAPTER 28 – Miriam

She'd been back and forth through the trees so many times now that Miriam felt like she was finally starting to see the forest like Kim did. Somehow, she just knew where she was, and which direction would lead outward. She saw subtle clues and landmarks that her memory quickly matched and oriented for her, keeping her on track without nearly as much effort as she'd needed before. That gave her more time to think, and more time to formulate.

More time to plan.

Miriam thrived on being truly alone. She didn't feel like herself any other time. Being around people kept her on her guard constantly, requiring her to anticipate every social possibility so that she could respond appropriately, to do her best to not seem like a complete freak. It didn't even work most of the time, but she felt sure that if people saw her when she was the very most her, they wouldn't even be able to relate. Everyone else seemed to derive some sort of benefit from social interaction, but Miriam often wondered whether she could subsist without ever talking to another human being ever again in her life. She thought she could.

One personality trait that would surely raise objection with most was her tendency to emotionally detach from almost anything. Somewhere in the woods, Macy sat alone and scared, but Miriam couldn't...

connect with that. She cared about Macy, in her own weird way, but she didn't fear for her life in the way she felt like maybe she should. Macy had survived Hogg Run in spite of a murderer and a mutant pig, both of which actively wanted to kill her. Despite the damage the dobhar-chús were capable of, Miriam believed Kim that they didn't mean harm, and wouldn't resort to attacks unless pushed. And Macy was the gentlest soul Miriam had ever met.

Yet, here she was trudging through the woods to save a woman she'd only just met. Fine. Miriam didn't even understand herself, apparently. Or perhaps she was just really good at triage.

The mission was over, really. The devil had been revealed to be a misplaced dobhar-chú, and with Kim's help, Miriam would have all she'd need to write a convincing report. She still wanted to gather up some physical evidence, though. Pictures, at the very least. Hair samples would be even better. And maybe, since Kawa had an injury anyway, gathering up blood wouldn't be too cruel. Damn. She should have thought of that before she'd left. The blood would tell them a lot about the creature's origins.

Miriam turned her attention to the mystery of how exactly the dobhar-chú made it to southwestern Washington state all the way from Ireland. She loved pondering mysteries more than anything else in the world.

Either the dobhar-chú existed in multiple places, or someone had brought them in. Intentionally? She struggled to think of a motive for something like that. Surely no one would derive benefit from introducing monsters into the local ecosystem. If they knew they had a mysterious cryptid on their hands, they would have gained greater rewards from turning it over to someone. Maybe not money. People didn't tend to pay well for cryptid proof—Miriam had learned that the hard way—but at least fame and respect.

No, these things got here without anyone knowing.

Up ahead, Miriam finally spotted the worn trail that led back to the parking lot. No more tromping through the thick vegetation to find her way. Now the path would be clear.

She pulled out her phone and checked her coordinates. Abby's contact would be another few miles past the parking lot, giving Miriam a lot of time. She thought about calling the authorities against Abby's admonition, but decided against it. Abby seemed so adamant, and if Miriam did call the cops, the dobhar-chú would be public knowledge too soon. She'd been hired to find it, catalog it, report on it. It wasn't for her to decide when the existence of this creature went public.

Before she put the phone away, she noticed the cell reception ticking back up as she got closer to civilization. Without Macy, Miriam lacked someone to bounce ideas off of; someone to help her solve the problem. Perhaps talking to herself would work. She had a better idea, though.

She brought up the phone app and punched in Tanner's number, having memorized it long ago. Miriam tended to memorize almost anything, and despite never needing the number thanks to current technology, somehow it still stuck in her head, perfectly clear.

It rang once, twice, three times. On the fourth, his voicemail picked up. Not even customized. Just a prerecorded lady informing her that the mobile customer was not available.

After the beep, Miriam dumped as much of the situation as she could in the short time frame given. She didn't really expect him to do anything about it, but at least someone would know their situation.

She finished by setting a time limit by which she wanted him to call the cops. That seemed like the best of both worlds. She'd get the authorities involved eventually — if necessary — but gave herself some time to get things sorted out. To save Macy and Abby. To assure Kim the dobhar-chú would be safe. That actually seemed the hardest task of all, because Miriam still didn't know how to protect the things once the world knew that they existed.

Lost in thought, the miles melted away. The sun tracked across the sky. The air was cool enough that Miriam didn't feel the heat of it, and the canopy protected her mostly from sunburn. Periodically she checked her coordinates until she was right on it...

...and then, over a fence, in the middle of a field, she saw a small plane. That had to be where Abby meant her to go.

She hopped the fence and started forward. A man stepped out of the pilot seat. Short, young, and energetic, he flashed her a wide smile lined with bleached teeth. His skin was pleasantly tan, his eyes piercingly blue. As she got closer, she realized he wasn't really that young. He just looked it, like some of those actors who never seemed to age.

When she got within about twenty feet, he hollered at her: "Hey there!"

No questions. No accusations. He seemed on his guard, but in the most jovial way possible.

Miriam closed the gap, didn't offer a handshake, and instead spilled straight into her purpose.

"Are you Radley?" she asked.

His smile evaporated almost immediately, his guard shifting from jovial to cautious.

"Yes, that's me," he said, offering a hand now that the introductions had become personal.

Miriam took his smaller hand in hers and shook it firmly. Two pumps, no more, just as her father had taught her. "You work with Abby, right?"

More cautious now, his eyes suddenly sharpened. His young countenance looked shrewder, almost dangerous, as he opened his mouth to respond, closed it, then started again.

"That's right. How do you know her?"

"Let's just say we're recent acquaintances. I met her near Misty Lake."

And there he was. Back to jovial. Though small, Miriam felt threatened by this guy's mercurial shiftiness.

"Ah. So you must be Miriam Brooks then?"

Now it was Miriam's turn to be surprised, only she was far worse at hiding it. "How did you know—"

"Doesn't matter. What's wrong with Abby?"

"I didn't say anything was wrong," Miriam said, still trying to find her footing.

"Well you're here. She's not. Something must be wrong."

"Right. So, yeah. She's hurt. In the woods. I have the coordinates. She said I should tell you instead of calling an ambulance."

If he was surprised, he didn't show it. He simply asked, "What happened?"

She couldn't tell him the truth. She didn't know how much he knew, and if he didn't know about the devil—the dobhar-chú—then she didn't want to be the one to clue him in.

"Not sure. A bear maybe? I found her in pretty bad shape. A lot of blood. She needs medical attention."

He nodded curtly, not showing surprise exactly, but at least a little bit of consternation.

"Thanks for the heads up. If you'll just give me the coordinates, I'll make sure she's taken care of."

Miriam popped out Kim's phone and relayed the coordinates to him, which he took down on a small notepad that he retrieved from the cockpit. How very old school.

"Thanks, Miriam," he said with another of his bone-white smiles. He tried to lock his gaze onto hers, but Miriam was quite adept at avoiding eye contact.

"No problem," she stammered. "I'm gonna head back. I guess maybe I'll see you out there."

He started to climb back up into the cabin of his plane. "Maybe so."

Radley saved Miriam the hassle of trying to extricate herself as graciously as possible, instead closing the door and removing himself from the situation. She turned and walked away, fighting the urge to look back. Something seemed off about that guy, despite his carefully crafted persona—or maybe that's what was off.

Her mind didn't worry about it for very long before meandering back to the dobhar-chú. The time away from the mystery had served her well: the answer hit her like lightning. She remembered something Kim had said—that the otter population had been nearly wiped out in the fur trade, and that they'd brought in otters from outside to reinvigorate the population.

Sea otters, she thought, which were far larger than river otters, but she'd bet her paycheck that those rehomed otters came from Ireland. It was easy to understand how they might have mistaken dobhar-chú pups for sea otters. Then it wasn't much of a leap to believe they'd found themselves inland, being freshwater animals.

That had to be it.

Miriam smiled to herself. A solid working theory that would definitely go into her report. More intriguing still would be that surely Ireland had some, too. If she could find a dobhar-chú there, then she'd really have something to be proud of. It wasn't often that cryptids were found, much less tracked back to their home of origin.

Lost in thought like this, musing about the possibilities, thinking about all the mysteries of the animal kingdom, Miriam almost forgot that Macy was lost in the woods.

CHAPTER 29 – Abby

When Abby regained consciousness, the cave was empty. She could only hear the dripping of water hitting the cave floor, some of it having seeped through from above and forming a puddle towards the back. The pressure in her bladder grew with each drip. It was time to get up. She'd be damned if she was going to wet herself.

She shimmied her shoulders, grimaced against the pain and then flexed her hands, her ankles. She leaned forward. Everything hurt, but she felt better than before. She planted her hands and lifted herself up, using the wall for the strength her weakened arm couldn't supply. Her legs threatened to give out, but didn't, reluctantly holding her weight enough for her to remain upright.

She clutched her side, instantly feeling her own blood. There could have been more, though. She thought maybe it had stopped, or at least slowed, and that meant she had a chance at continuing. She hobbled to the mouth of the cave and peered out.

No devil, but the girl was still there, her blue hair shimmering in the sun. With Abby unable to remain stealthy, it took Kim almost no time to look over and notice that she'd awoken.

"You're awake," Kim said.

Abby nodded, slipped and fell to her knees, barely catching herself before going all the way down. Damn this pain. She needed to get it together. She couldn't let this stop her from her ultimate goal. Not after so much sacrifice.

"Need something?" Kim asked.

"Bathroom," Abby eked out.

Kim crossed the distance between them quickly and ducked down under Abby's arm, helping her back to her feet. The going was slow, but Kim shuffled her towards the tree line.

"Where's the devil?" Abby asked.

"He left."

"And you didn't go with him?"

"I'm not leaving you until I'm sure you're out of this forest," Kim said. "I won't let you hurt them."

"The Director wants a dead devil, and he'll get it. From me or someone else. You can't stop it."

Kim remained quiet as they shuffled forward. Eventually they made it to a tree. Kim leaned Abby against it before retreating far enough away so that Abby had a modicum of privacy. Though it was painful, Abby managed to take care of her business. Her range of motion was coming back. Her ankles were protesting less. Perhaps she was in better shape than she thought.

"I'm done," Abby said.

Kim appeared quickly and took some of Abby's weight again.

"Why?" Kim asked as they shuffled back to the cave. "Why kill them?"

Abby tried to shrug, but didn't really make it. "It's complicated."

"They didn't do anything to you. Why punish them?"

Abby stopped, forcing Kim to do so as well. "Didn't do anything to me?"

Tears threatened as Abby drew strength from her painful past. "One of those things killed my fiancée. The only man I've ever loved!"

Kim glanced sideways. "Wait. You're..."

Abby took a deep breath, swaying as she tried to support her own weight, relying on Kim as little as possible. As she backed up, a glint caught her eye from the waistband of Kim's jeans. The gun. Abby suddenly felt invincible, adrenaline pushing away the pain enough for her to realize she still had a chance at this.

"I can stand on my own," Abby said. She moved her hand down from Kim's shoulder, across her back, then wrapped her fingers around the handle of the gun. She pulled it out and scuttled backwards, her feet tripping over one another and threatening to topple her to the ground. She held her balance, though, partially by extending her arms towards Kim, muzzle pointed at the girl's chest. Kim immediately put her hands up.

"I didn't know," Kim said. "We thought maybe you killed your boyfriend and made up the story about the devil."

Abby laughed mirthlessly. "I didn't make it up. We were camping. It came for us in the night. We ran. And it killed him right in front of me."

Kim's dark brown eyes glassed over. "That's... horrible. But, I know these creatures. They wouldn't have done that for no reason."

"Are you saying it's Ben's fault he was eaten by one of these... things?"

Kim shook her head quickly. "No, I'm not saying that. Maybe you threatened it by accident. You don't have to kill it."

"But I do. For me. And now, for my employer. I've never failed a mission. I'm not going to start now."

"But look at yourself. You can barely stand."

Abby saw the truth of the statement, but the adrenaline of the moment convinced her that she could muster through until the job was done. For Ben. For Beatty. There'd be time for medical attention after that. Once she had the catharsis of this kill, she'd finally be at peace. She couldn't remember what that felt like. To be hopeful and unburdened. She wanted it so bad, and this was her path. This is what she had to do to get herself back, and she would not let a few injuries stop her.

"Turn around," Abby said. Kim hesitated, so Abby tightened her grip on the gun. That was enough. Kim turned.

Abby considered pulling the trigger. She'd never killed another human, but it seemed easy enough. Easier than killing a rare tiger, or a charging elephant. She could put a bullet in this girl's back and have one less headache to worry about.

"Which way did it go?" she asked. Kim started to turn. "Nuh-uh. Point."

Kim pointed towards the tree-line opposite the cave, where Abby had taken her failed shot that had led to the pain coursing through her body.

"Are you lying to me?"

Kim shook her head.

Abby took a step forward, steadier than she expected, and pushed the muzzle of the gun against Kim's shirt. Her finger tensed on the trigger. She'd come this far for Ben. To avenge his death. Her muddled mind tried to justify killing Kim as a step towards that goal. As long as this girl was alive, she'd stop at nothing to frustrate Abby's efforts.

No. She wasn't going to kill a person. This whole thing started because a person had died. Instead, she lifted her hand in the air, brought her arm down, and hit Kim hard on the head. The girl crumpled to the ground, face first into the mud. This was the best option. The best way. Now she needed to find her gear, then the devil, then get the hell out of here and away from this life forever.

Strength returned with every minute. Abby was able to kneel and roll Kim to her back, at least. She'd wake up before long, and her friend would be back eventually.

With that taken care of, Abby looked around. The girl had indicated that the devil had gone into the woods across from the cave, but Abby didn't believe that for a second. She could see signs of the devil scrabbling up the hill next to the cave. She needed her gear first, though.

Her backpack was easy to find. She'd sat it down before she took the shot. She took up her canteen first and emptied the contents into her mouth, lapping up every drop with delight. That alone made her feel more energized. Next, the radio. She needed to check on Beatty and update Radley. She pulled it out, adjusted the volume and pressed the button.

"Radley, you there?"

His voice came back almost immediately. "Abby? So you're okay, after all?"

She considered how to answer that. "I'm... alive."

"Miriam Brooks came here, said you needed a rescue."

The very idea caused all of Abby's wounds to ring with pain, as if to remind her that yes, she absolutely needed a rescue. She even entertained the thought. If she bowed out now, she could return at full strength... hopefully after these cryptozoologists had skipped town.

Radley apparently didn't care for the silence. He spoke again. "I'm glad you're okay. I have some news for you."

"About Beatty?" Suddenly nothing else mattered.

"Yes," he said. "I heard from the nurse taking care of him, and..."

A pause. Too long. Far too long. Her heart was already beating hard, trying to give her enough strength to continue with her injuries, but now it went into overdrive.

"He didn't make it, Abby. I'm sorry."

The sorrow came first. Then the fear.

Then the anger.

It all flooded her so quickly, riding her adrenaline, that she only recognized the last one. First Ben, now Beatty. This damn creature had taken everything from her. She sank to the ground, the back of her radio hand against her mouth. Tears stung her eyes. The cool, humid air of the woods suddenly felt cloying and claustrophobic.

Radley again: "Abby? Are you there? Are you okay?"

His voice sounded distant. She didn't care what he said. Didn't register it.

Abby Wilson had experienced grief. More than many, perhaps. It had never caused her to shrink away. It had never caused depression, in the classical sense. It had only provided fuel. Turned her into a machine that fed on that large supply of grief. She didn't need more fuel. But Beatty had provided it, unexpectedly, to her. It felt the same. Exactly the same. No different than the night Ben had died.

Her mind tugged her back from the brink, reminding her that Radley needed an answer. An answer to a question she didn't hear.

"Um... I..."

"You can pull out now, if you want," Radley said. "No one would blame you."

If she hadn't been in shock, she might have picked up on the tone of his voice. The edge that implied the opposite of what he said. She didn't register that, though. She only heard the offer and considered the implications. No one would blame her. How could they? She'd lost two people she loved—yes, she loved Beatty, she couldn't pretend otherwise now. But she knew one person would always hold her at fault. One person would never let the failure go. And she had to live with that person every day.

"No." She said it with finality, acknowledging the truth of her path before she'd fully formulated it. "I'm okay. I can finish this."

"Alright. I'll call off the evac then."

"Roger that," Abby said. "I'll reach out when the devil is dead."

She turned off the radio without getting a response. It was against protocol to turn it off, but she didn't care. She was in this alone now.

She could finish this.

She *would* finish this.

CHAPTER 30 – Macy

Macy's stomach rumbled. Mama appeared out of the water carrying a mouthful of fish. The babies danced in circles, following her until she unleashed her haul and set them loose on devouring it. Macy didn't particularly like fish, especially raw, but hunger tempted her. The pups would probably share. They'd all gotten on quite well as they waited in this tiny grotto.

Food she could do without. She knew that. It was drink that she worried about. Without any of the skills or kit necessary for purifying her water, she'd been at least sifting it through her t-shirt before drinking from the lake. She had no idea if that was sufficient, but even if she drank up some sort of amoeba or something, surely it would be preferable to dying of thirst. In the grotto, there was no rain, the canopy above shielding them entirely from the outside world, so Macy made do with what she had. The thought of going out there into the woods, especially after the bullets, frightened her enough to stay put.

Macy didn't know the otters particularly well, but Mama seemed sluggish and lethargic, mostly sleeping while the pups played themselves to sleep. Papa hadn't come back, and Macy feared the worst. These creatures were huge, and maybe they could take a few bullets without going down, but surely he'd have come back by now.

She'd have to leave. She knew that. No one could possibly find her in this grotto, and if she didn't leave, she'd starve or die of thirst. She told herself that Abby wouldn't shoot her, but Macy remembered all too well being held captive and didn't want to repeat that either. Though, if Abby got her mark, maybe she'd left. Maybe the forest was safe again. Miriam was still out there somewhere. She wouldn't leave Macy behind.

Macy stood.

Now was as good a time as any to strike out. Sure, there were things to fear out there, but nothing worse than she'd already been through. She pulled up her arms and looked at the faint scars there. After Hogg Run, looking at them brought tears, but now she'd learned to use them for strength, as potent reminders that she could survive more than she thought—that she was stronger than she believed.

For months after, she'd worn long sleeve shirts and pants, sure that anyone who saw all the scars would shrink away from her, but now... now she wore a short-sleeved shirt that even showed off a bit of midriff. The scars on her bare leg were even larger and scarier, but she had barely given them a second thought. She'd come so far. She could do this, too.

She watched the pups devouring their fish buffet, then looked over at Mama. The monstrous otter looked at Macy, their eyes locked. Macy didn't know if a bigger animal meant a bigger brain. She didn't know what Mama could understand or see. Macy needed to go find her people, just like Mama needed to be with her own.

"I'm gonna go," Macy said. "I need to find Miriam."

Mama's ears twitched and her pupils dilated, as if she wanted to understand the words but couldn't quite make sense of them. It didn't matter. Macy moved towards the small hole leading out to the forest, wondering if she'd be able to push through without Mama's help. The pups chittered and chirped behind her, nearly done with their meal and just noticing that Macy was on the move.

"I'll miss you guys," Macy said, turning to look one last time. The pups trotted towards her, the larger of the two nipping at the leg of her jeans. Macy laughed and leaned down, stroking the pup across the head. Mama made a strange sound almost like a groan, but made no move to stop her. After petting the other pup, Macy gently pushed the larger away and turned to leave — for good.

She found the hole, got down on all fours and crawled through, surprised how easy the trail actually was despite looking completely and utterly grown over.

Before long she was out into the forest again. As she stood, panic set in. Something was off. Something was nearby. She scanned the foliage around her waiting to see something, anything, but came up with nothing.

Just nerves, Macy.

She took a step forward, stopped. Listened. Something rustling. Something rumbling.

Papa!

He came through the brush slowly, his back arching with each step. She rushed to him, but he backed away and growled, baring yellowed teeth. Macy swallowed hard. He was hurt. She could see blood. Bullet wounds. Even though she couldn't have done anything to stop what had happened, she felt somehow responsible just by virtue of having been present.

"It's me," she whispered, as if she could talk down an angry monster.

Papa rushed past her, giving her a wide berth, and buried himself into the wall of foliage, where he began inching his way towards the grotto.

Macy bit her lip. She'd been so sure that striking out to find Miriam was the right choice, but she worried for Papa. What if he needed help?

Reluctantly, she headed back.

CHAPTER 31 – Miriam

Miriam's face flushed as she processed the scene. Kim lay on the ground, unmoving and frighteningly still. No sign of Abby or Kawa.

Dammit.

Miriam knew this would happen. She scolded herself for leaving Kim behind. Rushing to her side, Miriam grabbed at Kim's wrist to check for a pulse. Before she found the rhythm, though, she saw Kim's chest rise slowly, then fall. Miriam exhaled, realizing only then that the breath had caught in her chest. Not dead. A quick scan of Kim's body showed no obvious signs of trauma. Certainly no gunshot wounds.

"Kim?" Her voice came out shakier than she would have expected.

Miriam sat on the ground and cradled Kim's head into her lap.

"Kim?"

Still nothing. She lightly patted Kim's cheeks.

"Kimiko?"

Kim's chest suddenly rose higher as she inhaled a deeper breath. Her eyes snapped open, pupils dilating. Fear apparent. She sat upright so quickly that her head almost clipped Miriam's chin.

After looking around, Kim pulled up her knees and rested her head on them. She groaned.

"That bad?" Miriam asked.

"My head," Kim said. She rubbed the side of her temple.

No sign of the gun. Kim had clearly underestimated Abby. Gotten too close. Given her an opportunity.

"Yeah. Getting pistol-whipped doesn't feel good." Awkwardly, Miriam reached out and put a hand on Kim's back, a little unsure of what to do after she made it that far. She decided to rub gently. "You'll be okay, though. Probably. I'm just glad she didn't shoot you."

If Abby had gone to the trouble of stealing a gun to escape Kim's guard, she had a plan. There could be no question that Abby meant to kill the dobhar-chú. Losing even one of the adults could spell doom for the population, even if there were others in the area, as Miriam suspected. The job wasn't to protect them, though. The job was to find them and prove their existence. Abby was about to do that in a completely different way.

"You were right," Miriam said. "Abby's going to kill them."

Kim turned her head to look back. "We have to stop her."

Miriam didn't like the prospect. She wasn't a hunter of people. She wasn't an enforcer of decency.

Who was she kidding? She could rationalize with herself all she wanted, but she was already committed to this, either through a need to protect the dobhar-chú, or to please Kim. Miriam wasn't quite sure which.

"Okay," Miriam said. "But we need to be smart about it. And we need to find Macy first."

Kim nodded. "Deal."

"We don't have weapons."

"Sorry."

"It's okay," Miriam replied. "But Kim, we really should consider calling the authorities."

"No. Then the secret will be out. People will come for miles. If they don't kill them outright, then their habitat will be eroded. We can't out them to the world. Besides, they're not even known animals, and that means they aren't protected."

"Yet. But they will be once the world knows they exist."

"That won't be fast enough."

Miriam wasn't sure she completely bought Kim's logic, but she did feel the passion emanating from her conviction. Wasn't the entire point of the expedition to out these animals to the world? It wasn't that Miriam didn't want to protect them. It was just that she and Kim had very different ideas about how to go about doing it.

"But what can we do? Let's say we stop Abby today. Let's say she leaves. She'll be back. She knows about them, and if she knows, someone else probably knows. Her contact, for one. We can't stem this tide."

Kim scooted herself around so that she sat facing Miriam now, her black eyes stern and cold. "Then we have to make sure they can't come back."

"We're not killing anybody. Not unless they present a direct threat to us."

Miriam wasn't shocked exactly, but she also didn't believe Kim could live with the consequences of what she was suggesting. In Rose Valley, Miriam had killed a man. One too far gone to save, perhaps, but a man all the same, and that had changed her. She could shoulder it. She'd managed to justify it, compartmentalize it, and live with the consequences, but she knew she'd never been the same since. It was that action that had finally pushed her away from her father for good. That finally gave her the strength to chart her own path.

Kim stared at her for a bit in silence, making Miriam uncomfortable enough to avert her eyes downward. Kim was mad. Fine. But murder? No.

Miriam offered a hand to Kim, helping her to her feet. She wobbled a bit at first, but quickly looked steady enough to move. What they decided to do with Abby might come to a head eventually, but finding Macy was first priority. Stopping probable murder could come next. Miriam didn't doubt her ability to stop Kim from doing anything stupid. Passion was no match for strength and training.

First, Macy. Miriam didn't even know where to start. Somewhere in this maze of trees languished a red-headed southern girl with a laughable amount of camping experience. It seemed an impossible task. Even with above-average tracking skills, the chances of finding Macy seemed astronomically low.

"Kawa went that way," Kim said, pointing up the hill next to the cave entrance.

Not what Miriam was looking for.

"Macy first, remember?"

"Oh, right."

Miriam wandered through the clearing. She could see signs of their presence. Scuff marks on the ground. A few partial footprints. In the cave, she could see a smoothed-out area on the ground where the dobharchú had slept. None of this was going to help her find Macy. In a forest this vast, surely Macy hadn't been at this exact cave. Neither life—nor Miriam's luck—worked that way.

"Sneakers, right?"

Kim's voice sounded muffled with Miriam in the cave, but she'd heard enough. She rushed to the mouth and peered out to Kim, kneeling on the ground.

Kim looked briefly up at Miriam, before looking down again. Her eyes carefully studied the ground. "I'm no expert, but I don't think these are hiking boots."

Looked like luck might have broken Miriam's way this time. Or perhaps, ending up in this place wasn't as coincidental as it sounded. Clearly, the dobhar-chú liked to den here. It was the only non-porous shelter Miriam had seen. With as often as it rained, that cover was valuable to dobhar-chú and humans alike. Macy would need shelter to avoid hypothermia, so it made sense that she'd seek out and find shelter from the rain.

Kim stood up and dusted off her hands, her gaze never leaving the dirt. She walked a few feet forward, following the tracks that Miriam could only barely see from her vantage point. She stopped, then laughed.

"Like I said. Kawa went that way."

Miriam went to where Kim had started, retracing the steps to verify her claim. Sure enough—though not always fully clear—it did look like a pair of sneakers had headed up the hill.

"Good job."

"Thanks," Kim said. "Seems I may know what I'm doing, after all."

Miriam couldn't tell if that was meant as a passive aggressive jab or the sort of self-deprecating humor girls her age tended to reach for. Based on her time with Kim thus far, Miriam decided on the former.

"Ok. Well if Macy went this way, then that's where we go."

"After you," Kim said, stepping aside and motioning up the hill.

Miriam walked past without hesitation, planting her feet and navigating the steep terrain. Finding Macy's trail put them one step closer to wrapping up this entire cluster of an expedition.

But also one step closer to having to steer Kim away from murder.

CHAPTER 32 – Abby

Pure willpower. The only fuel Abby needed to push forward. She at least knew enough to ignore what the blue-haired girl had told her. Now up the hill and into the woods, she felt confident she'd gone the right way. Scuff marks in the ground. Smashed foliage. The devil had come this way. Now it was just a matter of staying conscious long enough to find and kill it.

The gun seemed heavier than she remembered, but she put her faith in adrenaline and muscle memory. She knew now that errant shots wouldn't bring the thing down. She needed better aim. The head. She had to go for the head, then hope its skull wasn't too thick to penetrate. If she missed, perhaps she'd die. But what did she have to live for anyway? The oozing blood from her arm and the ache of her every joint, made her ready to cross the threshold of death.

Everything aligned when she heard rustling ahead. Ducking behind a tree, Abby watched as Macy crept towards a wall of vines and trunks, dropped to her hands and knees and crawled into a portal that Abby would have never seen on her own. Curious. If Abby couldn't have found it, neither could Macy, which meant that something had revealed the way.

Abby shimmied out of her pack and dropped it to the forest floor, checked her gun, carefully, slowly. For extra protection, she detached the pistol from the side of her bag and slid it into the back of her waistband. She took multiple deep breaths. She knew this was it. Her last chance. Either she or her prey would be taken out of the fight after this next encounter. Abby only had strength for one more push.

After she collected herself, she crept forward, looking down and choosing each step to avoid anything that might crack or creak. She didn't know how thick the wall of foliage was, and she didn't want to give away her position sooner than she had to. She channeled all her experience into each deliberate movement, her body sidelining the pain in service to the purpose that she'd spent years preparing for.

When she arrived at the tiny portal that Macy had crawled through, Abby crouched and listened. Macy's southern drawl floated out as she talked to someone, or something, but Abby couldn't make out the words. Crawling through would make her the most vulnerable, so Abby either had to be quick or quiet. She opted for the latter, moving to her hands and knees and squeezing through, surprised at how big the hole was. She moved in relative silence—at least to her human ears.

Partway through, she heard Macy's voice clearly: "What is it, boy? What's wrong?"

Abby took that the only way she could. Her position had been compromised by superior devil hearing. She sped up, caring less about the sound she made and hoping that she'd gotten close enough.

Feet shuffled by as she approached the exit of the tunnel, two of them clearly Macy's, and more of them the devil. Or devils. She couldn't be sure. She also didn't like her chances at fighting more than one, but she had no time for calculating the odds.

She stopped moving, leveled her rifle, aimed at one of the giant otter feet, and fired.

Scrambling and roaring ensued, but Abby didn't wait to sort it out. She surged forward again, confident that she'd landed a hit that could have potentially hobbled her prey. Something deep inside her nagged that she'd acted recklessly but she ignored it. She came out the other side of the hole just in time to see the cubs and smaller of the two devils dive into a pool of water across a small grove. The larger one remained, teeth bared, blood pouring from its leg where she'd already landed a hit.

It was ready for a fight.

Abby leveled the gun at the devil's head. It could charge if it wanted, but it wouldn't make it before taking a lethal shot. The devil made its move. Abby exhaled, squeezed the trigger, then flew sideways as something hit her.

Macy.

Abby quickly and easily pushed Macy aside, scrambled back up and jerked the muzzle up to meet her prey, but Macy had bought the thing time. Too much time. Before she could even get a solid aim, the warm wet mouth of the devil wrapped around her leg and upset the balance she'd just regained. She gripped hard to the gun. It was her only escape. As the devil dragged her across the ground, she tried to twist to find a shot, but didn't manage the maneuver before she heard a splash, before the coldness of the lake consumed her.

The teeth of the devil tore into the flesh of her leg, but she could hardly feel it. The freezing cold water of the lake almost immediately numbed any pain, or any feeling at all.

She tried to find something to hold onto with her free hand, but found only mud. She took a deep breath just as the devil dragged her under, muting her senses even further as she fought to escape. She couldn't do it. She had no leverage. But she held onto the gun. She had to. No matter the cost.

The devil kept her underwater for what felt like an eternity. Her mind raced, adrenaline keeping it hyper-focused even as she began losing air. She could hardly feel the bottom anymore, her fingers swiping right through mud. Her speed through the water increased. Was this thing smart enough to know that it could drown her? Surely it could hold its breath far longer than she.

She twisted and spun, trying to get a good bead, but the murky water prevented her from seeing anything at all, her eyes immediately burning from the detritus in the water.

Just when she thought she'd pass out, her direction changed suddenly. Up, she thought. Confirmed when she breached the water and flew into the air. She gasped for breath, her leg finally free. The gun threatened to slip from her hand, but she held firmly. Below her, she saw the back of the devil briefly before it disappeared beneath the surface. They were on its turf now, and Abby's disadvantages vastly outweighed any advantage her more advanced human brain may have granted her.

When she smashed back into the water, she scrambled to the surface, looking frantically for any sign of the devil upon her. Nothing. Other than the ripples caused by her own entrance, she saw nothing. It waited, though. She knew it did. Possibly two of them. They could rip her in half if they worked together. She needed to even the odds as best she could, and that meant breaking for the shore.

Slinging the gun across her shoulder, she dropped into a perfect form. Her legs offered what strength they could.

The lake was big. Too big. She only made it halfway before feeling water *swish* by her leg. Jaws crunched down on her midsection and dragged her under, as she held whatever breath she could. Again, she thrashed under the water, striking the jaws that gripped her. The teeth sank further into her skin. She begged silently for relief—begged herself to give up. Yet she couldn't. She wouldn't.

For Ben.

For Beatty.

She owed them every last ounce of her strength.

She tried for the gun, but couldn't get it untangled from her shoulder, and possibly the devil's teeth. Instead, she punched as hard as she could against its snout, the water lessening her momentum.

Then, once again, her direction changed, up, up and out of the water, flying through the air until she landed with a splash at least ten feet away from her exit. She gasped for air, fumbled the gun back into her hands, and waited. Clearly, it wouldn't let her make it to the shore. It came faster this time, jerking at her ankle and dragging her back under. She felt her bones crunching this time as its bite closed with more force. It must have been tempering its strength before. Playing with her.

Abby would've cried if not for her immersion in the cold lake. Even her legendary stoicism couldn't shake the pain she now felt. As she flowed through the water, though, she wormed her way around, trying to do enough of a sit up to aim the gun at the amorphous blob that she hoped was the devil's head. Water wouldn't slow the bullet down enough to prevent its lethality.

She took the shot.

Immediately, the pressure on her leg relented and she burst to the surface. Shaking her head to get the water from her eyes, she pulled the muzzle of the gun above the water, readying for another attack. But none came. Instead, she heard a *plop* as a dark mass floated to the surface of the water, still and unmoving. Had she done it? Had she really done it?

She watched carefully for any sign of movement. She saw no sign of life. Holy hell. She'd actually *done* it. The adrenaline keeping her alive still pulsed, but faltered, her head spinning. She had to get to shore before she passed out. Her victory would be hollow if she drowned.

Nothing stopped her from moving forward in the water. No movement. No splashes. No noises. She climbed onto the mud and grass and rolled to her back, gasping for breath.

She leaned forward to see what she'd wrought. The mass only floated. Still no movement. She couldn't believe it, though. After all that, the last shot had been too easy. Too quick.

A ripple of water lapped against the mud at her feet, drawing her eyes across the lake to a writhing, slinking form, moving towards the dead devil. It stopped there, though, making no movement towards Abby. She saw the giant otter-head pop out of the water, then turn the carcass over until it faced upward. She knew then that she had succeeded. She knew the face of the dead when she saw it.

The smaller devil let out a piercing howl that shook Abby to her core. Though a different species from one another, she had no doubt the meaning of that sound. Abby had made the same sound the night Ben had died.

Now they were even.

Taking another deep breath, Abby forced herself to her feet, wincing at the pain and careful to not make any more noise than she had to. Though the smaller devil seemed content to mourn, that sorrow would soon enough turn to rage.

Pop.

A gunshot. Abby fell back to the ground. Waited for another.

Only one, though. She glanced about the lake, spotted Miriam tackling the blue-haired girl to the ground. An unlikely ally, but Abby was all too happy for any help she could get. She had no quarrel with the scientists here to find the devil. Abby's job was done. The mission complete. Her life of hell avenged.

She stood back up, neither of the girls looking at her as they quarreled with one another. Abby reached for her radio, surprised to find it, and then called in for the extraction. One more trek out to the airfield. Then it would be over, and she'd never have to return to this god forsaken forest ever again.

CHAPTER 33 – Macy

The tears flowed freely as Macy processed what she was seeing. Papa was dead. She couldn't see the cubs, but Mama wailed as she mourned the murder of her spouse.

A gunshot knocked Macy out of her trance, drawing her attention to Miriam and Kim, now fighting each other on the ground. Then to Abby disappearing into the tree line.

Miriam had finally found her, just like she knew she would. Or had Macy found Miriam?

"Mir!" she shouted.

The girls stopped fighting. Both heads popped up and registered Macy.

Found.

But at what cost?

CHAPTER 34 – Miriam

Kim sat up in a huff, tears streaming. "She got away. You let her get away!"

"Killing her wouldn't have solved anything," Miriam argued.

"It would have made me feel better."

"It would have made you a murderer. You don't want that on your head. Trust me."

"Mir!" The shout echoed, but Miriam knew the voice instantly. Both her and Kim's head whipped towards the sound.

"Macy!" Miriam shouted back, waving a hand.

The path to each other was long, the lake snaking out and around in such a way that skirting the shoreline would take a while. But the distance across the lake at this point was relatively short. Swimming would be faster, albeit a bit cold. With Abby missing-in-action, though, Miriam didn't want to lose eyes on Macy if she could help it.

"Swim!" Miriam suggested.

Macy looked down at the water disgustingly, then glanced back up and nodded. Miriam knew she could swim. Macy had been a lifeguard in high school, and even though she'd done it mainly for the boys, it still meant a significant amount of training and practice in the water.

As Macy waded in, Miriam turned her attention to Kawa and his mate. She didn't think they posed a threat, but given the situation, Miriam wouldn't bet on it.

There was no movement from the dobhar-chú as Macy made her way across. She stepped out onto the shore in front of Miriam and Kim, shivering, her wet clothes clinging to her body. If the cold bothered her, Macy didn't show it. She closed the distance between them and wrapped Miriam up in a hug before Miriam could protest. Now they were both wet and cold.

"I thought I'd never find you," Macy said.

"I would have found you. Eventually." Miriam regretted having not started the search in earnest earlier.

A splash caused Miriam to pull away from the hug, in time to see Kim dipping into the water. Kim shuddered.

Miriam rushed forward. "What are you doing?"

Kim ignored her. Miriam stood in silence as Kim made her way out to Kawa's dead body. The mate floated nearby, on her back, still occasionally wailing. The scene was, of course, tragic, but Miriam hadn't taken the time to fully appreciate the effect it must have had on Kim.

As Kim swam through the water, Macy stood next to Miriam and whispered, "What now?"

Miriam only shrugged. What was there to say? What was there to do? The mission hadn't exactly gone the way she'd hoped, but neither was it a complete failure. The Devil of Misty Lake was real. Now they even had a carcass, which would yield years of research and information that would surely upend the scientific community. Sad, yes, but not fruitless.

So what next?

Go home.

Kim made it to the pair of dobhar-chú. Instantly, the female swam over and cuddled against her. Of course this one must have a name as well, but Kim hadn't shared it. Even Miriam couldn't fight the sadness of the scene. The best thing they could do now was to report, hope they could find another pod of them somewhere, and integrate them together. For the future of the species, it would be important to find this one a new mate.

Macy sniffled beside her. Miriam tried to stay in the moment, but could only think of the next step. The way to fix the problem, or at least mitigate the fall out. She knew no other way. She knew that made her cold, distant, and hard to relate to. Perhaps for the first time, as she sat here knowing that she should feel more strongly, she wondered if something was wrong with her. On a more fundamental level, beyond a rough childhood and an analytical mind.

She wouldn't leave Kim behind, though. Not knowing how long Kim might want to mourn, Miriam sat herself down on the bank of the lake and pulled her knees up to her chest.

Macy followed suit, then asked, "Won't that hunter be back?"

Of course. Of course she would. Why else would Abby have killed this thing, if not to take it as a trophy? It made no sense to kill it and walk away.

"Maybe."

"Doesn't seem like we should be here when she does."

"Do you want to tell Kim to cut it out and come back?" Miriam asked.

Macy glanced out over the water. "No. I guess not. Not yet."

Not yet. But soon. Abby didn't seem interested in hurting any humans, so Miriam didn't take her as much of a threat, but it still seemed better to be safe.

But for now, they would mourn, together.

CHAPTER 35 – Radley

Radley left before Abby made it back and called in a secondary pilot to be there to evacuate her. It wasn't often that a hunt happened so close to his backyard, and he wasn't about to miss the opportunity to participate in the extraction.

He landed his plane at the estate, this time parking it in a small hangar near the back of the property. Ms. Coleman waited nearby, now without a wheelchair.

She nodded curtly. "Sir. You asked to see me?"

Radley flashed her a smile that she didn't return.

"How's our patient?" he asked.

"Stable."

Radley moved to a door that led to an adjacent hangar, trusting that Ms. Coleman would follow. She did.

"Good. Keep him sedated and here until I get back."

"Sir. He needs a hospital."

Radley took in the helicopter in front of him. His true pride and joy. This thing had been used all over the world, but this would be the first time he personally flew the extraction mission.

"After we're done, we'll get him to one. Right now, I need as few variables as possible."

"Sir. How could he possibly ruin this?"

Radley didn't go into details with her. He didn't tell her that he'd lied about Beatty dying to ensure Abby would find the resolve to push through. If Abby found out the truth now, who knows what she might do. Radley didn't know her well, but he knew enough to know Beatty meant a great deal to her. He didn't intend to be anywhere nearby when she heard the truth. After the specimen was properly secured and Radley was safely back at his estate, he would release Beatty, who would surely find his way to Abby. And that was fine. Just fine. Then. But not now.

"Ms. Coleman." Radley spun and locked his cobalt blue eyes onto her deep brown ones. "I don't have time to discuss this. Just do what I ask, please."

He stopped short of telling her to "do her job," but knew that the sentiment came across all the same. He paid her handsomely for the work she did. She wouldn't give that up for one man's life. Especially a man like John Beatty.

"I'll be back this evening," Radley continued, her gaze having drifted downward. "Have my studio ready. This one is big."

She nodded, not raising her head. "Yes, sir. I'll make sure it's prepared."

"Thank you. I really appreciate everything you do here." And he meant it. He expected obedience from those he paid, but he wasn't a monster.

When she didn't respond to that, he continued. "You're dismissed. Thank you for the update."

She shuffled out, a few pegs lower than he'd found her. He had that way with people. It had served him well, working in the shadows, hiring people across the globe to fetch his prizes. Abby and Beatty had been one of his most reliable teams, but the Devil of Misty Lake might have done them in. It was a worthwhile trade in Radley's book.

Alone now, he went to work preparing the helicopter. He'd already called in the extraction team.

They'd meet him there with all the gear he'd need. He just needed fuel. Plenty of it. Airlifting a bear-sized monster over the Seattle metro area wouldn't be the most subtle way of doing it, but he'd be safely landed before anyone could track him down to question what he was carrying. His trip would be an oddity. Something interesting for people to mention over a glass of beer, maybe. A strange story, not unlike those told about the creatures he collected.

The devil wasn't the most exotic animal he'd ever snagged, nor the largest. But to Radley Furey, every procurement meant as much as the last one. His collection had no equal, and he took pride in all the "nonexistent" animals he'd managed to dig up over the years. It was a shame he couldn't share it with the world, but he wasn't after fame or recognition. He was driven by the act of collecting. Once the devil was stuffed and displayed prominently among his many trophies, he would move on to the next, then the next.

Satisfied that he was as ready as he'd ever be, Radley opened the hangar doors. The aircraft sat on a mobile helipad. All he had to do was get it out of the hangar. He did that with a nearby F350 he kept for the purpose, expertly attaching the hitch and maneuvering the helicopter quickly out of its berth.

He climbed into the cockpit and looked over the controls. It had been a hot minute since he'd flown this thing, but he had confidence in his piloting skills, and even more confidence in his success rate. He wouldn't fail.

Radley never failed.

He spun up the blades, took flight, and headed towards Misty Lake to claim his prize.

PART THREE:
The Director

CHAPTER 36 – Miriam

It was over. There was nothing left to do.

Miriam didn't like the outcome, nor did she shy away from the truth of it. They'd found the devil. With any luck, more of the species lived within a range the female could roam. The cubs could hopefully find a new population to mate with, and this rare species of incredibly large otter could continue to survive, as it had for hundreds or thousands of years. Nature tended to be persistent, she knew, though humans also had a knack for completely disrupting the natural course of evolution.

"We can't just leave him there," Kim whined. Miriam had come to respect Kim, and a part of her even liked the girl, but there was no point in complaining or arguing about something they couldn't change.

"That thing weighs hundreds of pounds. What do you want us to do?" Miriam asked.

"If we leave it in the middle of the lake, someone's gonna find the body. Then the secret will be out."

Macy jumped in, trying to help the situation. "Abby has the knowledge and the scars to prove its existence anyway. We can't stop what's coming."

"With any luck," Miriam added. "The female and her cubs are far away from here by now, hiding where they can, maybe even migrating to another lake."

"Usa. Her name is Usa."

Kim hung her head, her eyes still red, though finally dry. Her clothes hugged her body, still dripping from her sojourn across the lake to commune with the dead.

Miriam nodded towards Macy. "Come on. Let's go pack up camp and head back."

She started walking, not waiting for Kim. Conversation would no longer help. Now was the time for action. The time to accept the next step, even if it was a bitter one.

Macy followed dutifully. Reluctantly, finally, Kim brought up the rear. They walked in silence, Miriam picking her way through foliage. She'd become quite adept at navigating these woods, even though she'd only been there for a little while. Such was her knack. Her superpower. She would have preferred to have super strength to evacuate Kawa's corpse. Or super-empathy so that she could calm Kim's heart. Instead, she could only offer a clear head.

Once they arrived at the camp, all three pitched in to help take down the tents, and fill up the backpacks. The silence might have bothered someone else, but Miriam enjoyed the chirping of the birds, and the slight rustle of the branches overhead. She told herself that even though this trip may not have gone as planned, she would have others in the future. She would find more work. She would have to. She certainly wasn't going to run back to her father.

"Thank you." Kim's voice came strained and quiet. Miriam hadn't even noticed Kim approaching her. Miriam turned and locked eyes with Kim, struggling not to wither from the darkness of her gaze.

"I'm sorry," Miriam replied. She meant it. She didn't want things to have ended up this way. "I know you just want to protect them. And I do, too. I promise."

Kim gave a curt nod, almost sheepish. "I know."

Then, in a flash, Kim's hand wrapped around Miriam's, her gaze never faltering. "Seriously, though. I know you tried your best."

Miriam nodded, too distracted by Kim's touch to really pay attention.

"I think that's it," Macy said from across the way. "I think we've got everything."

Kim immediately dropped Miriam's hand, and spun around. So weird. Miriam had become pretty accustomed to awkward, but she was used to being the cause of it.

They headed out, Kim in the lead, with Macy hanging back until she was shoulder-to-shoulder with Miriam. Macy nudged Miriam with her elbow, widened her eyes and motioned her head towards Kim. Miriam didn't understand the meaning of it, causing Macy to roll her eyes and shake her head.

Wait. Did she mean...?

Miriam gave the implication no more thought. Kim was emotionally compromised, and besides, Miriam wasn't interested in girls. She had Gabe.

Before long, the path started to widen, the moss-covered ground turning to slick mud. Shoeprints crisscrossed over the landscape, leading to the parking lot where their adventure had begun. Miriam felt the tug of freedom. The allure of a reset. She couldn't wait to get on the plane to head back to Dobie. She very suddenly just wanted this sad, failed trip to end.

She turned to Kim. "So I'll get the report written up in the next couple of days. Do I give it to you, or...?"

As they walked out onto the paved, empty lot, Kim turned. "Oh. Um. I'll get you the contact information for the University. You can turn it in to the head of zoological research there. I've never actually met her."

Miriam hadn't met her either. They'd had a few brief conversations on the phone, and a few texts back and forth, but Kim was the only face that Miriam had attached to the job. She had assumed that Kim knew their mutual employer personally. How else would she have been chosen? It suddenly felt like something the two of them should have talked about before now, but somehow it never mattered.

Miriam's mind desperately wanted to turn this thing into a new mystery for her to solve, but she knew there was no merit to that. It didn't matter who'd hired them. A job was a job, and the back half of her payment wouldn't come until the report was submitted. The contract that she and Macy had hastily written, without any legal input, said nothing about success or failure, but Miriam vaguely knew there was a risk that they'd never see the full payday.

Macy kicked at the pavement. "So how are we getting out of here?"

The car and van were both gone, and Miriam estimated at least a ten mile walk to any sort of civilization.

"Uber, I guess?" Kim suggested.

A simple solution to a simple problem. Miriam looked at the gear they'd dropped on the ground. "An XL."

Kim nodded and pulled out her phone, pecking away at the keyboard. While Kim worked, Miriam took the opportunity to sit. Macy plopped down on the ground beside her.

"Our first job in the books," Macy said.

"Yep," Miriam said. "Not exactly what we planned, but we did find it. We saw a creature that few have ever seen. The stuff of legend."

Miriam hadn't taken the time to fully appreciate that. Proving the impossible was why she played the game, and she'd done that. She'd found a new creature. One docile and smart and unlike anything she'd ever imagined. Of course, without hard evidence, it might end up being just a story, the kind her dad had told her his whole life. He had so many expeditions where he almost found the cryptid. He'd see it, but didn't have the camera. He'd fight it, but it would run away. It was always something, and Miriam had long since written those stories off as tall tales. But perhaps such tales were part of the job. These cryptids had never been found for a reason.

Kim slipped her phone into the pocket of her shorts and looked towards the girls. "Okay. Gonna be about an hour, it says."

Made sense. They were in a pretty remote area.

Miriam patted the ground next to her, inviting Kim to join them. Kim did so.

"Ya know," Kim said. "I'm gonna miss you... two."

There was a pause, right? A quick glance towards Macy's half-smile confirmed it.

Miriam wanted to respond, but didn't, her mind reeling to find something that felt appropriate. She wanted to be suave enough to come up with something that acknowledged Kim's obvious hints while also not rocking the boat anymore than she had to. Alas, Miriam had no such talent for expertly crafted retorts.

She was saved from the conversation as a *chug-chug-chug* echoed across the parking lot. It was quiet at first, but quickly grew in volume until Miriam fully realized what she'd heard.

A helicopter, moving fast and low, zoomed overhead, swirling dust and kicking rocks. It's trajectory—straight for Misty Lake.

A coincidence, or a friend of Abby?

Without saying anything, Kim sprang to her feet and bolted into the woods. Macy and Miriam shared a look, and Miriam sighed.

Apparently, they were headed back into the forest.

CHAPTER 37 – Radley

Radley had his crew now, working the back of the helicopter as they untangled massive rope and fixed heavy-grade carabiners to the frame of the chopper. He'd picked up four of his most trusted employees, guys who had handled extractions for him all over the world. By comparison, this one would be almost child's play. They wouldn't have to transport the corpse across borders, evading customs and the law. They just had to airlift it to the estate. Easy.

Radley brought the chopper down into a hover over the lake, scanning the lake for his prize. The helicopter moved forward the same instant that he spotted it, gracefully coming back to a hover squarely over the lump of fur floating limply on the surface. Abby was true to her word. Good girl.

"All right. Here we go. Do your thing."

The team lead answered into the radio, "Roger that. Move out."

Two of the men rappelled out of the side of the helicopter with the grace of gymnasts, lowering themselves evenly until they touched down in the water. Both unclipped and the team lead pulled up their lines. Radley turned the controls over to the fourth man, his copilot, and made his way to the cargo area to be closer to the action. Expertly, the copilot held the chopper steady, hardly any wobbling at all. Radley was impressed.

Radley helped the team-lead hoist the large net out of the copter, then quickly steadied himself as they rose ever so slightly when the net hit the water. The men below went straight to work, unfurling the net, swimming it out to the length of the devil, then slowly but surely spreading it underneath the carcass. Next, the team lead tossed out a large tarp. It hit the water hard enough that Radley heard the *slap* against the surface.

The tarp was essential to extraction. His flight path would take him out over the suburbs of Seattle, and he couldn't very well have a giant otter on display. Indeed, even with it covered, he ran the risk of turning too many heads and inviting too many questions. But people had short attention spans. They would stop, look up, go "huh?", then move about their day shuttling their kids about or picking up their dinners. No one cared about anyone but themselves in the grand scheme of things.

Down below, one of the divers gave a thumbs up, his arm held high above his head. The team leader watched intently until the other diver did the same.

Go time.

Radley jumped back into the cockpit and assumed control of the chopper. Slowly, he pulled on the flight stick, easily feeling when the weight of the thing started to counteract the lift of the rotors. He was ready for it, adjusting appropriately until it started to lift out of the water. The divers would stay behind for a later pickup. Priority number one was to get the carcass out of the area before anyone else happened upon it.

Little by little, the tarp-covered mound rose above the water until Misty Lake supported it no more. Now to get above the trees. Radley moved up faster now, the weight of his load decided and fully accounted for.

Steady.

Steady.

Below, the surface of the lake rippled, wide enough to catch his eye and curious enough to halt his ascent. The other devil. It had to be.

The team lead's voice echoed into Radley's ears: "We need to evac our guys. They're sitting ducks out there."

Radley continued his ascent without a reply.

"Sir. Seriously. Another one of those things is down there. I can see it."

The copilot glanced towards Radley, "He's right, sir. We should lower back down. Let them climb onto the haul."

Radley shot a chiding look at the pilot. He flipped the switch on his headset, muting the voices of his team. This was the job. He paid them so much for two reasons—the risk and their silence. If they wouldn't offer the latter right now, he'd force it on them.

Moving up. Faster now. Radley eyed the tree line, guessing they had at least ten feet to go.

Without his headset on, he didn't hear the screams of his copilot as much as he felt them. Radley looked down just in time to see a devil vault from the surface of the lake and hurtle through the air, mouth wide, teeth bared. Surely, it couldn't jump high enough to...

The chopper jolted downward, tipping sideways. Radley fought with the stick, but the shock of the extra weight gripping his haul made it impossible to right the trajectory. Lights blinded him. Alarms sounded, barely audible through his powered off headset. Radley focused. Fought.

The weight abated, he started to regain control. His copilot lurched forward, frantically looking out the windows. It was only then that Radley realized they'd lost the team lead, who'd no doubt plummeted into the lake below. Likely fine, assuming he didn't get eaten by the creature beneath the surface.

The devil jumped again, and Radley knew he hadn't gained enough altitude to outpace it. He hadn't recovered fast enough. In fact, he hadn't fully recovered at all.

"Brace!" he yelled.

The copilot held tightly to the arms of his seat. The chopper jolted again. Radley knew he wouldn't win the fight this time. He no longer fought to gain control of the chopper. Now he fought to guide the landing—or crash—into something survivable.

He acquiesced, lowering the copter as best he could, but the weight had become unbalanced, tipping the chopper until he lost all control. They were in free fall.

Radley unbuckled.

The copilot looked at him in confusion, but Radley wasted no time saving a guy whose name he couldn't even bother to remember. Instead, he jolted to the cargo area of the helicopter, holding onto his seat, then the canvas straps attached to the side, desperate not to fall out prematurely. Everything a blur. The chopper spun faster and faster. His eyes lost focus as their altitude dropped. Though he would have preferred time to slow down, instead it felt like it was speeding up. As if he had no time to think or act or save himself.

He had a radio attached to his belt, but no weapon. He grabbed the nearest gun he saw—a tranquilizer gun—and steeled himself for impact. He saw water below and wasted no time, diving deep into the freezing waters of Misty Lake until he could feel the bottom. Until his ears ached from the pressure. The water reverberated around him when the copter hit, but he managed to escape the debris, swimming away from the wreckage as best he could.

Along the way, in his travels, Radley had spent a fair amount of time learning to free dive. He knew he could hold his breath for minutes yet. By then he could be far enough away from the wreckage and the devil that it'd lose track of him. Though, if it cared about catching him, it already would have. His paltry swimming would be no match for an animal very much in its element.

He pushed forward. The pressure on his lungs built. The cold of the water numbed his skin. He ignored it. He'd survived worse than this.

After what he guessed to be about two minutes beneath the surface, he knew he'd reached the edge of his limits. He pushed up, quickly kicking his legs, his lungs burning. He breached the surface and hungrily sucked in air. He turned his head in every direction, looking for any sign of the devil. Of his men. The chopper. He saw what remained in the distance, but found no evidence that he'd been followed. Or that his men had survived.

He quickly swam to the nearest bank, hoisted himself onto land and leaned over, hands on his knees, to continue searching for his breath. Radley was fit for his age, but he couldn't ignore the fact that he'd been on the earth long enough that his body couldn't always recover as quickly as he'd like.

The tranquil sounds of the forest were replaced by splashing, screaming, clanging, and the moaning of sinking metal. His crew weren't all dead—yet. But it sounded like they were well on their way. Radley spent no time worrying about how to save them. He knew when to cut his losses.

And he'd lost them for sure.

He wasn't ready to give up on his prize, though. He'd need a new plan if he was going to recover the carcass. Or maybe, just maybe, he'd hunt himself a new one.

CHAPTER 38 – Macy

Gasping, Macy vowed to herself that she would never to be in another situation where she had to run through the woods. She loved Miriam to death, but from now on, she'd stay home, relying on her computer and research skills. No more fieldwork. Ever.

Never *ever*.

She lost sight of Miriam briefly, but then saw Miriam pull up just enough that Macy could stay on the path. Macy should have just stayed in the parking lot. The nice, empty, safe, parking lot.

At some point, the hum of the helicopter grew louder. She could see it just barely as she bobbed between trees. It was almost certainly above the lake, though Macy hadn't discerned the purpose just yet, or why Kim had taken off into the woods as she had.

As she rounded the next tree, the helicopter turned sideways—then started dropping out of the sky. She couldn't even make sense of all the noises. There were screams in there, but she didn't think they came from Miriam or Kim. They sounded masculine. The engine of the helicopter whined and sputtered, and Macy felt sure she had been transported to some Michael Bay movie. She almost expected a forest-flattening explosion.

Suddenly, there were no more trees for her to navigate. She burst through the tree line and onto the bank of the lake in time to see the helicopter crash.

Ripples of water shot out in all directions, lapping against the shore with the intensity of a near-surfable wave. Kim and Miriam stood nearby, staring in awe, their eyes wide, mouths agape. Macy hadn't seen the whole thing, but her immediate concern went out to whoever was in the helicopter.

She surveyed the surface of the water, spotting only one man. A quick shared look with Miriam, and Macy knew what they had to do. The one thing the two of them had in common. Lifeguarding.

Miriam took the lead, diving into the water without hesitation. Macy braced herself for the cold and followed, where she kicked across the surface with expert grace. The sounds around her were hard to discern. Screams and splashes. The dying groan of the sinking helicopter. She pushed forward toward the chaos. She was always more capable when worrying about someone other than herself.

Kim didn't follow, no doubt uninterested in saving the men who'd done harm to Kawa.

Once close enough, Macy began treading water to spot the survivors, wanting to prioritize anyone who looked incapable of swimming on their own. She found her mark quickly. A man floating face down near the wreckage of the helicopter.

"I've got that one," Miriam said, impressively not winded at all.

Macy nodded as Miriam took off, then surveyed for someone else. The man she'd seen from the shore floated nearby, his eyes wide with shock.

"Hold on!" she yelled towards him. "I've got ya."

She started her swim towards him, but got knocked off-course by something in the water. It grazed one of her feet. She pulled up to right herself, just as she saw Usa's sleek outline pop above the water, cutting across the surface like a giant snake. At least she hadn't been hurt in the crash.

The man chattered ahead of her, emitting something halfway to a scream. A sound of panic.

"You're fine," Macy said. She dove back into the water just as Usa breached the surface, the man in her jaws. Macy stopped hard and looked up, the man's body flying through the air as Usa tossed him skyward. She hadn't anticipated this.

Usa fell back into the water as the man toppled downward, but he never hit the surface. Usa was out again, this time chomping her massive jaws across his midsection, the sickening crunch of her teeth meeting through his skin. Macy averted her eyes too late, seeing just enough of the carnage to make her stomach turn. The man's last gurgling scream shook her soul.

"Mama!" Macy yelled, temporarily forgetting Kim's name for the creature. "Stop it!"

Usa made no indication that she heard or cared what Macy had to say. She disappeared into the blackness of the lake, leaving her kill behind, a body nearly severed in two. It took a bit for Macy to find her head before snapping back into action. She'd failed this one, but perhaps there were other survivors. It didn't occur to her in the moment to be afraid of Usa. Usa wouldn't hurt her. Not after what they'd been through together.

A tarp floated nearby, outlining the form of Kawa's dead body. So these people had come to take away the body.

Friends of Abby, then.

She spotted an irregular lump near the outside of the tarp. Maybe just a part of Kawa's body, but maybe a person. She dove back into the water and surged forward. On a breath, she saw Usa arching out of the water nearby, close to her, circling her. Every few strokes, Usa crossed in front of her again, each of them getting closer and closer to one another.

Usa wouldn't hurt her.

When it became clear that Usa wasn't going to give her room to swim, Macy stopped and tread water, watching as Usa swam impressively tight circles around her.

"Come on, girl," Macy said, not really knowing if her voice would carry below the surface of the water. "It's okay. It's alright."

Her breath caught in her chest as she realized that Usa wasn't responding. These men had come to take her mate, and she was angry. Perhaps beyond recognition.

Usa wouldn't hurt her. Right?

Macy continued to tread water, suddenly afraid that any movement would trigger Usa into attacking her. Off to the side, Macy eyed Miriam as she emerged past a piece of the wreckage yet to sink. The man Miriam had gone for was now on his back, hopefully breathing, as Miriam kicked hard to drag him back to shore.

When Macy tried to get a bead on Usa's location again, she saw nothing. The otter had sunken into the murky depths below.

"Mir," Macy yelled. "Watch out! Usa!"

Miriam looked up, but Macy's eyeline towards her was almost immediately broken as Usa surfaced, sliding and slinking along with a speed that Miriam could never hope to outswim. Usa dove again, but Macy knew exactly what it meant.

Both Miriam and the unconscious man disappeared beneath the water without a sound, as if they'd never existed at all.

"Mir!"

Macy took off swimming towards Miriam's last location, giving zero thought to what she'd do once she got there. She closed the gap quickly, but as fast as Usa was capable of moving, Miriam and the man were long submerged. Macy searched desperately for a wake or a bubble, or Usa's slick black fur. Anything to give her a new trajectory.

Nothing.

Then, with a loud splash, Miriam surfaced only about ten feet away, gasping for breath. The man was gone. She sputtered and shook her head to flush the water from her eyes before looking towards Macy.

"Shore!" Miriam yelled.

Macy nodded, needing no more insistence before breaking out into a freestyle stroke the likes of which she'd never swum before.

Usa wouldn't hurt her. She'd gone after Miriam because of the man.

Macy listened for the splashing of Miriam's stroke nearby. Her stronger arms had closed the distance between them as they now swam neck and neck back towards Kim, who stood on the bank yelling, waving her arms. Macy couldn't make out everything Kim said, but the frantic gesturing told her enough: Usa was on their heels.

Usa wouldn't hurt her.

Then Macy disappeared beneath the frigid waters of Misty Lake.

CHAPTER 39 – Miriam

In her periphery, Miriam saw Macy go under.
Dammit!

Quickly, and with the efficiency of training and experience, Miriam played through her options. She couldn't dive for long, and even if she could, she wouldn't be able to see in the murk below. Usa was in a rage, defending her mate, exactly like the Irish tales. Diving in to help the poachers was reckless and stupid. Usa may have been docile before, but now she only saw red, and she couldn't discern friend from foe. She wasn't a dog, for god's sake. She was a wild animal.

Usa wouldn't listen to reason, but she would be driven by instinct. Miriam reversed course and pushed as fast as she could towards the tarp floating in the water. If Usa surfaced with Macy, Miriam didn't see it, focusing instead on her path, praying that her plan would work quickly enough.

She dodged helicopter debris, ignored another body floating in the water. She didn't let up until she came to Kawa's covered body. She pawed her way beneath, able to surface and breathe under the tarp. The hot, fetid air flooded her throat, making it hard to breathe normally, but it was enough. She wouldn't suffocate.

She made her way to Kawa's lifeless body. Usa would be able to detect underwater sound from very far away. Miriam took another deep, foul breath, dove under and slammed her weight into the carcass. She punched and kicked it. Over and over. Molesting the corpse of a cryptid had never been on her shortlist, but now it was the only thing Miriam could imagine that might give Macy a fighting chance.

When she could hold her breath no longer, she burst upward, back under the tarp for another strangling breath, then down again to continue her assault.

Come save your damn mate!

The currents beneath her suddenly swirled, yanking down on her legs. Usa had come.

Miriam kicked back to the surface, this time away from the corpse, making her way towards the edge of the tarp. She stopped short of the surface when something tugged on her leg. Not Usa. Not painful. Unable to see far in the murky water, she reached down to her ankle to find a rope tangled around it. Miriam thrashed instinctively as if she could kick it off, but found herself instead wasting precious energy.

She stilled her mind and felt the rope in her hands, memorizing the strands, studying where they crossed, forming a mental map that she could use to untangle herself the same way she might untie a knot.

The pressure in her chest started to burn, distracting her, though she kept her focus. Drowning would help no one. She twisted one particular crossing. Then another. She felt again. She was making progress. She worked her way through and around the rope, using her hands and her foot until it finally broke free.

She reached for the surface, as if her hands could breathe for her if they made it first. They couldn't. Her temples pounded, her head dizzy. She couldn't make it. She was going to pass out.

Air flooded into her lungs as she broke through the surface of the lake, her lungs and throat spasming. She coughed and gasped.

"Mir!"

Macy's voice echoed behind, but Miriam never got a chance to spin before teeth clamped down on her shin and pulled her back under the water. Her lungs almost immediately felt depleted, not having recovered. Macy had survived, though. At least there was that.

The speed at which Miriam traveled through the water boggled her mind. If not for the crushing pressure on her lungs and the oozing blood from her leg, she might have spent the time marveling at the sheer evolutionary magnificence that had allowed such a large creature to move at this speed through water. But instead, she pounded her fists against Usa's thick fur, hoping for some sort of miracle. Hoping that the blood frenzy would wear off enough for Usa to retreat.

Miriam lost all sense of direction. She didn't know if they moved up or down or laterally. Usa didn't seem to want to eat her outright, as the bite force of the initial clamp-down hadn't changed. It was almost as if Usa meant to drown Miriam, which seemed like a morbid way for an animal to kill its prey. But then, Miriam had seen no evidence that Usa wanted to eat any of the humans thus far, so it made some kind of sense.

Up. She thought maybe they were moving upward. Miriam's eyes burned as she tried to make out anything she could. The murky water was almost black, but she knew it wasn't entirely so, as the edges of her vision were darkening. But the center of her sight started glowing, brighter and brighter. Yes. They were definitely moving to the surface.

Miriam had already pushed her lungs as far as they would go. Though her chance of escape seemed close at hand, Miriam's body gave up, no longer able to survive on adrenaline alone. Her vision narrowed until she could see nothing at all, then her awareness started to get fuzzy.

Then—brightness. Air in her lungs. She hit the ground hard, skid across it and slammed into a tree. Her eyes struggled to adjust. She felt the *thud* before her eyes managed to focus on Usa, in front of her, slumped to the ground.

Dead?

No. Her midsection moved. Out. In. Out. In. If not dead, then what?

A man stalked out of the woods, a grin on his face.

Miriam leaned her back against the tree and tried to force herself to get up, but her body would have none of it. Her lungs begged for more air. She felt dizzy, and, worried that she might pass out again, she allowed herself to collapse at the base of a tree. The man ignored her, instead studying the huge, unconscious otter on the ground. He circled around it, his grin only widening.

She couldn't find her voice. She couldn't find her wits. She couldn't decipher what would happen next or what she should be doing. She closed her eyes. Her mind wavered, danced, told her stories about situations that weren't the ones in front of her. Dreams, maybe, that she pushed away. Her eyes didn't want to open, but she forced them to, looking up just in time to see the man towering over her. Before, he had been her height, if not shorter, but from the ground, he looked overbearingly large.

His smile turned into a frown as he shook his head.

"What am I going to do with you?" he asked, confidence dripping from every word.

Miriam figured he didn't want an answer.

This was a man who expected to win every fight. To control every situation. To rule over every domain. She'd only met him briefly, and though she didn't fully trust him then, she'd accepted that he was just an affable pilot who had a vested interest in helping Abby. Miriam no longer accepted that narrative.

She wanted to ask whether he intended to kill her, but she found no point. If he meant to do that, then he would. She'd lost this fight. This expedition. She had never really had any control of it to begin with.

He didn't make any moves to hurt her. The only weapon he had appeared to be a rifle, one she recognized all too well. Her father, Skylar, had had an arsenal of the very same tranquilizer guns. They were effective at bringing down even the largest prey. A shot from that would certainly knock her out, but wouldn't kill her. Well, probably not. Unless her heart slowed too much. Certainly a possibility.

Her mind forced her to focus on these mundane details as if they meant something. As if they would help her in this moment. But they wouldn't, and they didn't.

The man stepped a few feet away, pulled a radio from his pocket and began talking to someone on the other end. Miriam tried to follow, but could only focus on bits and pieces. He was calling for help, asking for specific supplies. Before he ended the conversation, though, her mind took her far away from the woods near Misty Lake, where she danced somewhere between the worlds of sleep and wakefulness, aware of her location and her situation, but unable to take any action.

Her ribs, though. They hurt like hell.

CHAPTER 40 – Abby

Abby could hardly convince her legs to keep moving. Her shoulders slumped. Her vision blurred every time she jostled one of her wounds. She'd seen the helicopter hover overhead, so she knew the extraction had already begun. She crossed the parking lot slowly, her boots scraping against the gravel as she took each slow step. The rotor of the helicopter faded into the distance now, barely audible above the wildlife and her own panting.

She'd come out nowhere near the trailhead, stopping to gather her senses and orient herself towards where she'd find Radley. He'd said he would stay until she'd done the job. He'd be there to take her out of this god-forsaken place, where she could recover from her wounds, figure out her next step, and begin her life of solitude.

She found the path and shuffled towards it. One foot in front of the other. Focusing on a future where she'd already recovered and didn't feel like screaming with every minute movement of her muscles. Her mind forced her to think of Ben and Beatty. She'd avenged them both. She could be proud of that. Though, she'd only killed one. Another remained. And the pups.

No. That path had brought her nothing but pain. Revenge hadn't brought peace or closure.

Thoughts like these swam around her head as she pushed forward. Eventually, she made it to the field where Radley had dropped her off, where she saw a plane waiting. It didn't look like the one they'd arrived in, though. No, this one seemed smaller, with different colored accents along the side.

A tall, skinny man waved at her from a distance, as if she'd miss him if he didn't make some sort of grand movement.

"Ahoy!" he yelled.

Abby wondered if he was British. Or maybe a pirate. She let out a sharp breath resembling something of a laugh.

He rushed toward her and helped steady her as they made their way to the plane. He talked and talked, his smooth accent providing a soft balm for her ears. British, then. Probably not a pirate.

"Sorry for the switch up," the man said. "Mr. Furey had somewhere else to be. He's a busy guy."

Was he? Abby knew almost nothing about Radley. He hadn't seemed like a particularly busy guy. He'd seemed like a two-dollar bush pilot, hired for his discretion. Not someone she'd be inclined to refer to as "mister."

"He wanted to help with the extraction himself, he did. So he sent me to pick you up. I hope you don't mind. I ain't as good as he is, but I'll get you where you need to go."

They reached the plane and he helped her up into one of the two seats in the cockpit. He handed her a headset before quickly jogging around to the pilot's seat, jumping in, and putting on a headset of his own.

The slight hiss of the radio crackled before his voice echoed in her head. "Where is it that you want to go?"

Abby took a deep breath, shot him a sharp look. "Where the hell do you think?"

He nodded quickly, sheepishly. "Alright then. Off to the hospital. Have a preference?"

Before she could answer, a voice came across the radio. The stern, sharp voice of a woman annoyed.

"Derek," the voice said. "Have you heard from Mr. Furey?"

"No, not a peep. Just picked up Ms. Wilson and heading up to Seattle with her to a hospital. Looks like she's had a rough go of it."

He hadn't asked what happened to her, and that alone seemed odd. Abby felt like she'd managed to slip behind the curtain of the organization she'd worked for all these years. She'd never met her employer, never met Derek or this lady on the radio. Yet, somehow, they all seemed important to the organization; more important than herself.

"Abby Wilson is there with you?" the woman asked, curiosity in her voice.

"That's right," he answered. "The hero of the hour herself."

"Let me talk to her," the woman said.

"She's here already."

Curiosity piqued, Abby spoke into her microphone with a dry, raspy voice. "This is Abby."

"Ms. Wilson. My name is Ginger Coleman."

The name didn't ring a bell.

"I work for the Director, as well."

"Oh okay. Nice to meet you, I guess. Is there a point here?"

The line stayed silent. Abby looked to her pilot who gave her a shrug and a shy smile of endearingly crooked teeth.

Eventually, Coleman responded, "I don't know how to put this, and now is probably not the best time, but I'm not letting someone die on my watch. Especially when they did nothing to deserve it."

That just left Abby confused. She didn't feel even remotely close to dying. Sure, she hurt every which way, and would probably be taking it easy for weeks to come. But death was not imminent. She had some gas in the tank, yet.

Abby chose her words carefully, slowly unfurling what she hoped was an appropriate response. "That's very kind of you, Ms. Coleman, but I'm going to be just fine."

"Not you, dear," Coleman replied. "John Beatty. He needs to get to a hospital, and you're the only person I can think of who might be on my side, here."

Abby's heart dropped. She gasped for air. Her eyes stung. And her lips turned up into a smile.

"He's alive?"

"Barely."

"But Furey said— "

"Mr. Furey lied to you, hon."

Abby tried to process it. Why would Furey lie?

Without waiting for any response from Abby, Coleman turned her attention back to the pilot. "Derek."

"Yes, ma'am."

"Listen to me, and listen good. I don't care what Furey told you to do. You come here. You get John Beatty and you take the both of them into Seattle for medical care. Do you understand?"

Abby couldn't help but notice the worry across Derek's face.

"But, ma'am, that's not what he told me to do."

"I don't care, Derek. He's busy with the extraction."

Abby didn't know the specifics of the organization. She didn't know who Coleman was in relation to Derek. She didn't know what the punishment would be if Derek followed Coleman's new orders. But none of that mattered for the purposes of Abby choosing her side. Beatty was alive. She wasn't alone anymore. Her life didn't have to proceed in solitude.

Derek and Coleman bickered back and forth, exchanging ominous threats and fears of reprisal. Abby took the time to scan the small cabin. She clocked the dials and controls. The flight stick. The maps. The tape holding together more of the plane than she felt comfortable with.

And a leather holster tucked next to Derek's seat. With a grimace, she reached across, grabbed the holster, dislodged the gun and pointed it at Derek's head—all before he even registered that she'd moved.

"Do what she says," Abby demanded.

Derek looked at her from the corner of his eye, his hands up in front of him. Derek didn't seem like the fighting type. He seemed more like the do-anything-to-survive type.

"Don't shoot me."

"Then do what Coleman says."

"Good girl, Ms. Wilson," Coleman said on the radio. Apparently, the conversation had given her enough context clues to understand the situation.

"Fine," Derek said with a sigh. "I'm starting the engine now. Don't shoot."

He lowered his arms slowly. Abby's finger tensed on the trigger. If she shot him, she'd have no way to get to Beatty, but Derek was either too scared or too stupid to realize that. The engine of the plane roared to life, shaking and rattling from nose to stern. The propellers started turning, slowly at first, then whirring into a blur.

"Do you have to hold it so close to m'head?" Derek asked quietly.

Abby pulled the gun away slightly, keeping the muzzle trained on him. "Okay. But if you take me anywhere other than Beatty, I will shoot you. Even if it means we fall out of the sky. I have had a very bad day."

Derek nodded. "Yeah, yeah. I got that, lady."

The plane surged forward down the grass-paved runway, picking up speed until the plane lifted into the air. It rocked and bucked, shaking and shimmying to the point that Abby felt sure the bolts would unscrew themselves.

"Okay, Coleman," Abby said. "We're in the air."

"I'll have Mr. Beatty ready for you at the end of the runway. Thank you, Ms. Wilson."

Abby didn't quite know how to respond to that. It was Coleman doing her the favor, not the other way around.

"Of course," Abby said. "See you soon."

Perhaps she could have a happy ending after all. Abby tightened her grip on the gun, looked at her pilot, and tried to temper the hope welling inside her.

CHAPTER 41 – Macy

Macy coughed and sputtered, water spewing out of her mouth like a fountain. Kim knelt over her, a look of concern fixed on her face.

"Are you okay?" Kim asked.

Macy considered the snide answer, but instead nodded and tried to sit up, quickly realizing she'd only manage the maneuver with some help, which Kim quickly provided. Macy took a deep breath. Felt the sting in her chest. She looked down at her lacerated shirt, relieved to see less blood than she expected. She didn't feel great, but this was a far cry from how beat up she was after Hogg Run.

"Where's Miriam?" Macy asked, still struggling for breath.

"I don't know," Kim answered. "I think Usa took her. Around the bend there."

Macy glanced off to a bend in the lake, a jut of trees blocking the view. Macy didn't tend to worry about Miriam. Even when things seemed dire, the girl always seemed to land on her feet. Still, that was no guarantee that she'd land on her feet this time, especially if maimed by a bear-sized otter.

"Help me up," Macy ordered. Kim followed the direction without question.

Once on her feet, Macy took stock of her body. Her legs seemed okay. Every step would be painful, but not impossible. Miriam had put her life on the line to save

Macy more than once. The least Macy could do was repay the favor.

"Let's find Miriam."

"And Usa," Kim responded.

Macy fought the urge to roll her eyes. She loved animals. Growing up in Rose Valley, she'd been surrounded by them. Dogs, cats, pigs, cows, horses, chickens, sheep, goats. She had equal affinity for all and never wished an animal to suffer, but that same upbringing had also taught her that, sometimes, animals had to be slaughtered. For food. For health. Animals' lives weren't to be toyed with, but neither were they to be valued above that of humans.

Not keen to get into the water again, Macy struck out along the shoreline, realizing that the path would be much longer than a swim, but also much safer. They were no match for Usa in the water.

"I just don't understand," Kim said, shaking her head. "They've never been aggressive before."

"Well, you've never killed one of their mates before."

"True."

Macy wasn't really one to try to solve any puzzles. She wanted to survive, plain and simple. Her ability to do that seemed to defy statistical chance based on her experiences in the last few years, and her strength to push on had proven stronger than she ever imagined, but it still seemed elusive and far from guaranteed. Saving someone other than herself was always easiest, though, and a quest to save Miriam emboldened Macy in a way that few things could. Each step became a little lighter, the pain a little less severe. Maybe Usa hadn't meant to cause permanent damage. Surely she could have snapped Macy in two if she'd wanted.

"I don't think anyone survived," Kim said as they walked. "I think they either died in the crash or..."

"Yeah..." Macy said, trailing off as she rounded a bend of the lake. "Dangerous work going up against cryptids."

"Shouldn't have to treat it like a fight."

On that, Macy could agree.

Kim suddenly grabbed Macy's wrist, pulling her to a halt. Kim raised a finger to her lips, in a silent *shh*. Macy strained her ears to hear something other than the rustle of the branches above. Other than the singing birds. She heard nothing at first, but then—

The snap of a branch. Loud and clear. A sound that could only come from something heavy tromping through the woods. Usa?

Kim held firmly to Macy's wrist, her grip making it clear that they wouldn't move until they heard something more affirming. They waited in silence. It seemed like an eternity, Macy's breath echoing in her ears, making her wonder if she'd become too loud herself.

Then, finally, a sound that certainly didn't come from Usa... but from a person.

"I'm... extraction..." said a voice. The hushed tone of the person made it hard to understand. It was clearly a man, though. Someone had survived.

Macy shared a look with Kim and shrugged. The path forward didn't seem entirely clear. In all the ruckus, they'd left behind most of their stuff. No guns. No radios. Nothing that could protect them from a guy who Macy would be willing to call a villain, or at least an antagonist with misaligned goals to her own. Certainly no one they could trust.

Macy took a risk and whispered, almost without a sound, "Leave him. We need to find Miriam."

Kim twisted up her mouth and looked into the woods with her almost-black eyes. She was so hellbent on making sure that the devils—sorry, the *dobharchús*—weren't found that she'd lost all good sense. But as far as Macy was concerned, that ship had sailed. They weren't going to overpower some cryptid hunter extraction team guy, and even if they did, then what? Kill him? Certainly not.

Kim held up a finger and mouthed *Stay here*. Macy sighed, but did as she was told, not terribly eager to break rank and end up alone in the woods again. Kim crept forward with barely a sound, as if her feet were made of cotton. She moved to the tree-line and cocked her head, listening for another clue, no doubt. Macy heard the whispered yammer of the man again. No further, no closer.

Kim advanced, into the trees now, still managing to move without even the slightest rustle of foliage. A few more steps and Kim disappeared, swallowed by the massive trees. Macy suddenly felt alone and exposed, but she knew she couldn't move with the silence of Kim, so she stayed still and quiet, regulating her breathing, trying to ignore the itch that formed on her nose, seemingly just to spite her.

Seconds passed by slowly. Macy heard the whisper of the man occasionally, but no other sounds for what felt like an eternity. Then the slightest rustle of a branch and Kim's blue hair coming back into view from behind the leaves and bushes. She moved faster now, which seemed to explain the noise, but still crept quietly enough that few would be able to hear.

Once out of the tree-line, she rushed forward back to Macy.

Kim swallowed hard, her chest heaving as if she'd run a marathon. Her eyes looked glassy, wet, and panicked.

Macy whispered, "What is it?"

"Usa."

Macy blinked trying to make sense of the one-word answer.

"He has Usa."

Macy couldn't believe it. How could he have a giant otter on a rampage? And maybe more importantly...

"Any sign of Miriam?"

Kim nodded. Macy's heart sank.

"He has her, too."

Macy's fight or flight response kicked in. She wanted out. She didn't want to be the hero again. She just wanted to call the authorities and let them handle it. But what if they didn't make it in time? What if something had happened to Miriam? Macy gritted her teeth.

"What are we going to do?" Macy asked.

Kim bit her bottom lip and closed her eyes for a few seconds, then opened them. "Ambush."

Macy tried not to look too incredulous, but failed spectacularly. "Are you kidding? We've got no weapons."

"He has a gun," Kim said. "Tranquilizer I think. He's not carrying it. He's talking on a radio. If we can get the gun, we can turn the tables, maybe."

Macy's mind snapped her back to Rose Valley when the town had gone out to hunt for the beast. Skylar Brooks had brought in tranquilizer guns and handed them out to damn near the entire town. In the end, none of those potent darts had managed to bring down the Beast. This was a man, though. Just a normal man.

Macy took a deep breath and nodded.

"Tell me what to do."

CHAPTER 42 – Radley

Radley knelt in front of the mousy-haired girl slumped against the tree. He visually inspected her wounds and saw nothing that alarmed him too much. Then again, hardly any wounds would really alarm him. And he didn't care much whether she lived or died. More importantly, he saw no reason to believe that she'd remain unconscious for long and that was cause for concern.

Never in a million years did he expect to nab himself a live specimen. It had never been his MO before. He'd always been perfectly happy to have the dead carcass to stuff and proudly display in his hall of grotesque wonders. But this opportunity had presented itself, and now he imagined all the things he might be able to do with such an amazing find. For the first time, he considered exposing his collection to the world, reaping the fame that would come from such a find. In the past he hadn't considered this much, but now could see the appeal in it. Truthfully, though, he had no use for more money, and if he outed what he knew, then they'd take it all from him in the name of science or eminent domain or some other government bullshit.

Having escaped the helicopter crash with nothing but the tranq gun and his radio, he had nothing with which to constrain the girl, but Radley was nothing if not resourceful. He glanced around the tree line until he saw a vine. It wouldn't be terribly strong, but then, the girl wasn't exactly in fighting shape. It might be enough to hold her, or at least slow her down enough that he could tranquilize her if he had to. He really didn't want to, though. Those things were meant for the likes of this magnificent creature, not a small girl. It could be enough to kill someone in the right circumstances.

He went to work obtaining as much of the vine as he needed, working it back and forth until it snapped away. He felt the heft of it in his hand, not impressed with the weight, but it would have to do for now. It took him almost no time to wrap the vine around the girl and tie it up on the other side of the tree.

With that taken care of, he turned his attention to the devil. Its belly expanded and retracted, slowly. Its eyelids occasionally fluttered. He'd shot it three times, which would have easily brought down a bear for at least an hour, but he couldn't guess at the metabolism of this thing, and despite its similar size, it had a very different body shape. All of that mattered. Like an anesthesiologist, he knew that a proper amount of tranquilizer was unique to every animal. Size was only part of the equation.

He looked at his watch, noticing for the first time that the screen had been cracked in the wreck. It'd been through many an adventure with him, and he hated to see it go. Nonetheless, the hands still ticked dutifully away. His crew would be there soon enough. They'd bring heavy duty netting and ties to ensure they could subdue the devil. Moving it would be another problem entirely. He'd likely be working on this extraction for days.

Moving to the face of the devil, Radley stroked the furry cheek. It was beautiful in its own way, but not cute in the way that a normal sized otter could be. Something about blowing up the proportions made it off-putting and terrifying. He ran a finger down its long, thick whisker and stared at its wet, black nose. His eyes processed everything, but his mind couldn't quite grasp what he had. It didn't seem real or possible. Much in the same way that marsupials like the koala or possum seemed like some weird animatronic approximation of a real animal.

How much would he have to feed this thing to keep it alive? He dreamed of the massive enclosure he would build on his property. The idea of starting a real life menagerie of legendary and forgotten creatures suddenly seemed like the most important goal of his life. Killing them and mounting them had all been child's play. He should have been doing this all along.

Startled, he spun just as the devil rumbled, a low growl that instantly raised the hairs along Radley's arms. Before he could register the threat level, he dove for his tranquilizer gun, prepared to pepper the creature with another few darts if necessary. But his gun wasn't there. He cursed under his breath and searched for cover, up or down. Soon, though, he realized that the rumbling devil hadn't woken, but rather emitted something more like a snore. He let out a deep breath, chuckling quietly at his uncalled-for fear.

His gun, though. That really had disappeared.

He peered into the woods looking for any sign of another person, but saw nothing. As he searched, the forest itself came alive, suddenly filled with the sound of thrashing. Limbs against limbs, feet against the ground, and the *swish* of pant legs rubbing against one another.

Radley dropped into a defensive stance, ready to defend himself with his bare hands if he had to. His muscles instantly relaxed, however, when one of his own men pushed into the clearing. The man looked as if he meant to speak, but his entire body went rigid as his eyes drank in the unconscious creature taking up the bulk of the space.

"Magnificent, isn't she?" Radley asked.

The man stood silent for a bit longer, his eyes running the length of the animal, then nodded and finally snapped his focus to Radley.

"Yes, sir," the man said. "Is this what we're extracting?"

"To start with, yes." Radley motioned towards the water, now obscured by the trees. "Then we have to get the dead one from the lake."

"Understood, sir. The rest of the team is on the way. I sprinted ahead to let you know we'd made it."

"Good man."

All the while, Radley never stopped his search. His eyes scanned the underbrush and the trees above. Someone or something had taken his gun, and he suspected they weren't safe.

"Give me your gun," Radley demanded.

"Yes, sir."

Radley didn't know the man's name, though he'd seen him a number of times. It had been a long while since Radley concerned himself with new hires. He had people for that, and trusted his lawyers and the considerable compensation to keep them quiet. It had thus far worked pretty well, but he did worry that if he expanded to live specimens, the amount he offered would have to go up.

Checking the safety, the man offered Radley his pistol grip first, which Radley took. He didn't have an immediate target, but if trouble came, Radley would take care of himself first. He'd never had much use for worrying about the safety of others—unless it also directly meant the safety of himself.

"Is something wrong, sir?" the man asked.

"I don't know," Radley replied. "Just keep your eyes peeled."

The man nodded.

Radley circled the clearing, waiting. Someone had taken his gun and he expected he'd find the culprit soon enough.

CHAPTER 43 – Miriam

The sound of two deep voices brought Miriam back to the world, her wits returning quickly enough to warn her away from making any sudden movements. She kept her eyes closed, gathering what information she could and trying to make sense of what she might see when opening her eyes. Based on the words and her own memory, she felt sure that Usa lay nearby. And it sounded like more men were coming, which didn't bode well for any escape attempt.

After the conversation died down, she listened for their footsteps, doing her best to guess their location, waiting for the opportune time to open her eyes enough to drink in more information about her predicament. Abby's contact, whose voice Miriam instantly recognized, shuffled off one direction, while the stranger went another. The latter seemed close. Too close for comfort.

She could hear Usa's labored breathing, and, if she turned towards the sound of the creature, detect the smell of rotting fish.

There. The stranger walked further away, his steps getting fainter. She took her chance and barely opened one eye, peeking to make sure she was in the clear. Both men had their back to her, so she took advantage of the situation to fully open her eyes and gauge the her prospects. She was attached to a tree with a makeshift rope of vines. She didn't doubt she could break it if she wanted, but currently she didn't have an exit plan that would make use of such an escape.

She closed her eyes, focused on slumping down best she could, and waited for an opportunity to present itself.

CHAPTER 44 – Abby

Abby looked down to see a massive estate with rolling, perfectly manicured green fields and walkways lined with expensive-looking statues. A flower garden flanked the side of a huge mansion, blooming in all the colors of the rainbow. She'd always assumed her employer was wealthy, but she didn't quite expect this. She'd figured out by now that Radley hadn't been entirely truthful with her, not just about Beatty, but also his real identity. All signs pointed to him being the enigmatic man who'd wired her money for her kills all these years. She'd finally met him, only to be immediately burned by him. It didn't bode well for their future working relationship.

The plane dropped altitude quickly, causing Abby to stretch her jaw to force her ears to pop. The world was suddenly jarringly loud, the plane's engine deafening her even through the headset she wore.

A small runaway stretched out in front of them as they closed the distance with the ground. Derek expertly lined up the nose of the plane with a dotted line down the middle of the pavement. The plane rattled with force as they landed.

Abby surveyed the airfield but saw no sign of Beatty, or a woman whose voice might be Coleman's.

"What now? Where is she?" Abby asked. Her direct address of Derek reminded her to raise the gun which had slowly fallen during the trip. He eyed it warily.

"She's probably waiting in the hangar." He pointed ahead to a large metal building. "Door's open already."

Abby nodded and waited as Derek maneuvered the plane into position, then slowly drove it along the tarmac towards the hangar. She didn't expect trouble, but she preferred to be prepared for it, so she focused on seeing anyone in the fields, behind the statues, or otherwise hidden from view. Given that Radley wanted to keep Beatty's health a secret, she couldn't rule out the fact that she might not be wanted here. There certainly must have been a reason she'd never met her employer.

The sun overhead dimmed as the plane rolled into the hangar. Abby still didn't see any sign of Coleman or Beatty.

"Where are they?" she demanded, tightening her grip on the gun.

Derek held up his hands, stammering, a bead of sweat on his forehead. "I don't know. I swear. I don't."

Props still spinning, Abby threw open the door to the plane and climbed out. Her body protested, forcing a groan and a wobble, but she kept her balance. The rumble of the engine echoed into the small space. She looked up at Derek and drew her finger across her throat. He took the meaning and killed the engine.

Ears ringing, Abby looked once again around the hangar, hoping for some sign of Beatty. She saw nothing. The hangar consisted of nothing but a giant room with one open end. There was nowhere for anyone to hide.

"You know the grounds?" Abby asked Derek as he jumped down onto the concrete floor.

"Y-yeah," he stammered.

"Where would they keep Beatty?"

"The infirmary, probably," he said. "It's in the mansion."

"Well, then," Abby said. "Lead the way."

He didn't seem keen on doing her bidding until she raised the gun again. Just the possibility of a threat seemed enough to get him moving, though. He walked towards the open hangar bay and out into the sun. The clouds had finally broken after days of dreary rain. The reflection of the tarmac flooded into her eyes so brightly that she could barely see.

Then she was running, back to the hangar. Her body reacted faster than her ears. Only when she'd dived back into the shade did she realize she'd heard a gunshot.

"What the hell, Derek?" she yelled.

The lack of response caused her to realize a lack of Derek. Looking out of the hangar doors, she found him, slumped against the tarmac either dead or close enough to it. He'd taken a bullet for her—though, she imagined, not entirely on purpose.

Gripping the pistol tightly, she peeked around the corner and squinted against the sunlight. She couldn't see well, but two men stood next to ten-foot statues of satyrs. She took a deep breath and calculated her options. She'd never hunted humans before, but she was a crack shot. She could certainly take out at least one of them, if not both, before putting herself in mortal danger. But she didn't want to kill. She just wanted Beatty.

She yelled from her corner, "I don't want any trouble! I just want Beatty!"

The men didn't give her the honor of a reply. Instead, she was answered by a *bang* behind her as the doors on either side of the hangar slammed open, revealing two more men dressed in black and ready for a gunfight. The term "surrounded" suddenly seemed like an understatement. She considered surrendering, but, given the situation, she had little hope of that ending well. So she acted.

Putting to use years of training, she glanced around the corner one last time, memorized the position of the men by the statues, and fired exactly two shots before juking to her left to protect herself from the retaliation of the ones in the hanger. Gunshots rang behind her, bullets hitting the pavement in front of her but none came from the front. It seemed she had hit her mark.

Knowing she didn't have much time, Abby surged forward towards one of the statues, ducking behind it just before another round of gunshots rang through the air. Bits of the satyr chipped off, but she managed to dodge another volley. One of the guards she had shot lay on the ground next to her. Clearly dead. She swallowed hard. This was a matter of survival. A matter of saving the man she loved. She didn't ask for this fight, but she damn sure wasn't going to give up now.

She leaned out to survey her attackers—only to immediately duck back behind the statue at the sound of another gunshot. Clearly they weren't going to give her any breathing room, so she reached around behind her and blind-fired two rounds before crawling forward a few feet, pushing up and sprinting to the next statue. They lined the entire walkway to the mansion, so she just needed to get to each one.

More gunshots rang out. None of them hit her. She expected more men to show up, but so far she only had to concern herself with the two giving chase. She blind-fired again, advanced again, one by one, statue after statue, somehow dodging fate with every move. Either those guys were bad shots, or she was faster than she gave herself credit for. She'd take either.

Before long, she found herself at her last bastion. There was nowhere else to hide between her and the mansion, and this run would be the longest by far. A few blind shots wouldn't give her enough cover for this one. She sucked in a deep breath, knowing that if she didn't move, they'd be on her too quickly. She fired behind her then took off in a sprint, weaving left and right as sporadically as she could. Gunshots rang. Grass and dirt flew up about her pant leg.

Up the stone stairs, she dropped down to a crawl, pushing left then right, then right again. Up the middle, she dove onto the porch and rolled behind a giant stone column flanking the front door. She'd lost count of the gunshots, but somehow she'd avoided them all to this point. Her lungs burned. The pain from all her wounds threatened to slow her progress, but she pushed on. She looked up at the door before her, wondering whether it would be locked. Out here, surrounded by nothing, she could only hope that locking doors was an unnecessary hassle.

First, she needed to shake the two guys bearing down on her, though. She used her location to her advantage, slowing her breath to listen. To get to her, they'd have to climb the stairs which would slow them down and mess up any chance of an aim. So she waited.

Nothing.

Clearly they hung back, waiting for her to make a move instead. But she wouldn't give them the satisfaction.

Like baiting the curiosity of a cat, she stayed still and quiet, the minutes ticking by, confident they'd start to wonder if she'd given them the slip entirely. She left them no choice but to investigate.

And eventually, they did. She heard the scuffs of their boots along the concrete sidewalk.

Still she waited, until the distinctive sound of shoes on concrete turned to the *thud* of boots on stairs. She gripped the gun, moved fast, and spun out, tracking her aim quickly enough to kneecap one guy, which was all it took as his fall brought down the other. Both tumbled backward. Hesitant to kill two goons who were just trying to protect the property, she backed into the door, tried the handle, and smiled when it opened.

Abby ducked inside the mansion, slammed shut the solid, massive wooden doors, then flipped every lock she could see.

CHAPTER 45 – Macy

Macy held the tranquilizer gun reluctantly, but with far more confidence than she would have before her new life as a cryptid-hunter. She crouched with Kim beneath a tangled mess of shrubbery so thick that she could barely see herself. Nearby, men trickled by. Some in pairs. One alone. Macy silently kept count.

Five. So far.

Kim crawled forward and stuck her head out quickly before drawing back in.

She held up a single finger to warn Macy of just one more guy coming. They couldn't be sure others wouldn't follow, but this was the plan. Wait for the last guy that they could see, take him out, and use his gear to free Miriam and Usa. It seemed like a good plan in an action movie kind of way, but not so much in a real world, Macy-might-actually-live-to-see-tomorrow kind of way. Nonetheless, it's what they'd decided. Macy didn't love that she was the trigger-man, but between the two of them, she'd at least fired a weapon before.

She worried that this action might cause her to take a life. She'd done that in Hogg Run, and had vowed never again. But this was a tranquilizer, not a gun, and these guys were big, strong men with thick muscles who easily weighed in far over two hundred pounds. If anyone could survive a shot from this gun, it was one of these fellas.

Kim held up three fingers, counted down to two, then one. Macy stood up, surprising the man approaching. He was absolutely massive. Close to seven-feet, muscles of legend. This man would not die from a tranq dart, Macy told herself. His eyes widened just as he reached for his sidearm, but by then a dart had already buried itself into his huge pectoral muscles. He managed to get his gun out, pulled it up to take aim at Macy, then blinked rapidly as he watched the gun fall from his hand and rattle against the forest floor.

Kim grinned as Macy shrugged back down into the bushes.

"Good job," Kim whispered, before crawling out on her hands and knees. It was only a matter of seconds before she returned with her haul. A pistol meant for killing. A knife meant for cutting. A stick meant for beating. And a coil of sizable rope that Kim had to drag back into their hiding place. None of these things felt particularly helpful against a giant otter in a blood rage, but she didn't figure these guys made a habit of fighting legendary creatures with a death wish.

"That leaves six guys at the camp," Macy said. "The lead guy, and the five that walked in."

Kim nodded while checking over the gun, fumbling with the safety and haphazardly ejecting the clip. She didn't know her way around the gun very well, and that worried Macy. Kim might just as likely shoot herself than one of the poachers, and that wouldn't serve anyone.

"We can't take six guys," Macy said.

"Not alone."

Part of the plan relied on a lot of luck, and a lot of assumptions, one of which was that the only tranq gun now sat in Macy's hand. Without it, they couldn't subdue Usa if she woke up, and if they had any hope of taking on this small platoon, they'd need the assist.

"You're sure none of them had one of these?" Macy asked, motioning to the one in her hand.

"Nope. Only pistols and rope."

This group had to be the first of many. They'd need more than rope to get Usa out of the woods. That either meant Macy and Kim had no chance, or that they had to act fast.

"Come on," Kim said, motioning as she crawled forward into another bunch of foliage. Macy followed behind, not nearly as quiet, but not so loud as to receive a reprimand from her guide-turned-freedom-fighter.

After a little ways, Kim motioned for Macy to stop. They'd drawn close enough that Macy's lack of stealth became a liability. From here, Kim would go on to survey the situation.

Macy waited. She felt alone and scared and, despite the dense coverage afforded her by the shrubbery, exposed. Yet she felt a spark of confidence that they'd somehow pull this thing off. It had all happened so fast that Macy hadn't really given much thought to potential other options, but now as she sat with her thoughts, she wished they'd just alerted the authorities instead. But that did mean Usa and Kawa would not just be unveiled, but announced to the world? A more preferable path would certainly be one where these monsters were kept hidden, but that went counter to what she and Miriam had gotten paid for, and seemed impossible anyway.

She pushed aside other options and the myriad of possibilities that played out in her mind. All she could do was focus on the now, and somehow that would work out. Whether skill or luck, she'd made it this far, and was finally starting to believe that she'd picked up a few tricks that helped her survive, even persevere.

As the minutes went by, though, and the time stretched on, she started to worry that something had gone wrong. Kim hadn't returned, and Macy had heard nothing but the faint chatter of the men. How long should she wait before doing something?

And, maybe more importantly, what would she do?

CHAPTER 46 – Miriam

Keeping her eyes closed, Miriam lost count of how many men might have arrived. Certainly more than she could overpower or even run from. Her ruse of pretending to still be unconscious barreled towards useless. Both her curiosity, and the hopelessness of her situation, drove her to finally open her eyes, slowly and part-way, preparing for some sort of retaliation or reaction.

Nothing happened. No one noticed. Opening her eyes fully, she quickly understood the reason. Every poacher there busied themselves with trying to secure Usa. They looped giant ropes across her body, tying them into huge knots and binding Usa's feet and tail. Two men worked on her jaw, tying a rope tight around it to ensure she wouldn't be able to open her mouth. All of this looked effective and practiced. These men may have never seen a dobhar-chú before, but they'd certainly dealt with large animals.

She found Radley right in the middle of the fray, barking orders while also doing his fair share of tightening, binding, and checking.

All of this would serve to keep them safe from Usa when she woke up, but getting her out alive would be another matter requiring some sort of vehicle.

Psst!

The sound penetrated everything else as something foreign and unexpected. Miriam twisted her head and quickly found the source of the interruption: Kim, crouched nearby, shielded by a smattering of low hanging branches and thick, green leaves.

A small smile crept across Miriam's face, much subtler than the Cheshire grin on Kim's. Miriam motioned to the vines wrapped around her shoulders, eliciting a quick nod from Kim.

Like a panther, Kim crept closer, skirting away from the camp to keep as covered as she could. Anyone paying attention would surely see her, but the grunt work of securing Usa kept them all busy enough to ignore any movement in the woods. Given the possibility of more dobhar-chú in the area, Miriam thought it foolish that they hadn't left a guard posted. Perhaps it wouldn't be a monster that foiled their plans, though.

Miriam felt the vines loosen before she even registered that Kim had approached the tree, hearing only a slight snap as each one broke beneath a large knife that Kim brandished. Kim reached around and touched Miriam lightly on the bicep, motioning into the trees. Miriam took the hint and, as silently as possible, followed Kim to cover.

Not a single one of the poachers noticed her escape. Apparently, hunting dangerous animals did not translate well into being captors.

Together, they moved through the underbrush, increasingly far away from the camp until they found a very relieved-looking Macy sitting on the forest floor, surrounded by bushes, a tranq gun in her lap.

"Mir!" she whisper-yelled.

Miriam didn't try to escape or shrug off the hug that came next, but she did wince a little. Between the three of them, Kim was the least battle-damaged.

The moment of elation quickly passed as all three girls sat in a circle. As bad of an idea as it seemed on the surface, Miriam knew they'd be going back to save Usa. After what had happened to Kawa, it had to be done. They couldn't let this creature be paraded out of the forest and exposed to the world in this way, by evil men with an evil purpose. Whatever they planned to do with this specimen, it would rob Miriam and the scientific community of the chance to properly study and protect this majestic quirk of evolution.

If they were going to be stupid enough to do this thing, they needed a solid plan.

"What do we have?" Miriam asked.

"Some rope," Kim responded. "Both this pistol and Macy's tranq, and this knife."

"Not a lot to work with."

"No, but enough," Kim said. "We need to free Usa. She'll help."

"Or she'll attack us like she did before," Macy replied.

Macy wasn't wrong. Usa's attack vector would be unpredictable and uncontrollable, if she fought at all. She was just as likely to slink into the woods and leave the three of them to face a handful of hunt-hardened poachers, a task they were not prepared or equipped for. The odds seemed poor, and Miriam preferred battles tipped in her favor.

"She won't," Kim pleaded. "Not this time. She knows the bad guys from the good guys now."

Macy rolled her eyes. Miriam sighed.

"She's a wild animal, scared and mourning," Miriam said. "I don't think we can count on that."

Kim stared defiantly into Miriam's eyes. "Fine. What's your plan then?"

Miriam didn't have one. Not one that would succeed anyway. Neither of her companions could track, aim, and fire fast enough to make any sort of an ambush work. The poachers would be far faster on the draw, and, assuming they had no compunction with killing, would put the girls on their backs before they had a chance to accomplish anything at all.

Miriam's preference was to subdue or take out the men, then carefully release Usa back into the wild in the least threatening way possible.

"We need a distraction," Miriam said. Her mind raced to find one.

"If only we had Kawa," Kim said.

Kawa was dead in the lake. The pups, likely hidden in a den somewhere, were far too small to be of any use in a fight. But maybe... maybe they didn't actually need a dobhar-chú? Maybe they just needed the poachers to feel the threat of one.

Miriam checked her front pocket and breathed a sigh of relief to feel the outline of her phone. Of course it had been through hell and back, but her feature requirements for a phone were a bit different than most. Number one on her selection list: ruggedness. As she slipped it out, the water coating the outside of the plastic shone in the cloud-strained sun. But nothing was cracked. A quick tap of the power button brought the screen to life. No signal, of course, but she didn't need a signal.

She looked at Macy and Kim, both bedraggled and injured. Neither looking particularly primed for a fight. But Kim would stop at nothing to save Usa, and Macy always had Miriam's back.

Miriam held her phone out to Macy, looked her friend in the eye, and revealed the plan that might just save them all.

CHAPTER 47 – Abby

The pounding on the door echoed into the cavernous foyer, as if Abby were standing at the top of the Grand Canyon. She didn't expect the door to hold for long, and she had a hell of a lot of house to search if she meant to find Beatty. She honestly didn't even know where to begin. It's not like houses had signs pointing to the different rooms of interest.

She started first by poking her head into a powder room larger than most apartments she'd lived in. Then into more of a formal living room, with bookcases stretching to the ceilings. Next a ballroom, she guessed. It was mostly empty with chairs lining the walls. She supposed one had to make up some use for every room in a house this large, even if that use never came in handy.

She moved across the foyer again and down a hallway. The pounding against the door had abated, which meant she needed to pick up the pace. Surely those guards had another way into the property, and it would only be a matter of time before they found her.

At the end of the hall, her eyes widened and her jaw dropped, her arms relaxing as the pistol fell to her side. On every wall, every shelf, every inch of floor space, she beheld some of the greatest wonders she'd ever seen, and Abby was a woman who had seen quite a few wonders. She recognized a few of them from her own kills.

She shivered as her eyes ran across the stuffed yeti in the corner. She and Beatty had tracked it throughout the Himalayas. She'd never been that cold before or since. In fact, seeking warmth on that trip was the first time her and Beatty ever...

Her focus moved to another creature, stretched above the windows for the full length of the room. A serpent of some sort, but far larger than any she'd ever seen or even heard of. Above it, a large monkey with the wings of a bat. Her eyes couldn't process all that she beheld. Half of it didn't seem real, but she knew that all of it was. She'd seen too much to believe otherwise.

All of this. This is what her life had been dedicated to since Ben's death. Killing these creatures just to sate her sorrow. Her guilt. Her rage. It all seemed stupid now. Reckless and cruel. She'd gone down this path to avenge Ben's death by gaining all the experience and skill she'd need to finally kill the devil that took everything from her that night at Misty Lake. Now she'd completed her journey, and she felt no better for it. She felt worse. Almost sick. She wished she could take it all back.

She didn't waste any more time feeling sorry for herself, though. She had a chance at redemption, or, if not that, at least a potentially new life with a new partner. She moved past the menagerie of cryptids and hit another hallway. She picked a door. Another bathroom. And another. Laundry room with more washers and dryers than she could count. This search had started to feel hopeless.

She pushed forward, inspecting a handful of rooms that held nothing but sickening opulence of wealth and greed.

And then, for the first time since she'd entered the mansion, she tried the handle of a door that didn't move. Locked.

Her first instinct told her to move on to the next room. Trying to get into this one would only waste time. But her curiosity nagged enough for her to lean forward and put her ear up against the door. At first, she couldn't make out anything of consequence. Then she heard a quiet *beep*. Silence. Another *beep*. It came at regular intervals, like a heartbeat.

And maybe that's just what it was.

Abby slammed her shoulder into the door, but it barely budged. Backing up, she tried again, this time eliciting a groan from her but not the wooden door. She gave it a third go with no success.

Fine. She switched tactics, aimed the pistol at the locking mechanism, then fired. The sound of the bullet zinged around the hall in a myriad of echoes until finally dissipating somewhere else in the house. The handle shook, then toppled from its place onto the floor. She took a breath, gripped the gun, and kicked the door inward, slamming it against the wall.

An older woman stood with wide eyes next to a hospital bed. And on that bed—

"Beatty!"

Abby dropped her guard and rushed to Beatty's side. Electrodes were attached to his bare chest, cords and cables snaking in every direction. A monitor nearby displayed his vitals. She glanced at them, but realized she wouldn't know for sure what they meant anyway. She bent down to hug Beatty's unconscious body, her tears spilling out across his warm skin.

"Ms. Wilson?"

Abby felt her body go rigid as she remembered the woman in the room with her. Abby ran the back of her hand across her face and sniffled before turning.

"Coleman?"

The woman nodded, deep crow's feet in the corners of her eyes. It was hard to imagine that this stern nurse had ever smiled enough to earn them.

"I'm relieved you made it," she said.

"What happened?" Abby asked. "You were supposed to meet us on the tarmac."

"They were listening in on our communications. Locked me in."

Radley and his goons certainly weren't playing around.

"How many guards are there? Abby asked.

Coleman shook her head hesitantly. "Not sure. A lot usually, but not all here at once. The director took a good number with him when he left earlier."

For the extraction no doubt.

"Okay," Abby said. "Well it's time to get out of here. I assume you know this place. There some sort of vehicle out of here?"

"Can you fly a plane?"

Abby shook her head. "No, can you?"

"No. There's a garage. Some vans, jeeps, cars. We should be able to find something there, but it'll be hard to shake the guards that way."

"We'll figure it out," Abby said, motioning to Beatty's prone body. "Get him ready to move."

Coleman looked reticent, but eventually started unhooking him from the machines.

"He'll wake up before long without the IV."

"We'll just get him out before that happens then."

Coleman moved efficiently, turning to Abby only when it came time to get Beatty into the wheelchair. The weight of his toned body made Abby shudder in pain, but she managed the maneuver. She didn't have a plan exactly other than out, but she trusted herself to come up with one on the way. Surely, some opportunity would present itself.

Abby checked her gun. The clip had enough rounds to put up a fight if she had to.

"Okay. I'm going out first. You follow. If guards show up, hide."

"Understood," Coleman said. For an old woman with no physical presence to speak of, she sure didn't seem scared. Abby briefly wondered what the woman had seen in her years working for Radley.

Abby stepped out into the hallway, gun first and swept both directions. She saw no one. She heard nothing, either, no indication of where any guards might be. She'd only left one able to walk, so with any luck she only had one to fight off. She felt confident she could win a one-on-one gunfight if she had to.

She planted each foot along the hallway slowly and deliberately, doing her best to keep her shoes from squealing, or the floor from creaking. When she got to the end of the hallway, she peeked out into the trophy room she'd gone through before. She saw nothing but the stuffed monsters.

She took a step out, heard a gunshot, felt the whir of the bullet, and thought for sure she'd made the last mistake she'd ever make. Still, her body reacted quickly, spinning back into the hallway before Abby had time to register that the bullet had missed. She peeked again. No sign of the shooter, but she knew he must be hiding behind one of those giant trophies.

Abby took a deep breath, gripped the gun, and prepared herself for a shootout in a cryptid trophy room.

What a day.

CHAPTER 48 – Macy

Macy's chest heaved up and down, but she looked down to where she started and couldn't help but be proud of her progress. High in a tree now, the forest seemed less oppressive than before. She hadn't climbed out of the canopy, but the undergrowth on the forest floor didn't exist up here, giving her a clearer view than she'd had so far of the forest.

She didn't love the plan Miriam had come up with, but as reckless as it seemed, none of them wanted to leave Usa to die.

Macy tried to see Miriam and Kim below, but only saw the occasional shaking of the leaves or rustling of a branch. She could have attributed such things to animals or the wind just as much as her friends, so it gave her no comfort that they'd managed to make it into position. She decided to give it a few more minutes to be safe.

The minutes passed by slowly, Macy constantly checking Miriam's phone to see how much time had passed. The forest seemed abnormally quiet, as if it swallowed the sound from all the living creatures within. Given her particular part in the plan, she couldn't help but wonder if somehow all the animals knew that, for right now, they needed to give her the stage.

After the clock finally ticked down, Macy opened the sound player that Miriam had pointed her to, made sure the volume on the phone was as high as it would go, then hit play.

CHAPTER 49 – Radley

Every man in attendance startled when the sounds of growling and yipping echoed through the woods. It was no animal that Radley knew well, and too close to the sounds he'd heard while escaping the helicopter crash and avoiding the devils. They'd already tracked two, and now, apparently, there was at least one more. Most of the rare animals he'd managed to get his hands on had been alone, rarely in a group. This truly did present him with an embarrassment of riches.

"Fan out," he said to his men. "Go in pairs. I'll stay here and guard the devil."

The girl had already escaped, but he chose not to sweat it. She wouldn't cause him enough trouble to warrant hunting after her. He didn't needlessly take life. After all, he'd gotten his prizes. He'd handle the fallout from the crypto team after the fact by paying off news agencies and greasing the palms of the authorities. Harder to do in the States, but still possible with enough capital.

His guards dispersed. Radley paced back and forth next to the sleeping devil, listening to the soft hum of its breath. He kept his muscles readied, their potential energy coiled and ready to snap into action. He could hardly contain the electric excitement pulsing through his veins. Three devils. One dead. Two alive. Amazing.

His ears alerted him to a sound. He stopped. Listened. Nothing.

Then, cold metal on the back of his neck. He put his hands up, his fingers still wrapped around the handle of his gun.

"Don't move."

The feminine voice behind him sounded serious, but he questioned whether she really had a gun. Perhaps she'd fashioned a fake one out of something.

He'd never been one to live cautiously. He ducked, spun, and knocked something out of the way. The same girl he'd tied up just minutes before now pointed a tranq gun at him loaded with the very same darts that had put the devil to sleep. They'd likely do worse to him. She hadn't even pulled the trigger, though.

He slowly pushed to his feet, his hands still up, but unwilling to let go of his gun. When he felt sturdy on his feet, he jerked the gun to point straight at the girl. She didn't flinch. He flashed one of his bleached white smiles, meant to disarm.

"My gun's deadlier than yours." It was a bit of a bluff. At his size, the tranq darts would likely kill him just as sure as a bullet.

"No, it's not," she replied. "I've used one of these before. I know what they're for. And I know what they're capable of. Best case scenario is we kill each other."

"I might live," he insisted.

"Maybe one dart, but I'll make sure to load you with two before I go down."

She seemed so cocky. Sure. He didn't expect it, but it gave him enough pause to resist the urge to do anything overly rash. The last thing he needed was to end this day with his own death.

CHAPTER 50 – Miriam

Miriam kept her face as impassive as possible, not deterred or swayed by the man's smarmy grin. He was more than a pilot, and she knew enough to take the threat of him seriously. Her survival depended on her own ability to convince him that she also posed a threat. At least for a few minutes.

Kim crept silently behind the man, her knife working slowly and surely on the ropes that kept Usa pinned. The creature hadn't stirred yet, but when she did, she'd have the best possible chance at escape. Hopefully without any more carnage.

"So what then?" Radley asked. "We stand here pointing guns at each other until my team comes back? I'll make you a deal. Walk away now, and I'll let you go. One of my guys finds you threatening me, and you're dead. This way is a better deal."

"What makes you so sure your guys are even alive?" Miriam asked. "You think they can fight off a devil with their training?"

"Oh, trust me, they're trained perfectly well to fight whatever monsters are in these woods."

"They're an extraction team. Your poachers have already left."

She didn't know that for sure, but she took the gamble that it was true. She'd seen no sign of Abby since Kawa went down, which implied that she'd completed the job. And if she had no hand in getting the carcass out, then someone else had to, and these guys fit the bill.

Somehow, Radley's smiled widened. "Smart girl. Still, I haven't heard any signs of a commotion."

On that, he was right. But then, she didn't expect to hear any commotion. Recordings of the devil would hardly put up a fight should they find them. Hopefully, Macy had found a hiding place safe enough to evade detection. Macy had already followed Miriam's clear instructions to only play the sounds for a few minutes. Enough to pique their interest, but not enough time for them to pinpoint the source of the sounds.

"Well, I guess we'll see how fast on the trigger I am, then," Miriam said, forcing confidence despite her heart pounding. "We're either both gonna die, or neither of us is. That's up to you."

Radley raised an eyebrow. "Oh? What's your counteroffer, then?"

"You leave. You and your team. Without the dobhar-chú."

"Is that what they are?" he asked. "I don't really know nearly as much about cryptids as I should."

Miriam fixed her eyes on his, waiting for his gaze to wander. She couldn't safely check on Kim's progress without his notice, and that meant she didn't know how much longer she needed to stall.

She got her chance to check when Usa huffed and shook her head, her eyes not yet open. The tranquilizer's effects had started to wane, though. Radley turned to look. Miriam rattled her gun at his face.

"Nope," she said sternly. "Eyes on me."

Radley seemed to respect the threat enough to stop his turn. Kim knelt frozen behind Usa, not nearly as hidden as she probably thought. Radley hadn't seen though, Miriam didn't think.

"So if I let the creature go, you let me go?" he asked. She didn't trust his tone. A man like this wouldn't make a deal that ended in him not getting what he wanted.

"Yes," she replied. "Simple. Just leave."

She watched Radley's mouth twist up in thought. "I'm going to have to consider that."

"Consider quickly," she said. "I'm running out of patience."

Mostly true, though she worried she would run out of time instead. His team would come back, and they would shoot, and as confidently as she stated her willingness to die, she really didn't like the sound of that outcome.

Usa huffed again, this time her eyes creeping open. Timing seemed to be working out in Miriam's favor.

"It's waking up," Radley said. "If I'm going to let it go, I need to remove the ropes now."

"That won't be necessary," Kim said from behind. Radley's smile melted.

He turned, ignoring the threat of the tranquilizer gun in favor of something that could tear him limb from limb. The wheels had started to turn now, and no matter how much Miriam preferred that Usa run off into the sunset, she was an uncontrollable force of nature. Usa slowly stood, her height easily eclipsing that of the three humans standing around her. She blinked her eyes, shook her head. Miriam couldn't be sure that Usa even knew that she was awake yet.

Miriam shared a look with Kim. For the shortest of seconds, Miriam considered aiming her tranq gun at

Usa and bringing the beast down yet again, but if she did, then Radley would certainly win. His men would soon discover that they'd chased a recording, return, then slaughter them all. At this point, the die had been cast, and Usa would do whatever was best for survival.

Kim started to back away slowly, into the tree line. Miriam took the hint and did the same. Radley stood there staring up at the creature that now stared down at him with laser-focused, beady eyes. Drool dripped from Usa's jowls. Her whiskers twitched.

Then...

Radley was gone in an instant, snatched up, chewed, swallowed. An unceremonious end, to be sure, but perhaps one that he deserved. He didn't even manage to scream.

Miriam's stomach turned. She'd seen death before, but this...

Usa bellowed into the woods, her cry echoing a warning to any who would cross her. Miriam took the hint, realizing now that despite whatever relationship Kim might have had with this dobhar-chú, it wouldn't be enough. Not now. The stories foretold of an extremely strong bond between mating pairs, and real life had proven the legends correct. This poor, previously gentle creature would never trust humans again.

And, maybe, that was for the best.

It was only a matter of seconds before some of the guards started pouring back into the clearing. Chaos and confusion reigned. Guns fired. Screams echoed. Usa turned into a tornado of fur and blood. Miriam would not make Radley's mistake. She turned and ran, leaving behind Radley's men to fend for themselves.

Kim appeared beside her after only a few long strides, panting, arms pumping, legs pushing hard. For the first time, Kim seemed scared, and that rattled Miriam even more.

"We have to get Macy," Miriam said, coming to a stop at least fifty yards away from the clearing. A small distance for a giant dobhar-chú.

Kim skidded to a stop just a few feet past Miriam, slapped her hands on her knees and gasped for breath. She nodded. "Yeah. Of course."

"Do you remember where she is?"

Kim stood and looked around, gained her bearings and pointed. "That way."

"Let's go."

Miriam took off in a run towards Macy's position, using the horrific death-sounds as a barometer for how much time they could afford.

None of this had gone how she'd hoped. The time had come to abandon all hope, get out of the woods, and finish the job.

CHAPTER 51 – Abby

Bullets tore into Bigfoot's chest, ricocheted off the hide of a sea serpent, and shattered the glass protecting certain artifacts, artifacts from wild creatures of lore. Abby ducked and fired. She'd nailed down the location of both of her attackers, and gratefully played the long game, hoping for a lucky shot, or a slip-up by one of the guards.

Coleman knelt behind Beatty's wheelchair, using him as somewhat of a shield. In calmer times, Abby might have objected, but Beatty's bobbing head made her worry that he wouldn't live long enough for it to matter. He'd begun to fight towards wakefulness, but even if he got there, he'd be no use in a gunfight. Not in his condition.

The shots slowed, then stopped entirely. Neither side had made any headway. Abby's ammo wouldn't hold out for many more shots.

"There's no other way out?" she whispered to Coleman.

Coleman only shook her head, her tight bun having started to unravel from the commotion. Abby needed a solution, and she needed it yesterday.

"Listen," she yelled around the corner. "I don't want to fight. I don't care what Radley told you, I'm not a threat. I just want to take my... friend... and go."

Neither of the guards answered, undoubtedly afraid to give away their locations.

"No one else needs to die," she pleaded. "I didn't come here to kill anyone. I came here to save someone."

Still no answer.

The hard way it would be, then.

Abby peeked around the corner. The crown of one guard's head rose just above a shattered display case, one containing the preserved specimen of a strange beetle. Abby hated all of this so much now. Each and every bizarre creature, whether she'd hunted it or not, represented a life—an industry—that should have never existed. She wondered the reasons that others had chosen her same path. Retribution? Vindication? Or maybe some of them for pure greed.

Radley Furey had paid her for years, and she never questioned any of it. She felt foolish.

She pulled up her gun and fired at the strange beetle. It splintered into a myriad of pieces, a priceless relic instantly destroyed, possibly to never be found in the world again. The bullet cut through the chitin and lodged itself in the wall on the other side. The man below shot up, took quick aim and fired. Abby hadn't returned to hiding, though. If she meant to end this thing, she needed brash action. Bravery or stupidity, or some mix of both.

The bullet hit her in the left shoulder. Pain exploded up her arm as she lost the ability to steady her own gun. But she'd prepared herself for that, instead holding firmly with her good arm and firing. Her aim hit true, hitting the guard in the chest and knocking him to the ground. Possibly dead, possibly maimed. She didn't have the luxury of caring. She ducked back into the hallway.

One down. One to go.

Coleman crawled from her hiding place behind Beatty's wheelchair. She hissed as she looked at the bullet wound on Abby's shoulder. After inspection, Coleman reported back.

"It went straight through. That's good. But we should get you back to the infirmary."

"That's a negative," Abby replied, trying to ignore how her labored breathing strained her voice. "There's only one direction to go from here."

Abby couldn't really tell how much she hurt. The pain of the bullet hardly seemed any worse than all the other pain she already felt, both physically and emotionally. She wanted to believe that, if they could just make it out, this would all be over, and that (possibly false) belief drove her forward.

"Stay here," Abby said.

She looked across the trophy room to the foyer on the other side. A wall would protect her if she could make it that far. She took the chance.

Stood up.

Ran.

As erratically as possible.

Bullets peppered the wall behind her, none of them nearly close enough to hit her. Even the best marksman had a tough time with a moving target, and Abby intended to make herself as elusive as possible. Unfortunately, her body disagreed with her intent. Her feet tangled up with each other and sent her tumbling within sight of her destination, enough that she was able to roll behind the wall of the foyer. She'd managed no new injuries, had wasted dozens of her opponent's bullets, and knew exactly where he hid.

She reached around and fired a blind shot, hoping to smoke him out or force a mistake. A short, orange bigfoot-looking thing toppled down towards the guard. Abby took the opportunity, spun out, aimed and fired. She'd tracked him true, but he dove behind another display case just before her bullet met its target. Abby sighed. This was getting tiresome.

She stepped out entirely from her hiding place, surged forward, and dove behind a display case of her own just as a bullet whizzed by overhead. Her opponent only sat a few feet away now. Less room for error. Less time for hiding. One of them would die soon. Abby only hoped she could keep her wits about her.

"Last chance," she yelled.

"You're hit," he said, finally deciding to respond. "Just give up."

"Then what?"

"That's for the director to decide."

"I'm not sure I trust his decision making skills."

The guard actually laughed. "No?"

"Are you really willing to die for a guy who doesn't give two shits about you? Look at your friend over there."

She could hear the guard's breathing, track his micro-movements. The conversation went silent.

"You just want to take your friend?" the guard finally asked.

"That's all," Abby replied. "And a car. To get us to Seattle."

"Ya know, I used to have a family," the guard said unexpectedly. "Wife left me. Took the kids. She even convinced the courts to strip my parental rights. I was never home. Kids barely knew what I looked like."

"That's a damn shame," Abby said, not managing to infuse her reply with much sympathy.

"I'll never get that back," he replied wistfully.

"No. Maybe not. But you can find something new. Just help me out of here. Get yourself out of here. Find a new path."

Silence again. Abby held firm to her gun, certain the guard meant to use the conversation as a way to sneak up on her.

Then: "The director took everything from me. And staying seemed like the only choice I had. The only way to make it all worth it."

"Hey, what's your name?" Abby asked.

"Devon."

"Well, Devon. Ever heard of the sunk-cost fallacy?"

A chuckle. "Yeah."

"Well I think maybe you're guilty of it."

"Maybe."

A distinctive *click* raised Abby's hackles. Then, the sliding of metal against the marble floor as a gun whizzed past her.

"Go. Just go," the guard said.

"Thanks, Devon."

Abby didn't wait for a response. She stood, scooping up Devon's gun, then nodded towards Coleman.

"You made the right choice, Devon. Good luck."

Out of her periphery she saw him stand. He smiled at her with crooked white teeth. He had a nose that'd been broken one too many times, and piercing green eyes that stood out against his close-cropped black hair. Abby had killed a lot of beautiful creatures. A handful of human beings. But not Devon.

Abby's heart dropped suddenly. Shoes clomped from somewhere else in the house. Two, three. She couldn't be sure. More guards. She sighed as three men came around the corner. Fresh suits. Fresh guns. Fresh stamina.

She cursed under her breath.

Beatty better damn well appreciate this.

They started firing before Abby could react. Coleman went down. Devon went down. They fired indiscriminately, peppering the trophy room with bullets, not even minding the sanctity of Radley's collection.

Not a single bullet hit Abby. She'd dropped to the floor without thinking, protecting herself at the expense of the only friends she had in the mansion. Beatty? Had they hit Beatty?

In a rage, Abby stood and fired back. One hit. Two hits. She spun the odds in her favor in only a blink of an eye, driven by years of self-loathing. She hated everything that Radley stood for. She'd always assumed this had all been her choice, and maybe, nominally it had been, but Radley had taken advantage of her weakness. Of her sorrow. Of her thirst for revenge. And as culpable as she was in all the horrible things that she'd done, she believed in that moment that Radley was just as much to blame.

The last guard managed to evade her third shot, closing the distance himself while providing his own cover fire. Abby had no choice but to retreat. His polished dress shoes scuffled across the floor towards her. She tried to anticipate which direction he came from, but she calculated wrong, and before she could react, there was the muzzle of a gun pointed at her face.

"Drop it," he said in an accent she couldn't place.

She complied. All that bravery. All that hatred. All for nothing.

"Stand up," he demanded.

"No," a strained voice came from behind. "Stay down."

A gunshot.

A perfect shot.

Blood oozed from the guard's forehead as he slumped to the floor. Abby gasped for breath, then turned to see Devon smiling at her with his crooked blood-stained teeth. He'd managed to crawl to another gun.

"Where was that aim when you were fighting me?" Abby asked, trying to lighten the mood.

Devon didn't answer, rolling onto his back. His green eyes stared up at the ceiling, unmoving and glassy. She moved to him as quickly as she could, but she knew deep down that she'd be too late. His own team had shot him without regard. That's the sort of person Devon worked for. That's the sort of person Abby worked for. That's the sort of person who couldn't be allowed to profit from their hard work.

"I'm gonna burn this place down, Devon."

She stood and rushed to Beatty. His eyes shot open. She searched his body for bullet wounds and found none. Coleman lay on the floor nearby. Abby attended her with a half-hearted attempt to find a pulse, but like Devon, this lady had risked everything to end Radley's tyranny. It didn't seem fair that Abby would be the one to survive.

"You're a lot of work," Abby said, as she started pushing Beatty toward the door.

He let out a sharp laugh, which brought a glimmer of hope to Abby's heart.

"You love me," he managed to get out.

"Yeah," is all she could manage in response.

She met no more resistance. With only a little searching, she pushed up a rolling door to reveal a collection of cars the likes of which she'd never seen. A board nearby held all the keys, perfectly labeled. Abby couldn't contain the tears of joy. She chose a van that would allow Beatty the room to lay down, if necessary, and loaded him up.

Starting the engine, she checked the dials... only to see that she'd need gas.

No matter, she'd seen the pumps outside. She could fill up in just a matter of minutes.

Pulling the van alongside the pumps, her mind started putting together one last plan. One last bit of revenge.

She peeked inside. "Hey, Beatty. Give me a few minutes, okay?"

He attempted a nod.

Nearby, she found plastic gas containers. She filled every last one of them. Two at a time, she carried them to the house. The minutes she promised Beatty turned into a handful more. She couldn't help herself. She didn't know where Radley was or when he would return, but she wanted to make sure that he had nothing to return to. She wanted to make sure he would have to start every hunt over again. She wanted to take away the one thing she knew he coveted more than anything in the world.

She emptied most of the gasoline into the trophy room, taking one last look at the wonders within. If she couldn't make sure Radley burned in hell, then she could make sure every last one of these dead, soulless creatures did.

She started the fire on Bigfoot's chest, his hulking eight-foot form having been knocked over in the fight.

The sasquatch went up in an instant, the blaze growing and growing, until it started to engulf every last piece of evidence. Sea serpents, bigfoots, giant thunderbirds. Abby didn't really know what they all were, and she didn't care. She just cared that they melted back into the legend from whence they came.

By the time she walked out the door of the mansion, more of it burned. When she got to the van, she turned to admire her handiwork. She doubted the entire thing would come down, but the trophy room would certainly leave nothing to recover, and she cared the very most about that. From inside the van, Beatty stared out, a stupid grin on his face.

She climbed into the driver's seat.

"Guess you're retiring?" Beatty asked, his voice stronger than before.

"We both are."

"Together?"

She looked at him and smiled.

"Together."

CHAPTER 52 – Macy

Macy more fell out of the tree than climbed down, but she slowed herself on each branch enough that the end result left her no worse for the wear.

Kim and Miriam stood guard below, ready to catch her. Once Macy's feet touched the ground safely, though, the two were off, leaving Macy to bring up the rear yet again. She pumped her legs as hard as she could to keep up, compelled by the sounds of gruesome horror echoing through the trees. Too many people had died on this day, and Macy shuddered to think she was partly responsible for the carnage.

The path out of the woods seemed strangely short this time, as if time had dilated to hasten their exit. Macy wanted to believe that the adventure had come to its conclusion, but she'd thought that before, then had to traipse back into the forest once again. This nightmare seemed never-ending and she wouldn't believe that it was over until she'd buckled her seatbelt on a Texas-bound flight.

"Just a little farther," Kim hollered from the front of the pack.

Her estimate proved accurate as all three girls burst out of the tree-line onto the asphalt of the parking lot. Macy gasped for breath, but still found room for a smile as she surveyed the scene. Police cars. Everywhere. And at the front, staring at them with those cool blue eyes and warming smile, Tanner. He'd come for them. All the way from Texas.

Macy found the strength to run a few more feet until she collapsed into his arms, his warmth instantly stealing away all her fear and doubt. God she loved him.

"You got my message," Miriam said from behind, not nearly as winded as Macy.

Macy heard Tanner's voice just above her head, her face still buried in his chest. "I did. Am I late?"

"Only a little," Miriam replied. "It's over."

The police immediately swarmed them, leaving little time to straighten out their story. Before being pulled away, Kim said only one word: "Bear."

Macy took the hint, recounting a tale of a rabid grizzly intent on killing everything in its wake. She told of a helicopter crashing into the lake for reasons unknown. She told of the unfortunate carnage that resulted from the survivors startling the bear. She didn't know if her fiction would align with that of Kim's, or whether Miriam would be willing to lie at all, but Macy had come around to Kim's way of thinking. The fewer people who knew about these creatures, the better. They weren't ruthless killers. They were relics of the past just trying to survive in a modern world that left no room for them.

It all went by like a blur. Ambulances arrived and threw blankets over her. They tended to the wounds of all three of them. Tanner stayed by her side through it all, clutching her hand. The whole ordeal really was over. She'd tell him the real story eventually, but for now it only mattered that he was there for her. She didn't need him to survive. She'd proven that multiple times over. But she wanted him near her. Always.

As the scene died down and the ambulances readied to take them to the hospital, the three girls closed in on each other and met up, perhaps for the last time before leaving Kim behind. Macy would miss her, as odd as the girl was.

With the cops now busy sorting out the mess in the forest, no one stood nearby to hear their conversation.

"What did you tell them?" Kim asked.

"Grizzly," Macy replied.

"Same," Miriam said.

Macy's eyebrows raised in surprise. Miriam tended to stick to the truth, believing lies to never be worth the cost. It'd be interesting to break down that decision with her in the future. Macy wondered if Miriam intended to give the real story to the University, or if she intended to collect payment on a stack of lies. Macy could go either way given the circumstances, but she doubted Miriam could see it any way but one.

"Thank you," Kim said. She meant it. Macy could tell.

Miriam didn't have a response. Macy replied, "Of course. It's the right thing to do."

Sometimes, lying could be the correct course of action.

"Well, listen," Kim said. "Keep in touch, okay?"

Macy nodded. Miriam stayed silent.

Kim continued, "And, Miriam."

Miriam looked up to meet Kim's dark gaze, as that Cheshire grin spread across her face.

"If it doesn't work out with you and Gabe, give me a call."

Kim turned away without waiting for Miriam's response, which turned out to be a look of confusion and shock. Macy giggled.

"You're just breaking hearts left and right, girl. First Gabe. Now Kim."

"Shut up," Miriam said. "It's not like that."

"Uh-huh."

Macy put her arm around Miriam's shoulder and walked with her back to the ambulance, where Tanner waited.

"You know it's okay if you like girls, right?"

Miriam didn't answer, leaving Macy to drop the subject, but not the amused look on her face.

"Ready to go?" Tanner asked as they approached.

"So ready," Macy answered.

Another exciting end to another unbelievable adventure. Macy started to think that maybe, just maybe, she might get used to a life like this.

CHAPTER 53 – Miriam

Miriam's leg bounced up and down. She sat on a stiff, unwelcoming couch in a room that seemed far too quiet. She tried to focus on the television in the corner despite having only closed captioning. The TV showed a burning husk of a house, the shadow of the helicopter filming the shot visible in the white smoke. She couldn't tell if any of the house remained.

Her pocket buzzed. She pulled out her phone to see a text from Gabe. He'd tried incessantly to get her to open up about the past few days, but every time she saw his texts, she avoided him. She told herself that she'd just hit her limit and couldn't bother to talk with anyone right now, but that provided little consolation. His texts almost made her mad, but that made no sense whatsoever, and she hated it.

Miriam pushed aside the complexity of feelings she couldn't understand, and instead forced herself to read the words on the television: "This mansion, owned by wealthy philanthropist Radley Coopersmith, went up in flames this past weekend."

The melting house gave way to a classy professional headshot of a man with a bleached white smile and piercing blue eyes, fine-line crow's feet forming at the corners. Radley Furey. Or, rather, as Miriam had just learned, Radley Coopersmith. Furey always did seem like too awesome of a last name to be real.

She continued reading: "The firemen have been unable to control the fire, and no sign of Mr. Coopersmith has thus far been recovered. It is unknown whether he was present when the fire started. Police are looking for any information about what started the fire, or anyone who might have information pertaining to a potential gunfight on the property."

They wouldn't find Radley there. If they ever found him at all, he'd no longer be in any recognizable form. It couldn't be a coincidence that his estate went up in flames on the same day that she squared off with him in the forest. She'd never know the full story, but she suspected Abby. Who else would have cared enough to get involved?

From the burning building, the scene changed to another helicopter shot, this one of Misty Lake. Debris stretched across the surface.

The captioning caught up with: "In a potentially related case, a helicopter—belonging to the same Radley Coopersmith—lost control and crashed in Misty Lake this past weekend. There have been a number of casualties recovered, all of whom are assumed to have died in or shortly after the unfortunate crash. Eyewitnesses reported hearing the helicopter go down, but the tree cover prevented anyone from seeing the reason for the accident."

They'd find the guards. The helicopter debris. The ropes and the tarp. But they wouldn't find Kawa. The debris had pulled him under, hopefully forever to the bottom of Misty Lake. Miriam took solace in that. She looked down at the bound report in her lap. Macy had gone above and beyond, creating a professional looking cover and taking it to the local printshop to bind it with a little plastic spiral spine. Their first official report to a paying customer.

Miriam expected everything to change after this job. Once she turned this report in along with the physical evidence she'd collected, her little cryptozoology venture would come to a head, one way or another. She couldn't be sure if it would mean more or less work, but it seemed hard to believe that all of the danger and fear and near-death came down to nothing but a few dozen pages bound by a minimum wage worker down at the local FedEx Office.

Since leaving the forest, Miriam hadn't spoken to Kim. The last few days had been a whirlwind of medical attention, report writing, and a whole lot of lying to law enforcement and medical personnel. Just three girls camping in the woods, unexpectedly waylaid by a roaming grizzly that had gone too far south. They'd never find the grizzly, but they seemed to take the reports seriously enough, intent on hunting down and subduing the bear that would surely have an unshakable taste for people.

Miriam picked up the report and riffled through the pages.

"Miriam Brooks?" a lady said from a doorway. "We're ready for you."

She grabbed her backpack and slung it over a shoulder, standing, report in hand. It held everything except the part with Abby and Radley and his goons. Pictures. Samples. Her backpack held the footprint cast and a thumb drive with the audio of the mythical devil of Misty Lake. In just a few short minutes, it wouldn't be a legend anymore. It would be real, and whether the world would know of its existence would become the sole discretion of the University of Washington.

"Please have a seat."

Miriam stood stunned for a second when she saw blue hair. The girl turned.

Kim.

Miriam's stomach did a somersault.

Kim didn't have that blinding smile today. She looked nervous. Maybe even angry. Miriam knew Kim didn't want her to do this, but she'd been hired to do a job and she had to tell the truth. She simply had to. For her own future. For the future of these creatures. Hiding them in the shadows only delayed the inevitable. Someone would find them eventually. Better her now than another Radley Coopersmith down the road, right?

Miriam sat. The woman took the chair across from her and sat at a large oak desk. She curled her fingers into one another before resting her hands on the table.

"Ms. Akana says that you had quite an adventure."

Miriam nodded. "Yes, ma'am."

"I'm glad that none of you were seriously injured. We hold no personal responsibility of course, pursuant to the contract that you all signed. But still, none of us expected this."

Kim answered before Miriam could. "Miriam's expertise proved invaluable, though. She knew exactly how to save us from the grizzly that wanted to kill us."

Miriam looked over at Kim, then down to the report in her hands. The report that would turn Kim into a liar, and surely sever any future relationship the two might have built. The report that would ensure that the hunt for the dobhar-chú would never end. She'd always believed that bringing such creatures to light would only protect them.

Miriam looked at Kim, their eyes locking on to one another. In Kim's black eyes, Miriam saw, clearer than ever, the path Kim preferred. Her way would protect the dobhar-chú as well, perhaps not forever, but for a while. It would give them a chance to propagate, move, adapt, hide.

What was the point of it all, really?

Did Miriam mean to be famous? Of course not. She abhorred the idea. She hated interviews and press coverage. She delighted in the science of it, and finding these cryptids meant that she advanced science. But now she could see how that advancement sometimes came at a cost. A cost that maybe she didn't want to be responsible for paying.

"Is that your final report?" the woman at the desk asked.

Miriam sat her backpack down in front of her, unzipped it and slipped the report inside. Instead she pulled out a second. Shorter, but bound just as nicely. She'd written it after, early in the morning. It contained no evidence of a dobhar-chú. No photos. No measurements of footprints, or descriptions of vocalizations. Even before coming face to face with Kim's solemn expression, Miriam knew that perhaps the cost she needed to pay was one of her own professional advancement.

And, in this case, Kim was right. She had been all along. These beautiful dobhar-chú needed to be protected, and that couldn't be done effectively if they were brought into the light for everyone to hunt. Wherever a scientist poked around, so too would someone looking to line their own pockets either with glory or gold.

It was a hard call. One that went against Miriam's instincts. She wanted to study them, capture them, breed them. It was the only way their survival could be ensured. But living in only captivity would do a disservice to this majestic species. Perhaps nature deserved to chart its own course sometimes, without the meddling of man.

Miriam zipped up her backpack, leaving the cast of the footprint inside, along with the few other scraps of physical evidence she'd managed to salvage. She sat up straight. Perhaps straighter than she ever had before.

"Yes, ma'am. You'll find my final report about the potential existence of the Devil of Misty Lake herein. I'm sorry we couldn't prove anything. It's my professional opinion that the stories are just that—stories. There are a lot of animals out there, and the average person just can't tell the difference, especially under duress. Otters, bears, raccoons, birds. They're all very intelligent animals capable of doing things that people don't always understand animals can do."

Kim's face lit up, and something in Miriam's chest suddenly felt lighter.

"I see." The woman thumbed through the report, stopping on a few pages and pausing briefly before moving on. She closed the report and sat it down on her desk, resting her palms on the clear plastic cover.

"I appreciate the hard work you've put into this, and, again, I'm sorry that it turned into a dangerous assignment."

"Just part of the job, ma'am. The thing about being a cryptozoologist is that most hunts are going to be failures, but that doesn't mean we give up the chase. It doesn't mean it's not worth pursuing. It just means we're looking in the wrong place for the wrong thing is all."

The woman suddenly stood, causing Miriam to do the same. "Very well. Your payment should be deposited within the next few days."

She offered a hand, Miriam gripped it and shook.

"It's been a pleasure working with you," Miriam said, casting a glance towards Kim. "And your excellent guide."

Miriam picked up her backpack, shared one last meaningful look with Kim, then walked out of the office. Her perspective on what it meant to do her job might have changed.

Possibly forever.

But in this, she confidently believed she'd accomplished a job well done.

EPILOGUE

Thirty miles north of Misty Lake, at the foot of the mountains, surrounded on all sides by trees and nearly impassable terrain, stood another lake so remote it only existed on satellite maps. The Native Americans knew of it, but steered clear, afraid of the spirits that lurked there and respectful of the power beneath the waters. The waters were clear and clean, full of all manner of fish. It stretched as far as the eye could see, with bends and pools and mossy overgrowth, and fallen trees providing wonderful hiding places.

In a word, this pristine lake was simply breathtaking.

Almost no one alive had seen it, and here Kim stood. She lowered her backpack to the ground, her shoulders aching from the weight of having carried it so far. She'd never guided a group through such grueling, treacherous terrain, and the aching in her muscles attested to the difficulty of the trip. But they'd made it to a place so distant and so remote that not even Kim herself was likely to ever return. Exactly the kind of place she wanted to find.

Behind her, she heard her group approach. Usa's breathing rumbled as the creature walked up beside Kim and nuzzled against her elbow. Kim responded by scratching behind her ear, causing Usa to lower herself to the ground, enough for the pups to roll off her back and run out into the water, their energy full from being carried most of the way.

"This is your new home," Kim whispered.

Usa's huge black eyes scanned the surface of the water. She let out a bellow that bounced around in the wet air.

"Do you like it?" Kim asked.

Of course, Usa couldn't answer, but Kim took it as an answer when the gentle giant lurched forward and lowered herself into the icy cold waters of this nameless lake. Kim knew that someone would find this lake eventually, but she hoped that day was as far off as possible. She hoped that Usa and her pups could live here in harmony. She prayed that, somehow, through the miracle of nature, other dobhar-chú would find their way to her; that she'd find a new mate and propagate the species, hidden from mankind, for decades to come.

Leaving would be hard. Kim didn't want to say goodbye. But it was the best way. The safest way. The only way. She watched the pups splash around in the water while Usa floated on her back nearby. The tears flowed freely, and Kim let them come. Miriam had left without knowing what would happen to Usa, but Kim couldn't tell her about this place. Or about this plan. If Usa and her pups were to remain safe, then it had to be Kim's secret. Forever.

She blew a kiss out to Usa, heaved her backpack onto her shoulders, and turned away from the lake. A bellow from Usa caused her to pause and turn. The creature had come back to land, the back half of her body still in the lake as she perched on a rock and stared at Kim.

"It's okay, Usa. You're okay."

They held the look for a while longer, then Usa slid back into the water. Kim took that as understanding. Acceptance.

Content with her decision, Kim disappeared into the forest, leaving the dobhar-chú to melt back into legend.

ACKNOWLEDGEMENTS

Turns out writing a book, like many other things, is very difficult during a pandemic. At the beginning, I thought it would be a great opportunity to lock myself indoors and complete multiple works, but I struggled to get even this one done. I'm not much of a people person, but so much of writing comes from witnessing life, in all its many forms, that being stripped of that robbed me of inspiration.

Nonetheless, the book is finished. As always, the team at Evolved Publishing stood ready at every turn. I'm eternally grateful to Mike Robinson, Richard Tran, and Dave Lane (aka Lane Diamond). Books go through a lot before they reach publication, and it is these gatekeepers that ensure my book is as enjoyable and attractive as it can be.

I'd like to thank Mistie Cogdill, now a published author in her own right, who has been here with me since the very first in the series, always eager to read and honest with her opinions. She helps breathe life into my characters. It's no coincidence that this book takes place at *Misty* Lake.

To my beta readers: Amanda, Sammie, and Rachael. These three give the best reader reactions, balancing a tightwire between fan and critic, always careful to consider my ego while simultaneously telling me everything I need to fix. I appreciate all that they do.

Right before I started this book, I received a random message from a stranger asking if I'd like to join a local writing group. I took the leap, joined The Revenants of Yore, and met three wonderful guys who contributed greatly to this book. Thank you, Samuel, Cameron, and Mason, for coming out of nowhere to provide so much value.

To my wife, Akaemi—I always must thank her. She's helped me along the way on every step of this journey, rooting for me, challenging me, and leading me when I got lost.

And of course, many thanks to the fans. I've moved to a new area of the country and just now started to venture out into the world to meet people at conventions, festivals, and markets. It's encouraging to see that here, too, I will find a home among my people.

Just one more book left in the series, folks. I intend to jump the shark as hard as I possibly can, so stay tuned.

ABOUT THE AUTHOR

J.P. Barnett grew up in a tiny Texas town where the list of possible vocations failed to include published author. In second grade, he worked harder than any other student to deliver a story about a tiger cub who singlehandedly saved the U.S. Military, earning him a shiny gold star and a lifelong appreciation of telling a good story.

Fast forwarding through decades of schooling and a career as a software engineer, J.P. Barnett stepped away from it all to get back to his first real passion. Years of sitting at a keyboard gifted him with some benefit, though, including blazing fast typing hands and a full tank of creativity.

As a child, J.P. consumed any book he could get his hands on. The likes of Stephen King, Michael Crichton, and Dean Koontz paved the bookshelves of his childhood, providing a plethora of fantastical and terrifying tales that he read way too early in life. Though the effect these books had on his psyche could be called into question, these masters of storytelling managed to warp his mind in just the perfect way to spin a fun yarn or two.

J.P. currently resides in Seattle with his wife and hellion of a cat, both of whom look at him dubiously with some frequency.

For more, please visit J.P. Barnett online at:
Website: www.JPBarnett.com
Twitter: @JPBarnett
Facebook: JPBarnett.Author
Instagram: JPBarnett.Author

WHAT'S NEXT?

J.P. Barnett always has at least one book in the works, including the next book in the "Lorestalker" series. Please stay tuned to developments and plans by subscribing to his newsletter at the link below.

www.JPBarnett.com/Newsletter/

MORE FROM EVOLVED PUBLISHING

We offer great books across multiple genres, featuring hiqh-quality editing (which we believe is second-to-none) and fantastic covers.

As a hybrid small press, your support as loyal readers is so important to us, and we have strived, with tireless dedication and sheer determination, to deliver on the promise of our motto:
QUALITY IS PRIORITY #1!

Please check out all of our great books, which you can find at this link:
www.EvolvedPub.com/Catalog/

Thank you!

Printed in the USA
CPSIA information can be obtained
at www.ICGtesting.com
LVHW041111031024
792758LV00003BA/270